"I don't know why I'm asking a stranger for help."

"Am I still a stranger?" asked Sean.

Moonlight illuminated Connie's face as she tilted it up toward his. Her eyes were the dark green of a woodsy pond beneath lashes that drew spiked shadows across the curves of her cheeks. "No, I suppose not."

Sean brushed his fingers over her narrow back, feeling the warmth of her beneath the thin layer of fabric.

"You've been very nice about us intruding on your vacation," Connie said, "but I know Pippa may become an annoyance, especially now that she knows your profession."

He looked at Connie's solemn face, with traces of sorrow she couldn't hide, and nodded. What else could he do, when what filled his mind wasn't the tragedy of losing her husband—or even the recent upset of his own ordered existence—but that he had an overwhelming desire to kiss her?

"I'll watch out for your girl," he said. Then silently added *and you.*

Dear Reader,

Would you participate in a vacation house switch?

The idea intrigues me. Aside from traveling to an exotic destination, there's the aspect of moving into another person's house. How do they decorate, what books do they read, which soap do they use, what's programmed on their DVR? On the other hand, would I want a stranger in my house, learning the same about me? Maybe if I was happily ensconced in a sun-baked hacienda or a vineyard villa, I wouldn't care.

Sean Rafferty of *Nobody's Hero* takes the plunge and lands in a picturesque cottage on a small island off the coast of Maine. Lucky guy!

Enjoy,

Carrie Alexander

P.S. Visit me at www.CarrieAlexander.com and sign up for my e-newsletter *Get Carried Away*.

NOBODY'S HERO
Carrie Alexander

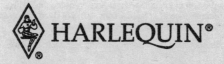

HARLEQUIN®

TORONTO • NEW YORK • LONDON
AMSTERDAM • PARIS • SYDNEY • HAMBURG
STOCKHOLM • ATHENS • TOKYO • MILAN • MADRID
PRAGUE • WARSAW • BUDAPEST • AUCKLAND

ISBN-13: 978-0-373-71504-6
ISBN-10:   0-373-71504-8

NOBODY'S HERO

This edition published by arrangement with Harlequin Books S.A.

® and TM are trademarks of the publisher. Trademarks indicated with ® are registered in the United States Patent and Trademark Office, the Canadian Trade Marks Office and in other countries.

www.eHarlequin.com

Printed in U.S.A.

ABOUT THE AUTHOR

Not only has Carrie Alexander given up on keeping her mountainous to-be-read stacks under control, she's lost count of how many books she's written. If she were ever to participate in a vacation house switch, she'd have to specify that only bookworms need apply. Carrie and her books live in a riverside cottage in the Upper Peninsula of Michigan.

Books by Carrie Alexander

HARLEQUIN SUPERROMANCE
1042–THE MAVERICK
1102–NORTH COUNTRY MAN*
1186–THREE LITTLE WORDS*
1239–A FAMILY CHRISTMAS*
1408–A READY-MADE FAMILY*
1455–A TOWN CALLED CHRISTMAS

*North Country Stories

To the Deadline Hellions bloggers and our readers,
for coming along on my strange writing adventures—
from rainbow manuscripts to deadline bats at 3:00 a.m.

PROLOGUE

SWAP YOUR VACATION HOUSE AT
HOLIDAYS AWAY!
Available July 21–Aug. 3, Osprey Island, Maine:

Quaint island cottage with splendid ocean view. Two
bedrooms, full bath, eat-in kitchen, fireplace, BBQ.
Enjoy kayaking, hiking, birding, boating and much
more in isolated splendor, sixteen miles off the
ruggedly picturesque Maine coast. Motivated owner
particularly willing to swap with Sunbelt location.

CHAPTER ONE

Pippa Bradford's Book of Curious Observations

JULY 21, OSPREY ISLAND, Maine. Latest subjects arrived at 9:17 a.m. on Jonesport ferry.

1. Bald man in trench coat, carrying briefcase, went straight to Whitecap Inn. Does not look like vacationer? (Check guest book for name.)

2. Couple met by Mrs. Sheffield of Peregrine House. Husband short and fat with gray hair and sunglasses, wife (or girlfreind?) tall with blond hair and high voice. Nice dressed, loads of luggage. Departed in silver Mercedes convertible, Mrs. S driving. Graves loaded luggage in pickup truck. Houseguests? High probabillity.

3. Pretty woman in purple shorts. Backpack. Got bike at Dockside Cycle. Overheard: one-day rental. Tourist—no more observation necessary.

4. Tall man with short dark hair. One bag. Jeans and baseball cap (Bruins). Sunglasses, suspicious limp. Walked to Pine Cone Cottage on Shore Road, took house keys from mailbox. Name on box is Potter. Resident? Future observation required.

SEAN RAFFERTY'S NAPE prickled. He brushed a hand inside his collar. There was no mosquito, nor stray hair from his grown-out law-enforcement buzz cut, but then he'd known that.

Someone was watching him.

He continued his limping circuit of Pine Cone Cottage's backyard. Behind a pair of tinted aviator sunglasses, his eyes were alert.

The sheltering wood was densely evergreen with a few spears of silver birch, bordered by ferns and underbrush. He took his time traversing the bumpy square of crabgrass and dandelions, waiting for the spy to give herself away. She wasn't nearly as sneaky as she believed.

Sunshine glinted off glass. He narrowed his eyes and searched the forest beyond the weathered picket fence of the vegetable garden. Hidden deep inside the pineconeladen branches of a blue spruce were twin lenses.

Pocket-size binoculars. They disappeared at his scrutiny. Branches bobbed as the lurker shifted position.

Sean stretched out the morning kinks, tilting his face toward the hot gold disk of the sun that had appeared over the treetops. He might have called out that there was nothing to see, nothing but a broken-down trooper with a bullet hole in his thigh and thirteen more days of emptiness to fill.

But he preferred the silence.

He'd found Maine's Osprey Island at a vacation house swap site on the Web. Desperate measures—his parents had been urging him to take their time-share condo at an Arizona desert resort. From previous visits there, he'd known that this time around he was in no mood to abide the other retirees' constant goodwill and inquisitiveness. They would want to commiserate about the shooting and his ongoing recovery. They would refuse to leave him alone, for his "own good." They'd probably even phone Patrick and Moira Rafferty with updates on their son's progress.

No, thanks. Peace and quiet was what Sean needed while he licked his wounds, not a resort filled with boisterous seniors in madras shorts and families of squealing, sunburned children.

One furtive child he could deal with. Even one with a penchant for sleuthing.

Sean settled into the lawn chair he'd moved to the backyard from the front, where there was an ocean view just beyond the road that bypassed the house. Two rustic thoroughfares, Shore and Cliff Roads, bordered the tiny island, following the coastline for the most part.

There weren't many cars but in his first day on Osprey he'd quickly learned that Shore Road was well traveled by both day-trippers and the seasonal locals, many of them creative types with two occupations—art and socializing. Two neighboring cottagers had already shown up at his door offering invitations, which he'd declined. Even in top form, he wasn't the cocktail-party type.

Pine Cone Cottage belonged to a woman named Alice Potter. She'd removed many of her personal belongings, including photos, so he had no idea what she looked like. From the modest cottage and her polite e-mails, he pictured a middle-aged lady, pleasant and plump. She owned a cat; he'd noticed a bag of kitty litter in a bathroom cupboard. No doubt there was also a close circle of island confidants, but no man, unless the voluble gent next door was not as gay as his beret.

The absent Miss Potter was currently fifty miles

outside of Phoenix, enjoying the desert's baking heat and the air-conditioned comforts of his parents' place. She'd written that she was looking forward to her first cactus.

Sean tilted back in the lawn chair, his neck still prickling. The girl spy had crept closer and was positioned off his left shoulder to watch him through the picket slats.

He gave her another minute, then suddenly twisted around. "Gotcha."

She gasped. Her red head popped up from behind the fence. She wanted to escape. He saw that in the angle of her body and the way she nervously clutched her schoolgirl tablet to her chest.

Instead, she stood her ground and screwed her round, freckled face into a knot. "You knew I was here?" Her voice was high and flutey.

"Of course."

Her eyes darted between him and the wood. "Who are you?"

"Don't you know?"

"Not yet."

He settled back again, closing his eyes and crossing his arms over his chest. "Then I'll leave you to find out."

That was stupid. Almost a challenge, when he wanted only to be alone. But the girl's solitary preoccupation was somehow amusing, at least for the moment. If she continued lurking, he'd have to put a stop to the intrusion.

He'd seen her several times already. First, trailing him from the ferry. Then poking into Alice Potter's mailbox at the end of the front yard's fieldstone walk. And once peering through the vine-covered kitchen window when he'd been putting away the groceries he'd picked up at the Osprey Island general store.

Few children seemed to live on the island. He imagined she was bored. And, therefore, overly curious.

His son, Joshua, had once been like that—bright and inquisitive. Before he'd turned into a prickly thirteen-year-old who hated his dad for living thousands of miles away. Although Sean regretted the miles between them, he knew there were even worse distances. Endless, uncrossable ones.

He shut his eyes tight, gutted by the thought of one particular child who would never have a father again.

Josh lived with his mother, a stepfather, two half sisters. That Sean's only son had a separate family outside of his father's was cold comfort, especially during the weeks when monosyllabic phone calls were all they shared. But comfort all the same.

The other child had no one left except a messed-up mother who'd screamed like a banshee over the body of her dead husband in the roadway. Sean would be haunted by the torn sound of those screams forever, by the lights of his patrol car illuminating the pool of blood on the pavement, but most of all by the sight of a small boy's face pressed to the back window of the family's car, taking in the entire scene.

That made two boys missing their fathers.

And *he* was responsible for both.

Sean's thigh seized. He winced and began to ruthlessly knead the tight muscles with his knuckles, letting the pain of the tender gunshot wound cut through the heavy layers of his guilt and regret.

Gradually the muscle let up. He exhaled, his head hung low on his chest, his eyes closed. Maybe the solitary, isolated cottage hadn't been such a good idea. Not exactly what the police psychologist had in mind when she'd told him he needed to work through his issues regarding the routine traffic stop gone tragically wrong.

Easier said than done, anyway.

When Sean finally remembered to look up, the redheaded girl was gone. For good, he hoped, doubting that he'd be so fortunate.

Pippa Bradford's Book of Curious Observations

CONTINUING SURVAILANCE of Subject #4. 8:47 a.m. Tuesday morning, Pine Cone Cottage, Osprey Island, Maine. No visitors or phone calls. Subject drank coffee standing at window, then went out to back garden. Patrolled perimeter. Picked up a pinecone, threw it into woods. Carried chair from front yard. (Sunbathing?)

This is boring and my bug bites itch.

Update: Mission aborted!!! Future observation at risk.

"SONOVABIRCH," Connie Bradford said when she saw the cluster of five-gallon English boxwoods, still not planted. She'd asked Bill Graves, the full-time gardener, to take care of it when she'd first arrived at the Sheffield estate to oversee the grand opening of the garden and maze she'd designed.

This was her biggest job ever. She'd begun work on the project almost three years ago, a scant month after her husband had passed away. But if she wanted perfection, she'd have to see to it herself.

Typical. She set aside her clipboard and picked up a spade.

Connie was halfway through the job when a trio

strolled out of the house onto the porch, which over-looked the sloping green lawn. "Connemara," called Kay Sheffield. Her slender arm waved back and forth in the brisk ocean breeze. "Hello! Come meet my guests."

Connie lifted a hand in acknowledgment of the summons while muttering "Oh, yay" to herself. She stabbed the spade into a half-dug hole and dusted her hands off on her pants. Time to schmooze. She'd wanted to step up her clientele, but hadn't counted on how much of her workday would be spent catering to the social niceties of the jet set rather than to their gardens. She was far more talented at coaxing forsythia into bloom.

"What on earth were you doing?" Kay asked as Connie approached. Connie felt disheveled in the presence of the well-groomed Mrs. Sheffield. The woman spoke through her nose with clenched teeth, a silly affectation she'd apparently picked up from old Katharine Hepburn movies. "We have Graves for that."

The gardener had been notably uncooperative toward Connie. She shrugged. "There's a lot to do before the party."

"I'm certain you can manage without getting your hands dirty." Kay turned to her guests, a squat man and a leggy blonde. "Harold, Jillian, this is Connemara Bradford, our up-and-coming garden designer. Connemara, Harold and Jillian Crosby. He's in real estate, she's in Prada." Kay tittered at her witticism.

"Hal," said the man, extending his hand.

"Connie." They shook briskly.

"No one calls me Jillian," the wife announced in a bubbly soprano voice. "I'm just Jilly." She, like Kay, was greyhound-lean, bottle-blond and clad in head-to-

toe designer labels. The two women might have been twins, except that Kay Sheffield was coolly beautiful while Jilly had an unfortunately long nose that shadowed her narrow lips.

"How do you do?" she asked in a more formal manner.

Connie smiled. "Quite well, thank you. I'm excited to be back on Osprey Island." While she'd made the trip several times from her home office in Bridgeport, Connecticut, most of her work for the Sheffield estate had been done at the desk and computer. A far cry from the early days of her business, when she'd designed suburban backyards, carting, digging and planting all on her own.

"This is my first visit." Jilly's buoyant personality bobbed back to the surface. She clasped her hands, the large rock on her ring finger almost clipping her chin. "The estate is just gorgeous. You're so lucky, Kaylene."

The pleasure on the other woman's face turned to restraint. "I go by Kay now."

Jilly's lips puckered around an *oops*. "Me and my big mouth." She winked at Connie. "We used to be Las Vegas showgirls together, but I'm not supposed to mention that."

Kay's expression was pained. "It's no secret," she admitted. "But you know Anders." Her husband. "He doesn't want to advertise my past."

Hal squeezed his wife's waist.

Connie decided she liked the Crosbys, even if they were an odd couple. "Would you like a tour of the maze?" she asked Jilly, who gave a flattering, "Ooh, yes!" at the prospect.

"Not yet," Kay commanded. "I want to keep it a surprise until the party. The opening of the maze is the event of the island's social season." Her mouth twitched.

"Not that the island has much of a season, according to my husband."

"Then I'd better get back to work. Saturday's coming up fast." Connie nodded, stepping aside as Kay swept her guests back indoors.

The woman was right, of course. Osprey would never make the list of society hot spots. Most of the small island's vacation homes were modest cottages, with only a handful of old-money mansions like Peregrine House scattered along the prime oceanfront acreage. The really fashionable people went to Martha's Vineyard or Newport Beach or the Hamptons.

The Sheffield home was an immense gray-shingled structure of the classic Cape Cod style, perched atop a narrow peninsula on the southeastern side of the island. The panoramic view of waves crashing on the cliffs was spectacular, but had left Connie with limited grounds to develop into the grand garden scheme the owners had requested. She'd designed a formal garden that followed the natural contours, with the octagonal maze fitted into the large open area created by a circular drive. For the upcoming garden party, they would set up a tent on the remaining stretch of flat lawn near the cliffs.

Connie returned to the boxwoods. As soon as she finished, the garden plantings would be complete. She'd have only the final touches to see to, which was no small task. Her clipboard lists were rife with notations on details and reminders that needed to be checked off before Saturday.

While she dug, Connie's thoughts turned to her daughter. Pippa was ten years old, an intelligent and inquisitive child who had grown too solitary and quiet since her father had passed away. Because Philip's treatments had frequently kept him from working, he'd acted as Pippa's primary caregiver during the day while Connie had been at school or work. His death from the leukemia two years ago had come after years of illness, no less difficult for being expected.

Connie was strong. The loss of her first and only true love still hurt badly, but she had finally reached the point where she could manage the sorrow. Pippa's continuing grief was her main worry.

Her daughter needed a boost. She'd hoped that a week on Osprey Island would at least get the girl outdoors. But so far Pippa had been more alone than ever, absorbed with scribbling in her notebook and rereading the few Trixie Belden mysteries she'd been allowed to pack.

Pippa clung to her precious Trixies as though they were life rafts. Philip had read the stories to her, one or two chapters a night. The tomboy detective—with her eager exclamations of "Gleeps!" and "Jeepers!"—had remained a part of their nightly ritual until the very end.

No wonder Pippa wasn't ready to let go of that strong link to her father. Connie didn't expect her to. She only wanted to encourage her child to move ahead with her life.

Connie straightened and pushed back the wiry strands of hair that had come loose from her ponytail. The sweater she'd put on that morning against the island chill had been tied around her waist for hours now. With the temperature heating up, the manual exertion had her sweating through her cotton blouse, as well. Determined to finish, she tamped the soil down around the boxwoods and went to find a hose to water them.

The gardener was nowhere to be seen. Graves had

resented Connie's presence from the start, especially after she'd brought in her own off-island workers to do the clearing and demolition of the old garden and its hardscape structures. He'd had it easy for years, doing only a minimum of upkeep to the grounds. Anders Sheffield hadn't bothered with the family's vacation estate until he'd married Kay, who'd soon begun to fancy herself becoming a proper New England grand dame. Thus the refurbishing had begun.

The current mistress of the manor didn't strike Connie as the outdoor type. Kay had never displayed a great appreciation for horticulture, either, but that wasn't Connie's concern. Her only responsibility was to turn the grounds into a showplace.

Hose in hand, she turned away from the outdoor tap and paused to take in the panorama of trimmed hedges and lavishly blooming flower beds. Four more days and she could turn in her final bill, then take time off at last to concentrate on Pippa.

Voices drifted from the open windows of Peregrine House. "I don't know why we have to go to all this trouble to impress your friends," huffed Anders Sheffield. He was in his fifties, more than a decade older than Kay, with two grown sons from previous marriages. Each successive wife had been taller, blonder and more beautiful than the last. The next one would have to be a six-foot Swedish supermodel.

"What about all the boring business associates of yours that we invited?" Kay responded in a lethally quiet tone.

Ice cubes clinked. Connie checked her watch. Early yet for cocktails.

"I don't need to impress them," Anders sneered. "They hope to impress me."

"Nothing impresses you. All the work I've done…" Kay's voice trailed off as the couple moved out of the room.

All the work I've *done,* Connie said to herself. Her only regret was that her thriving business had taken her away from Pippa, when the girl needed her mother most.

MIDMORNING WAS TOO EARLY for lunch, but Sean had nothing else to do. He got out a can of ravioli and cranked the lid off with the handheld opener he'd found in a kitchen drawer. He took a plastic fork from a box and ate the pasta cold, straight out of the tin. Not cold, he decided after a deliberate culinary evaluation. Room temperature. Almost tasteless, too, but the effortless cleanup was worth the sacrifice.

He threw out the can, the ravioli only half-eaten. His appetite had been lousy for a while now.

The lid of the trash swung shut. So much for lunch. Now what? The day stretched before him, empty and endless, with nothing but his thoughts to fill in the silence.

A long walk, he decided. The physical therapist had said walking would be good for working his leg muscles back into shape, as long as he didn't overdo it and reopen the wound.

"Not much chance of that," he muttered, his hand going to the misshapen dent where a .32-caliber slug had torn through his thigh. The island was less than three miles long, from the southernmost ferry dock to Whitlock's Arrow, a rocky outcropping that shot straight into the frothing surf of the Atlantic. He'd head north. The Potter cottage was halfway up the island, so a trip to Whitlock's Arrow would be no more than a three-mile jaunt, round trip.

Not an exceptionally long walk, but a good start. By the end of his two weeks, he'd be scaling cliffs.

The sun wasn't yet at its zenith, but it had grown hotter. Sean knotted a bandanna over his head, slid on a pair of sunglasses and took off down the lane. He followed the road north, moving at a clip that kept the occasional bikers or strollers from breaking his momentum with their cheery hellos.

The view was impressive, even though the drop to the ocean wasn't as steep on the western side of the island. Waves surged over the rocks; grass and wildflowers nodded in the breeze. He breathed the air—thick with brine and the pungent smell of evergreens—into the bottom of his lungs as he walked along Shore Road, coming to realize how grateful he was to be a long way from the job he'd previously lived for.

Gulls spiraled above the rocks up ahead, dropping down, then alighting in a flapping cacophony. The laughter of a group of picnickers sent Sean off the lane and onto the dirt paths that wound around the heart of the island, leading in no discernible pattern to various woodland cottages.

The hush was immediate. Towering pines closed ranks overhead, their interlaced branches blocking out all but intermittent patches of the vivid blue sky. Even the crash of the surf subsided until it was only background noise. The rhythmic pulse of the island.

Sean slowed, testing his pulse. He was out of shape. Getting blasted at short range by a crazed ex-con tended to have that effect.

A flash of reddish brown at the edge of a small meadow caught his eye. Too slow for a deer. Too tall for a fox.

He took off his sunglasses and polished them on the

hem of his plain white T-shirt, watching out of the corner of his eye as the same redheaded girl from that morning peeked out from behind a tree. Had she been following him the entire way?

He walked on, not glancing back until he reached a fork in the path. "Right or left?" he called.

After a short silence, the girl blew out a disgusted breath. "Whatsa matter? Are you lost?"

He didn't turn. "I'm taking you home."

A twig snapped as she stepped out onto the path. "I don't want to go home."

"I can't have you trailing me all over the island."

"How come?"

"It's dangerous."

She edged closer. "What's dangerous?"

He angled his head, taking a better look at her. She was short. Not abnormally, just kid-size. *Genius observation.*

The girl had pale, freckled legs and a round body. She wore shorts and an untucked T-shirt with pit stains. The binoculars hung around her neck and a spiral notebook was clamped under one arm. Her hair was fuzzy, drawn into stubby braids that barely reached her shoulders. Behind a pair of wire-frame glasses, her hot, red face was squished into a frown.

"You look like an angry tomato," he said.

Her mouth opened, then closed into an even tighter pucker. She shook off a few flecks of forest debris before shooting out her chin. "You look like a...a...peg-legged pirate!"

He remembered the bandanna on his head and laughed. "Fair enough."

Her small, chubby hand clenched a pen. "How come it's dangerous for me to follow you?"

"Just because." He moved off a couple of steps, but she kept pace. "Don't you have parents? Shouldn't you be at home?"

"My mom's working," she blurted, then looked sorry she'd given that away. Still, she added, "I'd just be alone there."

"You shouldn't tell that to a stranger."

She blinked. "I know."

He started off, taking the path to the left. "Don't follow me anymore. Go home."

He listened to her moving behind him, relieved when she turned onto the path that led toward the more populated southern end of the island. He stopped and watched as she progressed slowly, kicking at pinecones, glancing over her shoulder.

Her scowl deepened. "What are you doing?"

"Watching to see that you really go." He made a shooing motion.

She stomped off, but he wasn't convinced. He waited until she was out of sight, then followed, coming upon her almost immediately where the path twisted. She was scribbling inside her notebook, and looked up guiltily when he approached.

"I thought you were going home."

She shrugged. "I didn't say that. You did."

Spunky girl. "You can't keep following me."

"I wasn't. I was making—" She cut herself off by slapping shut the tablet.

"What's your name?" he asked.

"I don't tell strangers my name."

He nodded. "Do you live on the island?"

"For now."

"Will you stop bothering me if I tell you my name?"

She weighed the question, so he added an extra tidbit to tip the scales. "It's not Potter."

Her eyes got big. "Then you're a renter."

"More or less. The name's Sean Rafferty. I'm from Worcester, Massachusetts, originally, but now I live in Holden. It's a small town."

The girl smiled. "I was guessing Boston, 'cause of the accent."

"I've lived there, too. I'm on vacation for two weeks. And that's all you need to know." He made the shooing motion again, but it worked about as well on little girls as it did on his elder neighbor's cats. He pointed at the path, doing his best imitation of his first duty sergeant. Or his father, a decorated trooper who'd run a tight outfit at home. "Go. Now."

She went, reluctantly, looking small and alone.

Sean waited a couple more minutes, debating with himself while pine siskins hopped from branch to branch, nattering in chirps that punctuated his thoughts. A couple of teenagers came barreling down the path on mountain bikes, whooping back and forth harmlessly enough, but that settled it. Sean took the path to the right. He could just as easily walk down-island as up.

The girl soon realized she was being followed. She sped up, not liking it any more than he had.

In a short while, the path emerged from the woods and they were on the hard-packed dirt and gravel of Cliff Road. Beyond an ancient post-and-beam fence, sheer cliffs dropped into the booming surf.

After another quarter mile, the road veered inland again, losing the ocean view to a copse of pines. The girl scurried past gates guarding a couple of the larger island estates before turning between a pair of mossy stone pillars. A heavy iron gate that bore a scrolled initial *S* stood open. A plaque on one of the pillars read Peregrine House.

A poor little rich girl? Sean hadn't figured her for that.

The estate's gravel driveway led into a thick forest. The girl had already disappeared, but he could've sworn she'd turned off too quickly, into the woods. Maybe she was fooling with him, planning to double back.

He strode through the pillars, looking off into the woods, trying to pick up the girl's trail.

"Hey!" a woman shouted.

Sean halted at the start of a woodsy path so narrow it was almost grown in by the crowded foliage. He saw the peak of a red-roofed cottage among the trees.

A woman charged down the main driveway, spewing pebbles in her wake. Corkscrew curls of dark red hair bounced around her face, which was suffused with color.

He lowered his sunglasses, taking a good long look.

"Hey, you, mister," she accosted him. One fist raised. "What do you think you're doing, following my daughter home?"

CHAPTER TWO

SEAN SURRENDERED WITH his hands up. "Uh, hey. It's not what you think."

"Pippa?" the woman called. "Pippa, are you all right?" She aimed a finger at Sean before heading toward the overgrown trail. "Don't you dare move. I want to talk to you."

Sean remained frozen. She said *talk* the way his mother used to, when he and his brothers had been raising hell in the neighborhood and she'd resorted to threatening them with a talk from their father. The talk was usually a scolding, sometimes followed by a licking when the crime had been particularly heinous.

The girl had reappeared. "Jeez, Mom. Why are you yelling?"

So her name's Pippa, Sean thought, but his gaze was on the mother. With the wild red hair and the fighting attitude, she was the spitting image of her daughter. Except that the chubbiness around Pippa's middle had migrated in different directions in the mother, giving her an hourglass figure on a petite frame.

The woman gripped her daughter's shoulders. She bent to stare into the child's downcast eyes. "Are you okay, Pippa? Did this man try to hurt you?"

Pippa looked up with an owl-eyed blink. Her lower lip stuck out. "No, Mom."

"We only talked," Sean said.

"You *talked?*" The mother wheeled on him. "What are you doing, *talking* to a ten-year-old girl in the middle of nowhere? There's something fishy going on here." She looked ready to tear his head off with her hands, but she swallowed hard and turned back toward her child. "I'm warning you right now, buster. Stay away from my daughter."

"That's fine." Sean flicked his chin toward the girl. "You be sure to tell her to keep away from me, too."

The mother had Pippa in a headlock, crushed to her bosom. She threw him a look. "You can bet on that. And I'll also be talking to the Jonesport police about strange men who prowl the woods looking for..." She snorted. "Conversation."

Sean was running short on patience, but he jammed his hands into the back pockets of his jeans and re-treated a few steps so he wouldn't appear threatening. "I only followed her because—"

"Then you admit it." The mother clutched Pippa even tighter before abruptly releasing her. "Run up to the house now, Pip. I'll be along in a minute."

Pippa hesitated, grimacing as if she wanted to speak up. "Okay," she finally whispered, then turned and ran off.

The mother advanced on Sean, her hands clenched and her chest heaving. He couldn't help admire her ferocity, even if it was directed at him. He was Irish; he liked a woman with spirit. And the flaming hair didn't hurt, either.

"Do I get to explain before I'm condemned?" he asked.

She tossed her head back. "Go ahead. Try and worm your way out of it. I know what I saw—you creeping after my little girl, glancing around to be sure no one was watching."

He supposed he might have appeared furtive, although he was positive he hadn't crept. "I followed her only to see that she got home safely. I swear on my honor, that's all there was to it. No harm intended."

"Right." The woman folded her arms, regarding him skeptically. "And what about the 'talk'?"

"I caught her following me through the woods. She was lurking around my cottage, too, yesterday and this morning."

The woman's eyes flickered, betraying the slightest hesitation. "I'm sure. So you're blaming the victim?"

"There's no victim here. You keep your daughter away from me, and I'll stay away from her."

"You're claiming that Pippa was at your house?" She shook her head. "I don't believe it. Why would my girl be interested in you?"

"How should I know? You're her mother."

She frowned.

"Maybe it was some kind of game."

"I…" The woman drew in a breath, lifting her chin an inch higher. She couldn't have been taller than five-two, at least ten inches shorter than Sean. "I'll speak to her."

He nodded. "Good."

Her mouth thinned. "That doesn't mean I believe you."

"You don't have to, as long as your daughter tells the truth."

"Pippa doesn't lie to me."

Sean hoped not. "If you want me…" *to apologize for your tirade, perhaps* "…I'm staying on the west side, at Pine Cone Cottage, just off Shore Road."

"Wonderful."

She offered only the one sarcastic word, with no name, so he nodded and walked away, certain they'd meet again. Presumably under better circumstances. Osprey was, after all, a very small island.

CONNIE WAITED UNTIL they were seated at the dining table with their lunch—toasted cheese and tomato sandwiches—before she started in with the inquisition. Pippa was expecting it, and took a huge bite when her mother said, "All right. Tell me what happened."

"Mmph, mouth's full."

"I'll wait." Connie speared a dill pickle out of the jar. The juice speckled the table's watermarked wood surface, and she swiped it up with a paper napkin.

The Sheffields had installed Connie and her daughter in a somewhat ramshackle, long-forgotten guesthouse, as all the bedrooms in the main home were reserved for their VIP guests. Small and dark, the cedar-shingle house was hidden out of sight, in the woods not far from the front gate. The accommodations were summer-camp rustic, with thin, sagging mattresses, balky plumbing and flyspecked screens, but the privacy was wonderful. Constant exposure to the Sheffields worked Connie's last nerve. Anders Sheffield was an entitled snob with morality issues, and the lady of the manor was too unsure of herself to give him the boot up the butt that he deserved.

Connie had thought that the guesthouse setup was ideal. She'd be close enough to keep an eye on her daughter, even while she worked. It appeared she'd been wrong.

Pippa swallowed and went in for a second bite.

"Pippa."

She put the sandwich down. "Yes, Mom?"

"Were you at that man's house?" Connie was certain about one thing—her daughter wouldn't lie. Pippa's good conscience and the tendency to blush beet-red had always given her away. She'd learned not to even try.

"Not *in* it," Pippa said. "But I was nearby."

"Did you follow him?"

Her daughter's face was inching toward her plate as her shoulders caved inward. Gradually, over the past several years, Pippa had become more secretive and self-contained. Emotional conflict bothered her. She'd picked up the habit of cowering whenever she couldn't physically retreat.

"I guess so," Pippa whispered.

Connie winced, remembering the accusations she'd flung at the stranger. "Why?"

"I was observing him."

The notebook again. Connie sighed. "Pippa, I've warned you about that habit...."

The girl's head shot up. "I was bored! I read all my books. There's nothing to do here."

"I said you could go for a short walk. That didn't mean spying on strangers." Connie would have normally considered Pippa's spurt of temper and the venture outdoors to be promising. These days, it was tough to raise a child to be both bold *and* cautious.

Connie chose her words carefully. "This island may be small, but that doesn't mean it's safe for a young girl to be wandering around alone. Still, I want you to have fun here. Kid-type fun. You are *not* to get up to any of your *Trixie Belden and the Mystery of the*—the *whatever* mischief."

"Oh, Mom. Please? There's lots to see on the island. I won't bother anybody."

"Especially not that man."

Pippa sighed. She was good at doing that, in a way that made Connie feel like a tyrant.

"All right, Pip. I'll do my best to make some extra time for us to try a few island activities." Connie bit the pickle in half with a satisfying crunch. "But I want you sticking with me up at the garden for the rest of the day."

Pippa kicked the table leg. "Will I have to dig? Ugh."

"No, you won't have to dig. You can play in the maze if you like. As long as I know where you are."

"Okay." Pippa was fascinated by the maze; she'd studied the plans from their first inception, until Connie had drawn up an extra copy for her daughter to trace out the solution with her markers.

Pippa gave her a toothy smile and returned to her sandwich. She was like her mother that way—running hot and cold at the turn of a tap.

An only child, Connie had been smothered and pampered by her parents. As a result, she'd developed a strong need for freedom and independence, but also a hair-trigger temper. In her adult years, she'd been forced to learn to control her emotions and act as the rock of the family, particularly during the final years of her marriage. Even so, Philip had often teased her that she was only a dormant volcano, ready to burst forth at the first rumbling provocation.

She'd certainly gone off on Pippa's stranger. He must be feeling rather scorched.

Connie pressed two fingers between her closed eyes. She couldn't seem to remember exactly what the man looked like, beyond an impression of a lean body with wide shoulders and a fringe of dark hair sticking out from beneath his bandanna. He hadn't removed his sunglasses. She'd taken that as shady, but maybe she'd been wrong.

She didn't want to encourage Pippa's surreptitious sleuthing, especially after the "Case of the Locked Garden Shed" had led to a policeman showing up on her doorstep back home. Unfortunately, her own curiosity about the stranger was suddenly on a par with Pippa's.

Connie shoved aside her paper plate. "All right. Tell me. What did you find out about him?"

Pippa dropped the cheesy crust she'd been nibbling. "He came on the nine-fifteen ferry. I first saw him yesterday, when we were having breakfast at the harbor. Want me to get my notebook? I made lots of observations."

Connie had noticed her scribbling away at the time, but had overlooked it. "That's not necessary, Pippa." She picked up her can of diet soda. "Did you get his name? I should probably make a point of apologizing since it seems that he's not quite the degenerate I believed him to be."

"I didn't find out his name on my own, but he told me." Pippa looked sorry about that. She took pride in her growing ability to ferret out information. Too much pride. "It's Sean Rafferty."

Sean Rafferty, Pine Cone Cottage. Connie filed the info away before popping the top of the soda. She licked the fizz from her thumb. "And was he alone?"

"Yep. He *says* he's on vacation."

Connie's eyes narrowed. "How long did you two talk?"

"Only a minute. He knew I was following him and he told me to go home." Pippa frowned. "He didn't act like a vacationer."

"How does a vacationer act?"

"Happy. I think Mr. Rafferty is sad. Or maybe sick."

"What makes you say that?" Connie asked, although as soon as the comment had come out of Pippa's mouth, she'd realized that she'd had the same impression. Despite the wide shoulders, he'd been gaunt. He hadn't smiled once, even to reassure her when she was frantic and overprotective.

"Well, he limps. And he's restless. He ate his lunch standing up."

"Oh, Pippa. Were you looking in his windows?"

Pippa's head drooped. She gave a little nod.

"Good grief. That's so wrong I don't even know what to say to you." Connie set the soda can down with a clunk. She waved Pippa away. "Go on, wash up and get ready to come to the maze with me. You're staying within my sights for the rest of the day, young lady."

Connie took a few quick bites of her sandwich, regretting that she'd asked the questions and reignited her daughter's imagination. As well as her own.

She was on Osprey Island to achieve a garden design that would put her on the map. She had no time to become involved in one of Pippa's imaginary mysteries, especially a puzzle that might as well be titled *The Secret of the Handsome Stranger.*

THE NEXT MORNING, Sean made his second attempt at the walk to Whitlock's Arrow. The brisk salt air was invigorating, and by midmorning he was negotiating a tricky path down the cliffside to the shingle beach. Up top, he'd come across an island old-timer who'd offered directions, warning that while the close-up view was worth the trip, it was potentially dangerous once the tide came in.

Despite a few hairy moments when he slipped on the slick rocks, Sean landed safely on the beach. He sat on one of the outcroppings to rest his injured leg while watching the blue-green waves beat at the craggy stones of the point.

After a while, the constantly changing patterns of spume and the fecund smell of the tide lulled him into forgetting about himself. The shore was a world in itself, private except for the sightseers who appeared at the edge of the cliff to pose for photos. Some of them shouted into the roar of the surf, setting off the gulls and cormorants that speckled the rocks.

When the tide turned, Sean got up to go back. Along the way, he took a few extra minutes to explore the tidal pools formed by the water's recession. The microcosms of ocean life were more fascinating than he expected.

He'd been born and raised and gone to college in cities, then moved several times around Massachusetts during his career as a state trooper. He'd never much considered the rugged appeals of the country. After a marriage prompted by his girlfriend's pregnancy, vacations to Cape Cod with baby Josh in a soppy diaper and Jen complaining about her sunburn had been about as rural as he'd gotten.

He'd made the trip to Maine strictly out of desperation. He hadn't expected to enjoy it. He hadn't expected that the respite would truly help him recover.

Minutes flew by while he watched crabs scurry over the rocks and the delicate but sturdy anemones bob in the water of the tidal pool. Seaweed spread green tentacles through the shallows. Snails left glistening trails on the stones. He touched the elaborate white designs drawn on the black rocks, then licked at the crystalized sea salt left on his finger.

Only when he put a foot down wrong and his running shoe plunged into icy water did he realize how much time had passed. The tide was rising rapidly, already turning several of the formerly accessible rocks into mini islands of their own. He moved from stone to stone, traversing rivers that foamed white with each crashing wave.

A plaintive cry stopped his scramble up the cliffside path. He looked back the way he'd come, but saw only a white gull diving into the sea.

"Over here!"

He shaded his eyes with his hand and scanned the ocean. Huddled, shivering and wet, stranded on a steeply slanted rock that had become surrounded by the rising tide was the girl, Pippa. Sean's blood turned cold. There was no way for him to swim out to rescue her without being beaten bloody on the rocks by the incoming surf.

CHAPTER THREE

"DON'T MOVE!" HE SHOUTED, although clearly Pippa had no intention of moving. Flattened against the stone, she flinched each time the thunderous waves crashed and sent spray high into the blue sky. She was somewhat sheltered from the surf by adjacent jutting rocks, but her position grew more precarious every minute. The water crept higher, swirling with dangerous currents.

Sean shielded his eyes and searched down shore for help. He'd spotted a beached dinghy maybe a half mile away, but gave that up as useless. There was no time. Not even to climb the cliff in hope of finding tourists nearby.

A length of frayed rope lay twined among the stones on the beach. He grabbed it and backtracked, working out a route to cross the slippery stones. Several times he waded through the frigid water. Soon he was plunging in, swimming the gaps from rock to rock. Each time, the icy shock of it stole his breath and sapped another portion of his strength as he fought against the treacherous pull of the current. By the time he pulled himself onto the rock that brought him as close to Pippa as he could get, he was numb through.

The waves surged past Pippa's sheltered position and battered him full on. "Can you catch the rope?" he called, knotting a loop.

Her face was stark white, her lips almost blue. "I th-think so."

He threw the lasso, which barely had enough length to reach her. She lifted a hand but missed as a large wave broke behind her. The roped dropped into the rush of rising tide.

"You're fine." He reeled in the line. The waves lapped at her shins. "Try again."

Pippa got it on the third attempt and slipped the loop over her head and shoulders before clamping herself to the rock again. She closed her eyes and said, "Okay," through chattering teeth.

Not okay. He gripped the end of the worn rope, praying it was strong enough. "You have to climb down. Or jump."

She stared at the tumultuous gap between them. "In the water?"

At Whitlock's Arrow, the surf boomed as loud as thunderclaps. He'd read Pippa's lips more than heard her. "Keep hold of the rope," he yelled, hoping she'd understand. "I'll reel you in."

She looked down, then clutched at the craggy rock. "I can't!"

"You have to. I can't come to you." As it was, he could only hope he'd be able to catch her before the waves slammed her into the rock—or pulled her under.

She hunched her shoulders up around her ears and shook her head, her eyelids squeezed shut again.

"You can't wait!" he roared. He didn't give her time to think, just leaned farther over the edge of the rock and whipped the line taut between them, giving her middle a jerk. "Jump this way when I say go."

He'd been watching the waves. They came in escalating series of seven. When the largest one broke, showering both of them with foam, he barked, "Go!" and gave the rope another pull.

Pippa plunged into the water and was immediately swept sideways into the current, heading directly toward a half-submerged rock. The rope caught her up short. The sharp snap sent a jolt juddering up Sean's arm into his shoulder. She surfaced, white-faced and sputtering.

He pulled her in hand over hand, sliding dangerously low over the rock ledge, his thighs straining. The adrenaline that burned through him gave his numbed arms an extra shot of strength.

A wave descended as he reached in to haul her out. She was deadweight, and he had only enough time to press them both against the rock face, clinging like limpets as the icy water pelted them. When the waves receded he pushed her up and followed with a great heave, covering her as the next rush arrived.

Immediately he got Pippa moving, herding her along mercilessly until they were beyond the waves. They slumped onto the pebbly beach, and he pulled her roughly into his arms, chafing at her limbs to bring the blood up.

The sodden lump of her spiral-bound notebook fell out of the front of her windbreaker, along with her glasses. She reached for them.

He closed a hand over hers. "Dammit, Pippa. What did you think you were you doing, following me down here? Do you realize the danger you were in?"

The girl gasped for air. "D-don't tell my mo-mom."

He wrapped his arms around her. "You know I have to."

Pippa's shoulders shook violently against his chest. He felt as though he'd been cracked open against the rocks and emptied out, but still he cradled her, willing his warmth into the girl's small body even when he believed he had none left to give.

He wouldn't have this one's fate on his conscience.

CLEAR MIND, pure heart, gentle soul.

Despite Connie's best intentions, her lips tightened, her fingers curled toward her palms. Maybe it worked for some, but to her the mantra was a load of claptrap. She had way too much going on to forget for even a minute.

Breathe, woman. Relax and give it another go. You're on a picturesque island sixteen miles off the Maine coast. You can't get any more idyllic. The oms *should be rolling off your tongue.*

Connie had plunked herself on the ground outside the guesthouse. Her friend Lena swore by meditation, but then Lena was the sort of woman who kept a yoga mat in her desk drawer, which happened to be in her corner window office in the busiest business tower at the intersection of Boston's noisiest streets. Lena was the calm at the eye of the tornado.

Whereas tornado was Connie's middle name. When she made time for the gym, it was to take a kickboxing class. No *oms,* just right jab, left jab, kick, kick, kick.

Kay Sheffield, who'd yoo-hoo'd Connie from a leisurely breakfast on her seaside patio to say there was a touch of yellow in the maze hedge and that if Connie couldn't replace the section—yeah, sure, overnight— she might want to consider green spray paint? *Pow.*

The supplier who'd screwed up a gravel shipment, leaving Connie and her day workers empty-handed at the dock in the morning fog? *Punch.*

Graves, who'd absconded with several of her tools, even though they were clearly marked Bradford Garden

Designs, and had then said—to her face—that she must have lost them? *Bam, bam, bam.* Three lightning kicks, right under the chin.

Connie untangled herself out of the pretzel pose and leaned back on her hands to look up at the cloudless sky. Meditation wasn't working. No surprise. When Philip had been sick as a dog from chemo and she'd been half out of her mind, trying to take care of him and Pippa while beginning work toward her master gardener qualification, the only calm she'd known had been in their tiny backyard. Little by little she'd weeded, planted and pruned until the space had become a lush green paradise.

She'd always remember the quiet evenings in the garden with Phil, how he'd made her promise that she wouldn't give up on her dream, no matter what.

Connie squeezed her lids shut. If he could see her now, he'd bust with pride.

He'd also be terribly concerned about Pippa. He'd always known the right way to comfort their daughter without coddling her, while Connie couldn't seem to get it right no matter what she tried. She was either too harsh, to toughen Pippa up, or too open and easy, to encourage Pippa's independence.

Then again, everything was ten times more difficult without Phil. Whenever Connie thought she had herself under control and her life in order, she was reminded how alone she was without him.

Were her struggles the result of missing her husband, or simply the lot of every single working parent?

Probably both, she conceded. She didn't want to spend the rest of her life without a partner. In recent weeks, her loneliness had even led to a few thoughts about agreeing to one of Lena's setups.

But she hadn't been able to go through with it. Lena's men were business executives with sky-box connections to the Sox. Connie was a hot-dogs-in-the-bleachers woman. Only a rare man would pique her interest. None had landed on her doorstep.

"Mrs. Bradford?"

The sudden shout of her name was a shock. She sprang up as Sean Rafferty came around the corner of the house at a brisk clip. "Sorry to disturb you." He was out of breath. "I caught a glimpse and—"

"No, that's fine." She slapped the pine needles off her butt. "I was taking a break, is all." Why should that fluster her? "I, uh, didn't expect to see you again so soon, but since you're here, I ought to…" She stopped to inhale, which should have slowed her galloping pulse. "Apologize."

The man pulled up short, apparently speechless.

"I was wrong. I admit it. I jumped to conclusions about you, Mr. Rafferty, and I'm sorry. You're not a— a—" She gestured with both hands, trying to think of polite words rather than the blunt ones she was more accustomed to using. Watching her salty tongue around her new class of clientele was a job in itself.

"A monster?" he asked with a lift of his eyebrows.

"A child molester." A spade was a spade, even if it was in the hands of a resentful gardener like Graves.

"That's good, because…" Sean inclined his head toward the front of the house.

Connie groaned. "Pippa? Not again."

Pippa had still been sleeping when Connie had left the house to meet the early ferry. She'd set out cereal and a note on the kitchen table, instructing the girl not to wander off beyond the Sheffield estate. Since it was a big estate with much for an inquisitive girl to explore, she hadn't been overly worried when she'd found Pippa gone when she'd returned. For all her curiosity, Pippa was too cautious to get into dangerous situations.

At least, she *had* been.

While Connie's mind had raced, she'd also been staring at Sean, cataloging his features and build as if she might need to identify him in a lineup. The shoulders she remembered. Above them, his face was handsome, if gaunt. He had a good, strong nose and jaw. A sprinkle of gray in the clipped hair. His eyes were a solemn gray-blue, not dark the way she'd remembered.

She dropped her gaze, then blinked, appreciation turning to apprehension. "Why are your jeans wet? You're soaked to the skin!"

"That's what I've been trying to tell you. Pippa's okay, but she was caught out by the tide. I hauled her in."

"Pippa…was in the ocean?"

"No, she was on a rock." He conceded with a nod. "And briefly in the water."

"Where is she?"

"Sitting on your front step. Seeing as she was following me again when it happened, I think she's afraid to face you."

"Afraid?" Connie's head jerked back. "Because *I'm* the monster?"

"Maybe a tigress," Sean said with a small smile.

Connie resisted the urge to let out a low growl. Pippa was safe, that was the important thing. If there was anyone to blame, it wasn't Sean and it wasn't Pippa. It was her.

"PIPPA, PIPPA. WHAT WERE YOU thinking?" Connie's hands shook as she pulled a towel off the shelf. She clenched the length of terry cloth taut, then enfolded her daughter's shivering body. "I said over and over that you were not to go near the ocean without supervision. You've never disobeyed me so badly before. When I think what might have happened…"

Don't think it. She's safe.

Pippa bleated from the depths of a fervent hug, the third or fourth since her mother had rushed her inside and up to the bathroom for dry towels and a hot shower. "Oh, Mom."

Connie set Pippa back, knowing that despite her own culpability she must scold the girl. Mete out some sort of punishment. But that could wait.

"I'd rattle your bones if you weren't already shaking like a drowned kitten." Connie swept aside the mildewed shower curtain and cranked on the tap. "In you go."

Pippa stared, the towel clutched under her chin.

"Privacy." Connie bit her lip, remembering that her daughter was ten and growing up fast. No longer a little girl. But not a big one, either. "Right. Stay in the shower until the hot water runs out. I'll go brew you a cup of tea."

"Tea?" Pippa made a face.

"Hot chocolate, then, if I can remember how to make it when I'm so shook up."

"It's just chocolate and milk, Mom."

"Don't be a smarty-pants. You're in for it, you know. I'll have to ground you." But she already had, in effect, and that hadn't done any good. Before there could be a punishment, she'd have to find out why Pippa had disobeyed, what she'd hoped to gain.

Sean Rafferty.

He might know. Connie had left him on his own when she'd rushed Pippa inside.

He's probably gone, she told herself as she descended the cottage's narrow steps with a couple towels in her arms. A glance out the stairwell's porthole window revealed no sign of him, but then she found him sitting at the dining table, perched damply on the edge of a ladderback chair, his face pinched white. He looked as though he couldn't figure out why he was still there.

Suddenly, Connie knew nothing except that seeing him had eased her worry. As wary and edgy as he came across, she was instinctively comforted by his presence. *Go figure.*

"Towels." She thrust them at him. "You're shivering."

He stood and draped one around his shoulders, ignoring the wet denim clinging to his legs.

"Well," Connie said, pulling away her gaze. "Pippa's taking a hot shower. For a minute there, I was worried about hypothermia."

"She was chilled through, but the walk home warmed her up. I kept her moving. I'm sure she'll be fine." Sean rubbed his arms vigorously. "Since you've got everything under control, I'll leave."

"No, please stay. I'd like to talk to you." Connie put her hand on his arm to urge him down into the chair, then pulled away when the renewed warmth of his skin and the firm muscle beneath it came as a pleasant shock.

She rubbed the prickly hair on her forearms as she headed to the fridge. Holding a half-gallon container of milk and a squeeze bottle of chocolate syrup, she turned back to Sean. "Will you come to dinner tonight? I'd like to—" *Breathe, dammit!* "—express my gratitude to you." Despite the inappropriate timing, there was no denying she was aware of all sorts of things she'd like to do with him.

"That's not necessary," he said in a grave tone, and she dearly hoped he hadn't been reading her mind.

Her laugh sounded rusty. "Hey, c'mon. You rescued my daughter from the briny brink. A home-cooked meal is the least that I owe you."

He glanced away, raking a hand through his hair. It had dried into short porcupine quills. "It was nothing."

"It was huge. You're a hero in my book."

His face contorted. Only for a millisecond, but she noticed.

"Don't call me that."

"Why not?" She bent and clattered the pots and pans in the drawer under the electric stove more than she had to, then tossed her hair as she straightened. She shot him a smile over her shoulder. "Are you modest? Shy? Secretly a Mr. Limpet?"

"What's a Mr. Limpet?"

She poured milk into a saucepan. "A character from *The Incredible Mr. Limpet*. You don't know the movie?"

He shook his head.

"We watched a lot of oldies with Pippa when she was little," Connie explained. "*Mr. Limpet* was a favorite. Don Knotts played a wimp who turned into a heroic fish wearing glasses. The fish was animated." She paused, considering. "It was better than it sounds."

Sean rubbed a finger above his upper lip. "I'm not a wimp or a fish."

Connie grinned. "Not even a heroic one?"

"No."

"Seriously, though," she said and squirted the syrup into the milk. Not the best recipe for hot chocolate, but it'd do in a pinch. "What about dinner?"

He didn't answer.

She saw the beginnings of his frown and rushed on. "Sharing a little companionship won't hurt you. The island can be a lonely place. That is, assuming you *are* alone?" She stopped stirring. "Would there be a Mrs. Limpet?"

"Pippa didn't tell you?"

"I neglected to interrogate her." On that point.

"I'm here alone." He shifted his weight from one leg to the other, wincing slightly. "There's no fish wife."

With a chuckle, she resumed stirring. "Then you can come over. About six? Just so you know, I'm not promising a gourmet meal. My purpose is to find out exactly what happened with Pippa this morning."

"Then I can save you the trouble. What happened is that Pippa was spying on me again."

"I told her not to," Connie interjected. "Very firmly."

He nodded. "Even so, she followed me out to Whitlock's Arrow, on the north end. Apparently she climbed down to the shore after me, then was stranded on a rock when the tide came in." He rubbed his leg. "I didn't notice her until it was too late, or I'd have sent her home right away."

"What were you doing at Whitlock's Arrow?"

She got a shrug. "Walking. Exploring the shore." He met her eyes. "In complete innocence."

"I didn't intend to accuse you of anything. I'm just trying to figure out what's going on with Pippa. You seem like a normal sort of guy." *Normal? Maybe.* "What's so intriguing about you that she'd break the rules and—" she exaggerated for his benefit "—*risk my wrath?*"

Connie knew why he intrigued *her*—no mystery in that at all. In the fourteen years since she'd hooked up with Philip when they were both sophomores in college, she may have forgotten how strong the first sweet rush of attraction could be. But she was recognizing it now.

Sean's gaze took in her face, her hair. "Do you have a lot of wrath?" he asked, bemused.

Heat flooded her cheeks. Her scalp tingled. "My temper has been known to flare."

"Ah, yes, that's right. I remember now."

She snorted. "Hey, wait a minute. I wasn't completely off the mark about that." She tilted her head toward the ceiling as the sound of drumming water ceased. "A mother's got to be diligent, nowadays."

Sean retreated. "You're right, of course."

Connie poured the hot chocolate into a mug. "Want some? You got wet, too." She stared at his clinging jeans. "Shoot. I should have offered you a change of clothing, and instead I'm entertaining you with plot summaries of old Disney movies."

He waved her off. "Thanks, but I'm not fitting into any of your gardening togs. I'll go home to change." He dropped the towels on the back of the chair and moved to the front door, which still stood wide-open.

She followed. "I want you to know that I realize how lucky we were that you were there to rescue Pippa. If you hadn't seen her… If you hadn't acted quickly… Well, that's too horrible to consider. Words of gratitude aren't enough." She grasped the edge of the door. Swallowed the lump in her throat. "Pippa and I are indebted."

"A thank-you is enough." Sean stooped and picked something up off her doorstep, using his left hand. The knuckles of his right pressed hard into his thigh.

With a wince, he straightened and extended his hand. "You and Mr. Bradford owe me no more than that."

He thought there was a Mr. Bradford? Connie didn't wear a wedding ring, although that was because of her job rather than her marital status. She might have immediately explained that her "we" was a family of only two, but she was distracted by what Sean had handed her.

Pippa's sodden notebook. The answer, perhaps, to all of Connie's questions, even if she couldn't possibly read it without her daughter's permission.

"Thank you." She clutched the tablet to her midriff, even though it was cold and smelled of seaweed. She needed to hold on…to *something*.

Sean gave a short wave and strode down the path to the main road. Even with the pronounced hitch in his step and his damp, wrinkled clothing, he cut an admirable figure in the dappled sunshine—proud, angular and so very capable of the heroics that he denied.

Connie took a deep breath and pushed down the damnably persistent tide of attraction. She'd explain about Phil later, when and if Sean returned at six to take her up on the dinner invitation.

CHAPTER FOUR

"I MISS DADDY, TOO."

Connie's voice stilled the knock of Sean's knuckles against the door. He flattened his hand. The Sheffield guesthouse was such a small place that the redhead's voice was clearly audible through an open window. The only other sounds nearby were the birds in the trees and the wind through the pine boughs.

"And I'm sorry that I have to work so much. I'd be home with you if I could."

"I don't want you to be home with me." Pippa's voice, trying to sound belligerent, came across bruised. "I'm not a baby, Mom."

"You're not a teenager, either, so don't expect to have the privileges of one. When I say don't go near the ocean, I mean do not go near the ocean. Boredom isn't an excuse. Neither is curiosity." A metallic clang accompanied the words.

Sean supposed that she was banging pots and pans again. There was something familiar about that, and it didn't take more than a moment to scan past twenty years away from home to realize why. His mother had been a pot banger, too. His wild Irish rose, Sean's father had always said, even though the both of them had been born and raised in New England.

Connie gave Sean no maternal longings, that was for sure. Although as he listened, she continued a lecture that might have been torn from Moira Rafferty's book. The trouble he'd caused his parents growing up—they would have welcomed his dunking in the surf and tossed his siblings in, as well—brought a wry smile to Sean's face. He was forty, more than capable on his own, but his mother was still his mother. She'd been quite verbal about his decision to recuperate alone on Osprey Island instead of in the bosom of the noisy Rafferty household. It had been his dad who'd talked her into agreeing to supply their Arizona condo for the vacation house switch.

"From now on, you'll have no more opportunities to disobey me," Connie continued. "You'll be by my side during the rest of our stay on the island. And if for some reason that's not possible, you'll have a babysitter. The Sheffields' housekeeper told me she has a daughter who's available."

Pippa groaned.

Clang. "No complaining."

A long silence signaled the end of the discussion. Sean knocked.

More clattering from the kitchen, then Connie's voice. "Oh, my gosh. There he is, and I'm a mess. Look at my hair. Pippa, answer the door. And remember that you are not to interrogate Mr. Rafferty tonight. He's our guest, not a suspect in one of your made-up mysteries."

Sean dropped his smile as the door opened. Pippa looked at him with her eyes rounded behind a pair of wire-framed glasses. The temperature was pleasant, but she was dressed in jeans, socks and tennies, with a long-sleeved sweatshirt under the faded Camp Arrowhead

T-shirt that stretched across her middle. Her hair was braided so tightly her forehead looked taut and shiny.

Sucking in a large, wet sniff, Pippa wiped a finger beneath her freckled nose. "Hullo. My mom says I have to thank you for rescuing me."

Connie appeared and clamped her hands on her daughter's slumped shoulders. "That, my darling child, is not the most gracious way to express your appreciation." She squeezed then released, and Pippa fled gratefully into the shadowy interior of the cottage.

Sean held out three bottles of beer. "Wine might have been more appropriate, but this was all I had." He hadn't thought of making a trip to the island's general store until it was too late.

"Thanks." Connie took the clinking brown bottles, holding them against her breasts with one arm as she gestured him inside with the other. "I like a cold beer better anyway. But why three? One for Pippa?" She chuckled.

He entered. "Nope. Three's what I had left from the six-pack I bought when I arrived."

"Beer will go nicely with the clam chowder."

There was a moment of awkward silence while he looked around. Between the thick stand of trees and the narrow leaded-glass windows, little light reached the guesthouse even during the day. By evening, it was ill-lit by the few lamps in the house, bulbs shining dully from beneath heavy pleated shades. Lurking under the homey scent of dinner was an odor of mildew, as if the cottage had been closed up for years.

Sean hadn't seen the estate house yet, but he'd bet it was about a thousand times more luxurious. He began to wonder if Connie and her daughter were poor relations.

She must've read his face. "I know it's not much, but it's got a certain rustic charm, don't you think?"

He nodded, considering the paint-by-number pictures framed in Popsicle sticks and the heavily scarred mahogany table as she led him through the dining area that adjoined the kitchen. They stopped at the open doorway of a living room wallpapered in a field of flowers darkened with age and water spots. The room was crowded with too much cast-off furniture, including a threadbare Persian rug and an antique hutch stuffed with mismatched china.

He looked at Connie. "How come you're not at the big house?"

"It's filled with guests for the party. No room for the employees."

"Oh," he said, getting it at last. "You're an employee."

Pippa, who was curled into a plaid wing chair in the corner, glanced up from her book.

"I'm the Sheffields' garden designer." Connie peered up at him from beneath the fluff of her bangs. She'd scooped her hair high on her head and pinned it into an attempt at a schoolmarm bun type of thing, except that her hair was too curly and had escaped in an auburn froth. She looked like a rooster. "You know about the maze, right? The garden party?"

He shook his head. "I only arrived two days ago. I haven't been socializing much."

Till now. On the walk over, he'd asked himself why this invitation was the only one he'd been willing to accept. As uncomfortable as it was to admit, Pippa's loneliness had reached him. But Connie was the real draw.

"Then you may not realize that Anders and Kay Sheffield are the cream of Osprey Island society. The cream of New England, too, since it seems that they're planning to ferry over half of the region's population for the party. It's this Saturday. We're unveiling the maze that I've been working on for the past few years." Connie tilted her head at him, waiting for his reply with raised eyebrows.

He nodded.

"I redesigned and refurbished the estate's old maze from the time it was built in the 1920s," she prompted. "Kind of a big deal. The entire island is talking about it."

"I see."

One side of her mouth went up. "You're not impressed."

"I'm sure I would be if I saw it."

"I can wangle you an invitation to the garden party."

"Thanks, but I didn't come to the island to mingle," he said, ignoring the fact that he was doing just that.

"Why *did* you come?" She moved out of his line of sight to put the beer bottles on the table, returning with the front of her ribbed white cotton tank sporting three damp splotches that revealed the outline of a lace-edged bra. He looked away. Then back again. Her neck and bare shoulders were slender but strong, cinnamon freckled.

"Just a vacation," he said with a shrug. "I'm on leave from my job."

Connie's eyes were fixed on him, as bright and inquisitive as her daughter's. "Which is?"

"Which is what?"

Her mouth puckered. She knew he was stalling. "What do you do for a living?" she asked distinctly.

He gave in, knowing where this would lead. "I'm a Massachusetts state trooper."

Pippa's book dropped to her lap. Connie said, "Oh, boy."

"What?"

"My daughter's been a crime hound ever since she started reading the Trixie Belden books."

"Trixie who?

"She's like Nancy Drew."

Pippa scoffed. "But better."

"Nancy Drew, huh?" Harmless. "Isn't that sort of…"

"Old-fashioned?" Connie shrugged. "I suppose so, but my husband and I were always a little retro, not to mention poor. We haunted a lot of yard sales when Pippa was young. One day Phil brought home a set of Trixie Beldens."

"It's not my fault she won't let me watch *CSI*," Pippa said morosely from the corner.

"That's much too gruesome for a ten-year-old." Connie nudged Sean's arm as she brushed by. "You tell her. I'll get dinner on the table."

He said nothing. He wasn't thinking about Pippa and her mysteries but about Connie's missing husband. Phil.

I miss Daddy, she'd said, and he'd first thought that meant during their island stay. But the vibe was wrong. Probably not a case of divorce, either. Her tone had been mournful, not bitter.

He looked at Pippa, considering her lonely neediness.

Was Mr. Bradford dead?

Oh, shit.

Pippa pushed her glasses up her nose. She narrowed her eyes. "Do you solve crimes?"

"Not so much. I patrol. It's more a situation where I'm arresting suspects in the act, or right after the act." He refused to let his mind stray to that last, fatal traffic stop. "But once in a while I land in the middle of an interesting case and I get to do some investigating."

He'd tried to sound acceptable to a ten-year-old. Still, she sank back into the depths of the chair.

"I, uh, wear a uniform. The blue shirt and tie, the blue striped pants, the flat trooper hat. You know, the whole deal."

Pippa squinted. "Then you must not be a detective. Aren't they plainclothes?"

She was a smart one. He was a lieutenant. The next promotion would have been to detective lieutenant, but that was now derailed, perhaps permanently. A hard pill to swallow, given that his father had retired from the MSP with honors and that both of his older brothers and one sister were thriving in their law-enforcement careers, as well. His father wouldn't express shame, wouldn't express disappointment, over the way things had turned out for Sean.

But he'd felt it all the same because, no matter what the circumstances, no matter how necessary the shooting had been, there was no denying that Sean had failed. Yes, he'd gone by the book. The other man had fired first. There'd been no recourse but to defend himself and the mother and child. Still, in the back of his mind would always be the *what if*.

What if he'd done something, *anything,* differently— and prevented the fatality? What if another load of guilt hadn't landed on his shoulders?

Pippa was waiting for an answer. "A detective?" he repeated. "No, I'm not a detective."

"Too bad. Detectives are cool. I might want to be one."

"Then you'd better brush up on your surveillance skills. The object is to observe without being seen."

Pippa's face flamed. "I wasn't seen *every* time."

He gave her a point. "And it's hard to blend in on an island. Not enough cover."

"Do you do surveillance?"

"I have."

She leaned forward. "Would you teach me?"

"Oh, no, you don't," Connie said from the doorway. Behind her, the table was set with a steaming soup tureen, a large green salad and a basket of rolls. "Absolutely not, Pippa. You're in enough trouble as it is. Mr. Rafferty won't be encouraging your nonsense." She gave him a walleyed look. "Will he?"

"I…"

Pippa slid out of the chair. "Don't call it nonsense, Mom. That's not nice."

"Right you are." Connie set her hands on her hips. "Then Mr. Rafferty will not be encouraging your *preoccupation*. How's that? Better?"

"You're s'posed to support my interests." The girl sidled past Sean, her book—a vintage edition with a blond female on the cover—clutched to her chest. "Dad wouldn't be so mean."

Sean caught Connie's expression, a wince followed by relief. Maybe her husband wasn't dead, then.

"No, your dad would have been right there with you, making up stories about what Mr. Rozenkranz kept in his locked garden shed." Connie shared a fond smile with her daughter before glancing back to Sean. "Sorry. We've got issues. I'm afraid your being a cop is only going to stir the pot."

He held up his hands. "Don't worry. It's not something I'm looking to talk about."

She furrowed her brow before smiling. "Okay, then!

We'll have a nice New England chowder dinner without law and order as a side dish. How does that sound?"

"Relaxing," he said, and meant it.

Pippa dropped into a chair with such force she rattled the utensils. "Boring."

Connie's smile was determined. "Excellent. Just the way I like it."

Sean didn't believe her for a minute. The woman couldn't be boring no matter how hard she tried.

"I CAN'T HELP NOTICING your limp." Connie brushed away a tree branch that threatened to spring back at her face. Sean's hand flashed out to catch it. She looked over her shoulder at him. "Were you injured in the line of duty?"

He gave a reluctant nod. "Gunfire."

Her eyes widened. "How horrible."

"Yeah. Horrible." A touch of his hand to the small of her back got her moving again. He didn't want her watching him, especially with such a compassionate expression. "I'd stopped a car driving erratically, and the driver came out shooting."

He paused, uncertain how much he wanted to say. "Turned out he was an ex-con with a history of drug and spouse abuse. I took a round in the thigh before he went down."

Connie clenched her teeth. "Was anyone else hurt?"

Sean couldn't respond. Physically, the man's family had survived. But emotionally…? The loss of a father, even one who wasn't the best at the job, was not something a kid recovered from easily.

Connie glanced at his face and shuddered, obviously assuming the worst.

"I'm sorry that happened to you," she said softly as

they stepped out of the woods onto the manicured grounds of the Sheffield estate. Up ahead, Pippa trudged across a sloping lawn striated with shadows, heading toward the tall hedges of the maze. It looked ominous in the darkness, a gothic bulwark. Ornate cast-iron lampposts flanked dual entrances, on opposite sides of the maze.

"I'm trying not to dwell on the incident." He managed to swallow what felt like a stone in his throat. The dwelling was debatable, but certainly *incident* was too nice a word for the horror of seeing a man dead on the pavement—killed by Sean's gun—the wife streaked in her husband's blood as she wailed over his lifeless body.

Luckily, Connie was no longer watching his face. Her concern was with her daughter, who turned and waved at them to hurry. "Please don't mention the shooting to Pippa. Her imagination is already overdeveloped."

He wouldn't have, of course, but...

"It might do her good to realize that real police work isn't like a schoolgirl mystery."

"Maybe so." Connie frowned as Pippa disappeared into the maze. "Except that she's only ten years old and has already been through enough."

"I understand."

Connie started across the lawn. "Actually, no, you don't." She stopped suddenly and he had to pull up, his palm once more landing on her back, between her shoulder blades. He would have removed it, but she turned toward him with such a look of stark vulnerability that it was all he could do not to pull her into a comforting embrace.

A moment passed before she gathered herself to speak. Her shoulders squared. "I should have explained that my husband passed away. Leukemia. Two years and ten months ago, but Pippa hasn't been the same since his death. Probably never will be."

Connie's voice was low and swift; Sean inclined his head to catch every word.

"Her sleuthing is all tangled up with Phil's memory. He was the one who read her the Trixie books. And so this preoccupation with you…" Connie shook her head. "At first you were one of her 'suspects.' Now, well, I'm not sure what's going on in her head, considering your job. But I wanted you to have some idea—a warning, I guess—of why she's attached herself to you."

"I see."

"Has she said anything to you about—" Connie cut herself off. "I don't know why I'm asking a stranger for help."

"Am I still a stranger?"

Moonlight illuminated her face as she tilted it up toward his. Her eyes were dark green beneath her lashes, which drew spiked shadows across the curves of her cheeks. "No, I suppose not."

He brushed his fingers over her narrow back, feeling the warmth of her beneath the thin layer of fabric. They'd had a nice conversation over dinner, speaking only of normal things, like the weather and the island, the baseball season, where they'd been raised and gone to school, how much Pippa would enjoy the fifth grade if she gave it a chance. The girl hadn't been persuaded.

"You've been very nice about us intruding on your vacation," Connie said, "but Pippa may become an annoyance, especially now that she knows your profession. I'll do my best to keep her from invading your privacy. If she does, send her on her way. But be a little gentle about how you do it, okay?"

He looked at Connie's solemn face with the traces of sorrow that she couldn't hide, and he nodded.

"I'll watch out for your girl," he said. Then silently added *and you,* although if asked he'd have sworn that he didn't want the responsibility. And that he might never want the responsibility again, even if that meant quitting his job. He'd already let down enough people to fill a lifetime of regret.

"I'd be grateful. I suppose I worry too much, but considering what happened this morning, I feel justified. Unfortunately, my work's kept me from home too often. The trip to the island was supposed to bring us closer, but instead…" Connie sent Sean a rueful glance. "She's latched on to you. And is still carrying that damn notebook everywhere."

"What's with the notebook?"

"She writes down her observations. I don't read them."

Sean grinned, a little. He'd been a curious child, too. Not even his mother's threatening to snip off his nose with her sewing scissors had stopped him from poking into business that was none of his. "She's a smart girl."

"Too smart for her own good." Connie stepped away and called out to Pippa, telling her not to go deeply into the maze. She glanced from the hedges to the Sheffields' large shingle-style house and back to Sean. "Pippa's studied the plans at home and been through the maze a hundred times since we arrived, but never at night."

They had arrived at the entrance. The outer wall of boxwood hedges was seven feet tall, forming a solid bank in the dark. "It's impressive."

Sean could see Connie's pride in her work as she surveyed the formal gardens and maze. "I don't want to disturb the Sheffields, so we shouldn't stay long enough to walk it. But I wanted you to have a look."

He stepped inside the entrance and glanced down the corridors stretching away in three directions, criss-crossed by deep shadows. The openings onto the various courses appeared black. He flinched when Pippa appeared out of one of them, waved, and then was gone again, the soft crunch of her footsteps on the gravel path rapidly diminishing.

"How did you do this? I expected it to look newer. Shorter, I guess. Don't mazes take years to grow?"

"The Sheffields didn't want to wait that long. I worked with what was already here, clipping and re-planting, and we shipped over mature hedges to complete the new sections."

He whistled. "Must have cost a pretty penny."

"They can afford it. He's in finance." Connie lifted her chin toward the house, where music and laughter drifted from the terrace. The guests were having cock-tails by the sea. "We should go."

"Yes," Sean said, but he'd become intrigued in spite of his penchant for straight lines from A to B. He took the left-hand path and walked a short distance. "Is this a labyrinth or a maze?"

Connie followed. "You know the difference?"

"I remember solving maze puzzles as a kid. Laby-rinths have only one entrance/exit."

"We have two. It's a maze, not a labyrinth, which are unicursal, meaning they have only one path to follow. They're walked more for contemplation and insight, while mazes are a puzzle to solve. There are wrong turns, dead ends and always a goal to reach."

They had walked farther into the maze as she spoke,

with her following his lead without prompting him toward the correct turns to take. He led them to a dead end, where a statue of a garden nymph stood on a plinth, winking naughtily at them.

"Ah," Sean said. "I thought that taking only left turns was the way to solve a maze."

Connie smiled. "Not this one. I had to work within the parameters of the old design, and I didn't have as much acreage as I would've liked, but I still managed to design the maze to be as difficult as possible." Her eyes glinted with challenge. "All the more rewarding when you reach the center."

He looked at her, and around them the night seemed to swell and throb, as deep and mysterious as the sea. The sounds of the party and the relentless surf carried on at a distance, but he and Connie seemed enclosed in a bubble of silence and privacy and welling awareness.

He would have kissed her if she hadn't suddenly turned sharply away. She lifted her head, apparently hearing a sound his blood-filled ears had blocked out. "Pippa?" she called. "Are you near?"

The response was faint. "I'm here. At the center."

"Stay there." Sean caught the underlying thread of fear in her voice. "We're coming to get you."

CHAPTER FIVE

"WHAT DID YOU HEAR?" Sean asked under his breath as they sped through the maze.

Connie knew the pattern inside and out, and yet her heart raced as she cut a turn short, stopped, looked to the left, then to the right. The maze was laid out in an octagonal pattern. The paths were straight, but the turns were sharp, not a ninety-degree angle among them. Until now, she hadn't realized how menacing the arrow-like edges of green could seem, especially at night.

"I don't know," she said, moving on quickly. "Probably nothing." Her stomach revolted. "Maybe a footfall."

Sean squeezed her shoulder before saying in a raised voice, "Pippa, are you there? Gosh, I hope we're not lost." His tone was light, and Connie was grateful.

Pippa made no response. Was she gone? Playing a game?

"What's that?" Sean asked, trying to see over the top of the hedges. The splashing sound was maddeningly near, but unreachable, an effect Connie had engineered to frustrate the maze walkers.

She directed him to a turn that seemingly took them in the opposite direction. "It's the fountain at the center. We're almost there." His expression was dubious. "Trust me."

"Of course," he blurted after an awkward silence. "You know the way."

"Pippa?" she called. "Answer me."

Silence.

Connie rushed along the remaining path, and there was Pippa, standing beside the fountain with her eyes dancing and her hands clamped over her mouth. Her red hair fluffed out around her head, lit by the moon into an aureole. She giggled as if their run through the maze had been a good joke.

Connie patted her pounding chest. "*Pippa*. Why didn't you answer me?"

"I couldn't! I didn't want to ruin it for Mr. Rafferty."

"Well, you gave me a scare." Connie took a seat on one of stone benches interspersed with the topiaries and floral border that rimmed the center octagon. "I told you not to go so far." She wiped sweat away from the neckline of her tank. She didn't know why she'd become so frightened. Where had her motherly instinct gone when she'd been practicing meditation while her daughter was almost drowning at Whitlock's Arrow?

She stared at the two center entrances. "There's no one else in the maze, is there? Did you see anyone?"

Pippa flicked her fingers in the pool in the base of the fountain. "No, Mom."

Connie summoned a smile that felt as if it had been strained through a sieve. "I thought maybe one of the guests had snuck in for an advance tour."

Sean was watching her curiously. She closed her eyes for a moment, taking deep yoga breaths to calm herself. *Don't be silly. There was no one, and even if there had been, what was the harm? You've let Pippa's wild imaginings get to you.*

Connie stood and gestured briskly to round up the others. "Let's go. I really don't want to explain to the Sheffields why we're running the maze at midnight."

Sean checked the glowing dial of his watch. "It's only a few minutes past nine."

"That late? Pippa should be home in bed, especially after the day she's had." Connie looped an arm around her daughter's shoulders as they retraced the route through the maze. She strained to listen, but the sounds of their own footsteps were all she could hear.

Her eyes went to Sean. He must think she'd gone nutty, racing through the maze that way. She wouldn't have suggested the tour in the first place if he hadn't dropped his guard and their dinner together hadn't grown so cozy. Connie had been surprised by Pippa responding so openly, even admiringly, to Sean. She wondered if both of them were more prepared to let a new man into their lives than she'd believed.

"You really ought to see the maze in daylight," she ventured lightly. She wanted to show off for him.

He glanced back before returning her gaze. "I wouldn't mind solving it for myself."

Her blood warmed under his lingering, speculative look.

"I like the maze at night," Pippa said. "It's more spookier."

Connie pinched the end of her daughter's nose. "Enjoy it while you can, goblin. You won't be back, not in the dark."

They'd reached the far exit, where the lanterns gave off a comforting glow. Between them and the maze, the lights from the house stretched across the lawn. Beyond their reach, however, the woods seemed impenetrably thick. A garden shed was the only structure that gave civility to the wilderness. A rattletrap pickup was parked nearby, half-hidden in the woods. Graves's truck was always breaking down.

Unless it hadn't. Connie shivered at the thought of the dour gardener lurking in the dark.

"Do you still have your flashlight, Sean?" He'd brought one with him for the walk back to his cottage. Outside the village area near the harbor, the island had no streetlights.

"Yes." He pulled it out of his back pocket and clicked it on.

The narrow arc of light made the surrounding area even blacker, but Connie marched forward, determined not to give in to the heebie-jeebies. Pippa didn't need to see that.

They reached the guesthouse without a problem, and Connie sent Pippa up to bed. She waited until her daughter had reached the top of the stairs before turning to Sean with what felt like two extra tongues in her mouth. "I've got dessert, if you'd like to, uh, stay for a bit." Awkward. She was so out of practice.

He seemed cautious. "Sure."

"It's store-bought blueberry pie, but I can warm it up. And there's ice cream."

"Can I have some?" Pippa yelled from upstairs.

Connie called back, "I'll bring you a plate," before shrugging at Sean. "Sorry. There's no privacy in a house this small."

His gaze traced her lips. "Too bad."

She bolted for the kitchen. She'd once had boyfriends lined up in the hallway outside her dorm room, but it had been fourteen years since she'd settled on Philip Bradford as the love of her life.

She didn't know what to do with a man anymore, particularly a reserved, reluctant man. The type she used to tease and flirt into submission.

"Get hold of yourself," she muttered, scooping vanilla ice cream onto the pie.

Sean was sitting in the living room. She set two pie plates on the coffee table and excused herself to run up with Pippa's dessert. Her daughter had gotten into her pajamas and settled into bed, a narrow twin tucked under the eaves. *The Mystery on Cobbett's Island* was open on her lap.

"Here's your pie." Connie gave Pippa a peck on the forehead. "Brush your teeth after you finish, and then straight to sleep. No staying up late. You've read that book a half-dozen times already."

"It's my favorite. Trixie and Honey and their club go to an island. They get to sail and have a clambake and find a treasure map." Pippa dug into her pie, forking up huge bites. "I never thought I'd be on an island, too, just like the Bob-Whites."

"That doesn't mean there's also a mystery to solve."

Pippa grinned with blue teeth. "But there might be."

"Or you might invent one." Connie shook her head. "Don't borrow trouble, Pip. I've got enough going on."

She was at the door when Pippa stopped her. "You kinda like Mr. Rafferty, don't you?"

Connie nodded. "Don't you?"

"Yeah, he's okay. But I wish you'd let me ask him about crime stuff. How am I gonna learn?"

Since it was so good to see Pippa's enthusiasm, Connie acceded. "Maybe it'll be okay if you ask him a few questions. But don't be a nuisance. And no more following him around, you got that?"

"I can be his sidekick instead."

Oh, dear. Connie could imagine Sean's reaction to acquiring a four-foot, redheaded ball of questions as a constant companion. "I think you're missing the point, Pip. Mr. Rafferty seems to prefer his own company."

Pippa pushed her glasses up her snub nose. "But he stayed for pie."

That he had. "Yes, and I'd better go and keep him company. Good night, Pippa. Don't forget your prayers." Every night, without exception, Pippa asked God to bless her daddy. Hearing her little girl's plea used to break Connie's heart anew each time. Gradually, the harsh sense of loss had been replaced with warm memories tinged with aching sadness. They would never get over Phil's death, but maybe they were both finally ready to move forward to a future much different from the one they'd expected.

"I won't." Pippa licked her fork. "G'night, Mom."

A blue mood clung to Connie as she returned to the living room until the sight of Sean, lean and long-limbed and stretched out on the couch, jolted her out of it.

"You waited for me." She sat across from him, in the plaid chair, and picked up her plate. "Please dig in. The ice cream's melting."

They had dessert without discussion. Connie searched for something to say. She was intensely curious about his past—particularly the details of the shooting that he'd avoided—but she suspected he'd bolt if she got too pushy.

"Mmm-mmm, Maine blueberries," she finally said when her slice was reduced to crumbs and a few blue stains on the plate. "Is there anything better?"

He speared the last bite of his pie, eyeing it with

relish before popping the sweet morsel into his mouth. "Store-bought, you said? Sure tastes like homemade to me."

"Well, I guess it is, but not by me. You can buy fresh pies at Suzy Q's Bakery, the cute little shop next door to Lattimer's. I highly recommend their muffins, too."

"I'll keep that in mind."

She ran her eyes across him. "You could use a few extra pounds."

"Hospital food," he explained. "And I'm not much of a cook when I'm on my own. I do cans and takeout."

So his injury was that recent. Connie made an impulsive offer. "Come over for dinner anytime while you're on the island. I like to cook for—for people." She'd almost said *a man*, but felt strange about that at the last second. She hadn't cooked for any one man in particular, other than her family, since Phil.

"Aren't you busy with the garden?"

"Only wrapping up the final details, and then there's the party on Saturday. I always make sure I'm home for dinner with Pippa. Family meals were important to us when Phil was alive and I've tried to keep that going, even with just me and Pippa left." Connie furrowed her brow, aware that while she talked a good game, there had been a few too many late days at work in the past year.

"You miss him."

"Of course. But I'm not—*we're* not—" Her face knotted while she tamped down an unexpected spurt of grief…and guilt. "It's been almost three years. As impossible as it is to believe when you're in the worst of your grief, time mends. You adjust. You learn to live again."

"That's good to know," Sean said in a tone so distant it was almost as if he hadn't spoken at all.

Her gaze flew to his face. He was deep inside himself, but his pain was raw. Recognition struck her like a blow. She knew that pain well. She'd lived it.

"You feel guilty about the shooting," she guessed. As she'd vowed not to press him, the words were as gentle as she could make them. "You know what it's like to live through tragedy."

His features hardened. "Yes, but it's not the same as what happened to you. I didn't lose a family member or a loved one. The man I shot was a criminal. He might have killed me if I hadn't acted."

"That doesn't mean you can't feel sorrow for him."

"It was—" Sean winced. "His family. He had a family."

"Ah-h."

"A little boy." Although Sean's voice was clipped, very close to detached, the eyes he raised to hers betrayed his desolation. "He was in the car."

"Oh, no." Connie began to understand why Sean seemed so torn up inside. Her heart ached. "I'm so sorry for him, but you couldn't help that. You weren't responsible."

Sean shook his head. He pulled back. "It's late. I ought to go."

Connie rose with him. "Don't go." She reached out a hand, caught his arm. "Look, I'm sorry. I didn't mean to turn this into a pity party. Stay and we'll talk about nicer things, like, oh, I don't know…summertime and schoolgirl shamuses."

"Schoolgirl sham— What? I don't get you."

She chuckled, even though humor felt out of place. "That's something from Pippa's books. She goes around saying she wants to be a schoolgirl shamus like Trixie. A girl detective."

Connie sat, hoping that Sean would follow suit. She filled the room with chatter to lighten the mood. "We've had an interesting time of *that,* I can tell you. The past spring, Pippa thought our neighbor was fencing stolen goods out of his garden shed, all because she saw a couple of leather-jacketed guys leave with a microwave and CB radio. Apparently in the 1950s world of schoolgirl shamuses, anyone who wears a leather jacket is a hood."

"Did you explain profiling to her?"

"I pointed out that everyone wears leather these days." Connie picked up her coffee cup. Finally, Sean sat and did the same. She smiled at him over the rim. "Mr. Rozenkranz caught her in his shed with a flashlight and her notebook, taking down serial numbers. It turned out he was buying and selling items on eBay."

Sean nodded. "Uh-huh. Ninety-five percent of the time, the obvious explanation is the right one."

"I wish you'd explain that to Pippa. She's gone past normal curiosity to inventing wild scenarios about everyone we meet."

"Yeah, I noticed. She's a handful."

"I haven't been as strict with her as I should have, I suppose. She was so withdrawn after losing her father that the interest in detecting seemed like a good thing. At least it was something to occupy her, you know?"

"She'll get over it," Sean said. "The overenthusiasm, I mean."

"How did you become a state trooper?"

"Family tradition. My father was a decorated member of the force, and I've got three older siblings on the job, as well. Dylan, the youngest, is the only rebel. If you call being a computer analyst radical. He does play in a rock and roll band on the weekends."

"Then you're not the oldest. I wouldn't have guessed that."

"Nope, I'm number four out of five. What about you?"

"I was an only child. But I had two boisterous male cousins who lived on the same street as us. I was younger, but I wanted to hang out with them all the time, except it was a struggle to keep up and be heard around them and their friends." Although her cousins lived in separate states, many miles away, they were still close. Both had been there for her every time she needed them in the past several years. They doted on Pippa. She called them her uncles.

Sean looked at Connie approvingly. "I'll bet you managed."

"Sure." Her grin was cocky. "I held my own."

"Pippa's got a lot of you in her. She'll do okay."

He sounded so certain. "I didn't know you two had gotten to know each other that well."

"I wouldn't say that. It was an astute observation."

"Astute?" Connie laughed. "Well, whatever it was, I'm encouraged. Pippa used to be more outgoing. Maybe she's getting some of that back." In her heart, Connie knew that her child would always bear the scar of losing her father.

"Tell me," he said, leaning forward to set his mug on the table. He left his elbows on his knees. "What frightened you, up at that maze?"

She covered her face with a hand. "I feel foolish about that. I'm sure it was nothing."

"No, don't let second thoughts curb your first reaction. Tell me what happened."

"All right." Connie rubbed her forearms. "All I know is that first, a feeling that we weren't alone came over me. Then I thought I heard a footstep. Just one, which was the odd part, as if the person was being stealthy. What would it matter if someone else had been in the maze, walking it the way we were?"

"It wouldn't, unless they weren't supposed to be there."

"Exactly my thinking at the time. Now I realize it was probably one of Kay's guests. She wants to keep them out of the maze until the unveiling at the party, when she'll do the whole cutting-of-the-ribbon thing, with a prize for the fastest to complete the maze." Connie shrugged. "The noise I heard had to be a houseguest, looking for an advantage. I overreacted."

"You thought Pippa was in danger."

"That's putting it too strongly. Mothers worry—a lot. Plus, it was dark. I just wanted Pippa with me."

Sean nodded. "Okay. That makes sense."

The house creaked. They both jerked up their heads to listen, then Connie laughed. "Now we're all doing it! Next thing, we'll be joining Pippa on the trail of the Mystery of the Midnight Maze."

"It's still not midnight," Sean teased. "But it *is* getting late. Time for me to head back to Pine Cone Cottage."

Connie followed him to the door. "How long are you planning to stay on Osprey?"

"I've got the cottage for two weeks."

"Lucky you. When I saw how beautiful the island was after my early visits, I looked into the housing situation in case I wanted to return for a real vacation. There are so few cottages available. There's the Whitecap Inn, but it's booked all season, a year in advance."

"No kidding?" He opened the screen door and stepped down into the pool of light cast by the outdoor fixture, an old-fashioned hanging lantern like the ones at the maze and the front gate. "I guess I really was lucky, then. It was only about three weeks ago, right after I was released from the hospital, that I came across the listing on a Web site that arranges house swaps. Vacations Away, it was called."

Sean stopped, but she nodded for him to go on. "Alice Potter, the owner of the cottage, is spending the two weeks at a luxury resort condo that belongs to my parents. It's got everything—restaurants, golfing, riding, swimming, night clubs, a spa."

"Fancy. Why didn't you use *that* instead?"

He wrinkled his nose. "I know too many people there. I was looking for privacy and quiet."

The unspoken words were tangible: *Time to heal.*

Inside and out, Connie had come to believe.

"I understand." She let the screen door close between them. Being thrown together in a heightened situation had escalated her emotions, maybe even her attraction to him. Now was a good time to pick up on his broad hint and take a step back. "Which means I probably should apologize again for Pippa's intrusions." She pursed her lips. "And mine."

A brown moth pattered at the mesh. "That's okay," Sean said easily. "I didn't mind."

Connie was surprised at that. At first she wondered if he was only being polite, but he looked flummoxed by his own words.

"Actually," he added, "I've enjoyed it."

"I'm glad, because we're certain to run into each other again. Osprey is a very small island."

"I'm certain we will." Sean put one hand up against hers, touched her fingertips through the screen, then pulled away. He glanced into the forest. "Thanks for dinner."

"Thanks for the rescue." For a couple of seconds,

Connie felt as if her heart had stopped—but, no, it hadn't. She was fine, just fine. Everything was normal. Ordinary.

Extraordinary, she thought as she watched Sean leave, following the wavering path of the flashlight.

Suddenly everything was magnified. The spicy, woodsy smell of the outdoors had sharpened. The sky glittered with a zillion stars. Sean Rafferty thrilled her, and she could feel herself coming alive, or at least more alive than she'd been for years. Conscious of every heartbeat, of the shape of her lips, even the tingling roots of her hair.

Oh, Phil!

Pippa Bradford's Book of Curious Observations

QUESTIONS TO INVESTIGATE:

1. Who was in the maze? I heard him before Mom did. Could have been a woman. Mom says a houseguest and she's probably right. I think somebody was learning the maze pattern so they could win the prize at the party. But what if that wasn't it? What if Mr. Sheffield buried something important, like maybe even a body, in the maze while it was all dug up? Now that Mom's done, no one will dig under the hedges again for years and years, like maybe a century. It would be the perfect grave.

Check on Missing Persons!!!

2. Is Mr. Rafferty really a policeman? Mom believes everything he said, but he could still be a criminal for all we know. Or he might be on the island undercover to track someone down. Why did he want to see the maze in secret instead of at the party? What if his real name isn't even Rafferty? He could have bonked the real Rafferty in the head and gave him

amnesia so he could take his place in Pine Cone Cottage, like in *The Mystery of the Missing Heiress.* Except I don't know why. Continue survailance.

3. Does Mom have romantic feelings for Mr. Rafferty??? I couldn't tell for sure because I had to run and jump back into bed before Mom saw I was eavesdropping, but I think they might have kissed when he was leaving. That's just gross.

CHAPTER SIX

A SOFT FOG HUNG at the edges of the harbor and surrounding streets. Connie felt as though she and Pippa were walking into a watercolor painting as they descended the hill toward Lattimer's General Store. Except this painting had sound effects. The lap of the waves on the pilings and rocks was punctuated by the clanging buoy and the gulls' raucous cries as they wheeled above the arriving ferry. Its horn cut through the misty morning postcard scene.

"There's the first boat," Connie said. "Let's hurry."

She took Pippa's hand and swung it as they sped up to beat the crowd of incoming tourists. She was pleased that her daughter was still young enough to enjoy a public display of affection from her mom. Some of Pippa's classmates were already acting like teenagers, with skimpy outfits, cell phones, designer purses and the snotty attitudes that often seemed like a required accessory. Every day that Pippa stayed a little girl was a precious thing.

Connie gave her daughter a brief, hard hug as they climbed the wooden steps into the store. As soon as the maze job was through, she'd devote all of her time to Pippa. "The Sheffields have invited us to stay over in their guesthouse for as long as we like, after the party.

Do you want to? I can put off my other clients for an extra three or four days."

Pippa bounced up and down. "Yay!"

"We'll do everything together—clamming, hiking, picnicking." They entered the store and waved to the proprietors, Edgar, a gruff old salt, and his equally taciturn wife, Lou. "We can rent bikes and take a kayak lesson and sleep late…" *Invite Sean over,* Connie added impulsively at the first sight of him standing near the cash register. He was *not* her reason for extending their stay. But he was a pretty big bonus.

"Can we have a clambake, like the B.W.G.s did on Cobbett's Island?" B.W.G. stood for Bob-Whites of the Glen, Trixie Belden's club of mystery mavens.

"I don't know about that," Connie said, distracted by the butterfly wings batting around her hollow stomach. She wanted to blame them on lack of nourishment. Low blood sugar. Party nerves. Anything but what it was. She couldn't accept that Sean might be the rare man she needed, but hadn't been looking for. Not yet.

Pippa spotted Sean and bounded over to him. "Hi, Mr. Rafferty." She poked her nose into the basket he'd rested on the edge of the counter. "What are you buying?"

"Pip, that's intrusive." Connie hurried over and caught her daughter by the braids, using them to steer the girl toward the aisles jammed with a variety of goods, from just-picked fruit to leather shoelaces. "Here's our list. Go shop."

"Morning, Pippa," Sean said easily. "Connie." His slight grin tilted to one side. "I picked up a dozen blueberry muffins at the bakery next door. Someone told me they were good."

"So are we," Connie answered. "I mean, getting the

muffins." The fresh baked goods would sell out fast as soon as the day-trippers disembarked the ferry and swarmed Suzy Q's. "We're planning to go and sit on the harbor wall with our breakfast. Want to come?"

Sean slid his wallet into the back pocket of his jeans and took the brown bag of his groceries, the white box from the bakery and a tall, lidded paper cup. Even the Lattimers, who avoided the mainland and its newfangled inventions like the plague, had seen the profit margin in charging double for a latte as opposed to an ordinary coffee. Finally he said, "I've got nothing else to do."

Connie blinked.

An instant later, Sean winced. "Sorry." He replaced his basket in the stack by the door. "That didn't come out right. What I meant was that I'm free to linger over muffins with you and the gulls for as long as I'd like."

"Not if the gulls have anything to say about it." Feeling ridiculously giddy at his warmer response, Connie turned away. "I'll get Pippa. We'll do our grocery shopping later."

In minutes they were sitting with their legs dangling over the stacked-stone seawall, choosing muffins from the bakery box. Connie doled out napkins and a bottle of juice for Pippa, who'd plopped herself in the middle and was chattering to Sean about digging for clams.

"You look for the bubbles in the sand. But I don't know, I think I'd rather dig up a diamond than a slimy old clam. Trixie and Honey did, but that was in the Wheeler's gatehouse, not at the beach."

"I doubt a diamond would turn up." Sean rubbed a finger over his top lip, trying not to smile. "But maybe you'd find an ancient gold coin if you were very, very lucky. There *are* shipwrecks in these waters."

"Don't encourage her," Connie said with a laugh. "Anyway, given the level of income along Cliff Road, a diamond ring lost on the beach is more likely than a pirate treasure."

Pippa flipped open her notebook to the first page, where she'd written down all of the Trixie Belden mystery titles and made checkmarks by the ones she'd read. "*The Mystery of the Ghostly Galleon* is number twenty-seven. I don't have that one yet."

"We live our life according to Trixie," Connie said to Sean over her daughter's head.

"Right," he said, still mystified by the obscure references to the girl detective. He angled to read the notebook's rippled cover. "Pippa Bradford's Book of Curious…?"

Scowling, Pippa clutched it to her chest. "Observations."

Connie squeezed her coffee cup. *Don't tease her, Sean. Please don't tease her.* Pippa took herself seriously and was gravely disappointed in adults who dismissed her interests as silly and childish. Even her mother walked a fine line between discouraging and encouraging, particularly in Pippa's eyes.

"Observational skills are very important to a detective." Sean pointed at the wharf. "Study that scene for sixty seconds, Pippa. Then close your eyes and tell me what you saw."

"I've done this game before, lots of times. Time me."

Sean raised his watch. "Go."

While her daughter stared intently at the activity on the wharf, Connie broke off a chunk of muffin and popped it into her mouth. She could feel Sean looking at her, but she kept her face turned toward the sea. Sunshine danced on the water.

Too soon, she told herself. *Too fast.* She'd moved quickly with boyfriends before her friendship with Phil had grown into romance. *That* was what she should be looking for—if she looked at all—not an instant attraction.

Sean was holding out a plump blueberry muffin. "Have another."

She realized hers was already gone. There were crumbs all over her sweater. "No, thanks," she said, brushing them off. "I'm finished."

Finished? Not even. For a moment, she'd almost had herself convinced she was a goner, and with very little encouragement from Sean. But what did she really know about him, except that he was kind to children and on the right side of the law?

"Time," he announced. "All right, Pippa, close 'em and tell me. I want details."

"Oh, boy." Pippa squeezed her eyes shut and took a deep breath. "The ferry is named *The Blue Jenny* and its serial number, or whatever you call it, is SRG1855F. A man in a green shirt and jeans was coiling the ropes on the dock and there were two boys with fishing poles..."

Pippa rattled on. Sean kept nodding. Connie shut her eyes. She tilted her face as if she were simply basking in the sun. Inwardly, her mind was racing.

Details? I'm thirty-three and a widow. I have a little house with a big mortgage, a daughter who is finally coming out of her shell and a business that keeps us afloat, but just that, even though my prospects are good.

She glanced at Sean. *Maybe even very good, if I don't get too far ahead of myself.*

I miss my husband. I'll always miss him. But I have to admit that there's something about Sean, something that reaches inside and twists me into knots every time I look at him.

Mothering instinct, she tried to tell herself. For all his competence and control, he was a wounded bird.

But she knew that wasn't it, not entirely. There was no decent explanation except plain and simple attraction, whether or not she was ready for it. So why not count the next few days as a time to enjoy herself? After working so hard, she was entitled, and there'd be plenty of time for Pippa after the garden party, as she'd planned.

There was no rule that said she had to fall in love with the first man since Phil who gave her Houdini knots. Especially one who'd made his preference for solitude clear.

"Not bad," Sean said, sounding as though isolation was the last thing on his mind, "but can you stand up to questioning?"

Misgivings tugged at Connie. *Stand up to questioning? I'd rather not. Because then I'd have to admit that I once had a husband who was brave and kind and loving and there's no way on God's green earth that I can ever replace him.*

The knots tightened briefly before giving way. *Certainly not with Sean.*

Unaware of her inner turmoil, he went on, addressing Pippa. "What color are the boat buoys tied to the pilings? What about the bait bucket? How many smokestacks does the ferry have?"

"How many? One, of course! I think it's one." Pippa's face scrunched in concentration. "The buoys are...blue. The bucket is white."

"Take a look."

"They're red," Pippa blurted. "Red stripes. But I was right about the stack and the bucket." Her head bobbed. "How'd I do?"

"Better than average." Sean's eyes went to Connie. "I should have tested your mom, too. But I don't think she was concentrating as well as you."

Pippa giggled. "Were you, Mom?"

Connie's cheeks felt warm, like a beacon of guilt. "My mind wandered."

"You should practice like me, in case you're ever a witness to a crime and have to testify in court."

"I'm not planning on that, honey, but if it should happen I'll cope. My vision's twenty-twenty."

"Pippa's right," said Sean. "Most eyewitnesses are notoriously unreliable."

"See, Mom?" Pippa scrambled to her feet, brandishing her notebook. "I'm gonna go to the wharf and look closer. Can I, Mom?"

"Yes, you may, as long as you promise to keep out of the way of the fishermen."

Sean watched Pippa skip away before he turned and squinted into the sun. "She's got spirit. My dad would say it's the ginger hair."

Connie blinked. Sean was right. Pippa was more like her old self since they'd come to the island. As a mother, she was thrilled with the change, but…

"Phil used to call her Pippa Pepperpot." Connie used her husband's name deliberately. To keep him present. To remind herself. And Sean, also, if he thought it would be easy to take on a widowed mother and child.

He probably hadn't.

"Cute."

Connie glanced at Sean. "Thanks, anyway, for not

giving her the brush-off." She crumbled the remains of her daughter's muffin and tossed it to the gulls. They converged, squawking greedily. "My mother keeps asking when Pippa's going to play with fashion dolls or dress hair like the other girls."

He took out a pair of sunglasses. "Is that what girls do?"

"Most of them." Connie leaned forward on her arms to watch the water lap at the wet mossy stone. His sunglasses made her nervous again; she couldn't tell where he was looking. "I was a tomboy despite my mother's best efforts to turn me into a china doll." She swung her legs. "I liked dodgeball and street hockey and digging in our garden with my dad. I was so disappointed to get figure skates for Christmas when I dreamed of being the first girl to play in the NHL."

"I lived for hockey as a kid. Did you play kick the can?"

"Till nightfall, and sometimes longer, if my mother didn't realize I was still out." Connie's smile thinned. "Pippa stays indoors too much." She'd clung to her father, especially in his last few years, then holed up like a wounded animal after he'd passed on. "That's why I thought this trip would be good for her."

"I guess it was." Sean gestured. "Look at her."

Out on the wharf, Pippa was in the middle of the action, walking and talking with a man who lugged a lobster trap toward the ramps that led to the moored boats. Probably looking for clues to pirate ships or smuggler's bounty.

"Yeah," Connie breathed. She blinked away a film of tears. *That*—her daughter—was what she should be concerned with. Not an island flirtation. "Look at her."

After a minute, Sean said, "She can come by my place anytime."

The offer was startling. Connie blinked hard, supposing that he felt sorry for them. "Thanks and all, but you might want to reconsider. You do realize that you've become Pippa's hero, right? She might not leave you alone."

"I already said, I'm no hero." He softened the bluntness. "At least I don't seem to be her suspect anymore."

Connie chuckled even though Sean's curt denial continued to bother her. Why did he recoil? Was it only because of what had happened on his job, or was it a personal issue, too? "I'm not guaranteeing *that*. Pippa sees mysteries everywhere."

And Sean, solitary and less then forthcoming, was potentially a good puzzle to solve. Maybe more for Connie than her daughter, despite her best intentions.

She knew he hadn't fully dealt with the shooting incident, so feeling less then heroic made some kind of sense, given his burden of guilt. Still, she suspected he'd been more of one than he allowed.

Someday, if they ever got to really know each other, she would share her hard-earned knowledge that the mental recovery always took longer than the physical. But that it helped to have a hand to reach for, a steady arm to lean on.

She pulled up her legs, remembering how she'd felt shattered from Phil's death, even after she'd dragged herself out of bed and gone on with the outer trappings of life, much to the relief of her family and friends. "I ought to go and collect Pippa so we can head home. I've got work waiting."

Sean helped her to her feet. "I'll get this," he said, collecting the remains of their breakfast.

Connie dusted off the seat of her khaki cargo pants,

wishing she'd packed nicer clothes instead of practical ones. The pants weren't stylish. They made her look a little too squat and lumpy, but the extra pockets were handy on the job. The rest of her wardrobe was equally hopeless. She'd lost the impulse to dress "cute." The one nice outfit she'd brought along was Lena's.

At the wharf, she and Sean crossed paths with the Sheffields. Connie made introductions.

"We're on our way to our yacht," Kay said in her pinched "lady of the manor" voice. On several occasions, Connie had heard her slip and yell at the staff in a down-home Texas accent. "Going shopping on the mainland. I simply must have a few new things for the weekend events."

Anders twisted a heavy platinum watch at his wrist, bored. "Women."

"Oh, Andy," Kay chided. "You know you love to indulge me."

"You like to indulge yourself." He glanced at Connie. "I hope the rest of that pile of gravel will be out of the way by this afternoon. We have more guests arriving."

"I'm having the last of it spread today at the center of the maze. As we speak, in fact." She'd given orders to Graves to oversee the workers she'd hired, knowing he couldn't be counted on for the physical labor. "I'm just about to head off to check on the progress."

"The garden must be perfect." The wind caught at the silk scarf Kay had tied around her hair. "We're holding a dinner party this evening at Peregrine House. Please come, both of you." She ran an appreciative eye over Sean. "Cocktails and nibbles at eight. We'll watch the sunset from the widow's walk, then go downstairs for a casual buffet dinner."

Sean muttered something that sounded like a refusal, but Kay insisted. "You must be there. We're always desperate for fresh faces on this boring old island, and besides, Connemara needs an escort. You'll do very well." She glanced at Connie. "Don't you agree?"

Anders hurried Kay away before Connie and Sean were forced to answer. She half expected him to back out, but he turned to her with an amused expression.

"Connemara?"

"Oh, that. My full name. I guess Kay thinks it sounds more impressive or something. She can be pretentious."

"She tries hard to be," he observed, watching the Sheffields pick their way toward the marina, apparently squabbling as they went. Kay's raised voice briefly caught on the wind. "Don't accuse me when you're the one who gave away my..." She tried to flounce off but could only totter down the ramp in her high heels. Their yacht was anchored in deep water, and they would have to take a launch to reach it.

"She's going to gouge holes in the deck with those shoes," Sean commented with a trace of disdain.

"There's Pippa." Connie waved to her daughter on the wharf and called, "Time to go!" Reluctantly, Pippa put away her pen, closed the notebook and trudged toward them.

"About the dinner party." Connie kept her hand up, shading her eyes. Sean's head turned. Behind the dark lenses, he was apparently studying her. Her stomach, full of blueberry muffin, still managed to flutter. "You don't have to go."

"I'll pick you up a few minutes before eight, *Connemara*." His smile deepened the hollows below his cheekbones. "My good old Irish da' would never approve of me ditching a girl named after a district of the Emerald Isle."

PEREGRINE HOUSE was an immense structure covered in cedar shingles weathered to a soft dove-gray. With a massive central hall, double wings and a widow walk on the mansard roof, it loomed over the southeastern cliffs, offering a spectacular overview of the Atlantic side of the island, from the high point of Whitlock's Arrow toward the southernmost bay of the harbor.

Leaning over the railing of the widow's walk, Sean scanned the thick forest that hid most of the village from view. Feeling rather grumpy about his impulse to play Connie's gentleman escort, he said, "I'd feel like a king, too, if I lived here."

Connie glanced away from Anders Sheffield, who'd greeted her and Sean with a bluff hello and handshake before dismissing them. "The master of all you survey?" she asked lightly.

Sean's gaze traced her face. She was startlingly pretty in a scanty floral dress with a moss-colored sweater tied around her neck, but it was her eyes that drew him. They glowed in the early evening light like the rows of hurricane lamps placed along the lip of the railing. "Something like that."

"And I'm only a serf."

"No, *he's* a serf." Sean pointed at the figure riding a lawnmower toward the shed tucked away among the trees. Graves, the gardener. "You're a…"

"Jumped-up serf," Connie said with a laugh, taking a cocktail off the tray of a circulating waiter. She handed it to Sean and reached for another. They clinked glasses. "To those who serve."

He looked around them, at the upscale party. *So* not his style, according to his ex. That it was a style she'd wanted to be accustomed to went a long way toward explaining their divorce.

He shrugged. "The maids? The waiters?"

Connie nodded. "Why not?" But then she added, "To those who serve and protect," while looking at him with her large eyes.

Gulp. That did him in, as surely as anything could. He'd always been a sucker for the pure of heart, especially a woman who was willing to show genuine, unadorned emotion, even when it wasn't fashionable.

"Protect from root rot," he said. He'd come to Osprey for solitude, not solace. He didn't want to *feel*. He sure as hell didn't want to let someone new into his heart.

Connie blinked. "Root rot, huh?"

Sean sipped. He didn't recognize the cocktail, but it was as cold and sharp as an icicle. The inside of his throat was seared. A good explanation for the grating sound of his voice. "Right. Root rot."

"Yes, and black spot. Very bad, that black spot." She chuckled, prodding him. "I hope you don't have black spot. Lift an arm, let me see."

"My black spots are well hidden."

At least, he'd thought they were. She had a way of turning over his leaves to let the sunshine in.

Playfully, Connie poked a finger into his chest. "Never mind. A squirt of fungicide would cure you."

"Or kill me."

"Not you." She took a tiny sip, then puckered her

glossy lips in thought, making them look like a ripe, dewy raspberry. "You've got deep roots."

He laughed, feeling less than comfortable. He didn't give a fig about the party and its ritzy guests, but perhaps a little too much about Connie. "Uh, hey there, I'm not the one named after the old sod."

"I was actually named after the ponies, if you can believe it. Irish Connemara ponies—they're tough and sturdy. My mother was laid up during the final month of her pregnancy, and she and Dad watched a documentary on TV. He insisted the name would make me strong." Connie smiled into the martini glass. "The family joke is that I'm lucky they didn't watch a show about the potato famine instead. My cousins still sometimes call me Spud."

"Spud, huh? That's cute."

She wrinkled her nose. "I hated it, growing up."

They moved away from the railing, took napkins and hors d'oeuvres from a different waiter. "Not so bad," Sean said after downing a mouthful of salmon topped with caviar.

Connie concentrated on the flavors. "Mmm…I could get used to it."

A woman turned. "Yeah, well, try the bluepoint oysters first." She made a face. "Even with the horse-radish, it's like swallowing mucus. And those gooey little rubber things? Jellyfish. Seriously."

Connie snorted laughter behind a crumpled napkin. "Good evening, Mrs. Crosby. I'd like you to meet Sean Rafferty. Sean, this is Jillian Crosby, an old friend of Kay's."

"Jilly. Everyone calls me Jilly." The tall blonde stuck out her hand and shook his with a firm grip. "My hubby,

Hal, is around here somewhere. We're from Vegas. What about you?"

"Worcester, Massachusetts, originally," Sean answered, feeling the need to straighten his already upright posture. The woman seemed liable to say anything, but he rather liked her for that. The hard, shiny facade of most of the guests had put him off. Likewise, it bugged him that Connie seemed to want to impress them. It shouldn't have, seeing as that was her business, but it did.

Jilly tilted forward on her high heels, running a quick, evaluating eye over him. "Wooshter? Never heard of it, but you two look like the only fun couple here." She glanced around at the other guests before lowering her voice. "What a bunch of stuffed shirts. Now I know why Kay begged me to come. Someone's got to liven up this joint."

Connie started to say, "We're not a coup—" but was interrupted by Jilly.

"I'd suggest we liberate a bottle of Cristal and go streaking buck-nekkid through the maze, except then Anders would seriously kill me. He and Kaylene have already had one go-round today, so I'd better not cause another." Jilly giggled, perhaps having already liberated one cocktail too many. "But I *am* dying to get into that maze."

Connie smiled politely. "Have you sneaked a peek yet?" Sean knew she was thinking of the previous night's unidentified trespasser.

"Nope, but I took a real good look from up here." Jilly strolled to the railing and leaned over it, swaying like a reed. "Is that cheating?"

Sean looked down, past the slate roof and the formal garden to the shadowed maze. At this lofty vantage point, the overall pattern was clear, although the angle and the growing darkness saved the correct route from being obvious without intense study. "How much of the maze will you remember by tomorrow morning?"

"Good question!" Jilly lifted her cocktail and laughed loudly, drawing a glare from Kay. "So maybe I ought to ink me a cheat sheet on my palm the way I used to in my high school history class." She squinted at them, waving a hand. "Either of you got a pen?"

Sean patted the inside pocket of his sports coat. "Sorry, no."

"Not me," said Connie, and Jilly wandered off, calling at random for a writing utensil until she ran into a suited man who appeared to be under fifty. He offered her a cigarette instead and soon she forgot all about her plan.

"Didn't you want to object?" Sean asked Connie. "You seem protective of the maze's secrets."

"I'd rather Jilly won the prize than the rest of them." Connie dropped to a whisper. "Because she's right. These people are stuffed shirts."

The corners of his mouth twitched. What relief—she wasn't like his ex-wife. "Then what are we doing here?"

"I thought you wanted to come."

"Not especially. I thought you did."

She hesitated. "It *is* my job." A shrug. "Although not my favorite part. I'm still an earth-grubber at heart." The waiter swooped a tray under her nose and she took a tiny cup of fluted crust, then looked closer beneath a sprig of green herb. "Oh, no. It's the jellyfish." Her mouth drew into a sour pucker. "I just can't."

He laughed. "Toss it over the railing."

She looked tempted. "Someone might see."

"Allow me." He took the tidbit and made a motion toward the railing that turned her eyes into saucers. Her alarm became delight when he popped it into his mouth instead. One crunch and he bit into a salty, rubbery goo.

His stoic expression must have broken because she hurriedly passed him a drink. "Wash it down." She was smiling. "Don't tell me you're not a hero. That was absolutely chivalrous."

"No, that was called taking a bullet for…" He stopped. "I was…only trying not to embarrass you."

Connie looked at him sympathetically. He hated sympathy. He didn't want it, or deserve it, yet he'd gotten way too much of it. Osprey Island was supposed to be his refuge from all of that. He wished he'd followed his first instincts and kept to himself.

When he was alone, he had no one but himself to account for. With Connie, nice as she was, there was a high probability that what started out with a simple gesture, like swallowing jellyfish, would end as badly as the rest of his commitments. Divorce, separation, death, disappointment.

Not the sort of track record she deserved.

Connie took his hand, oblivious. She turned toward the short railing that capped the half wall of the widow's walk. "It's getting late." While most of the sky remained a deep cobalt-blue, the treetops had begun to shimmer in the subtle golden-pink glow that filled the western horizon. "Sunsets must be really pretty on your side of the island."

"I, uh, I guess I haven't noticed." Too busy wallowing in misery. Self-indulgent misery.

Enough of that.

Connie squeezed his hand. "You should look."

"I am," he promised, keeping his gaze high when what he really wanted to look at was her. Instead, he released her hand and did a one-eighty, fists shoved in his jacket pockets as he ignored the other guests and the elegant setting in favor of the raw minimalism of the ocean. Blue-bottomed cumulus clouds hung low in the sky, mounded high on top like meringue on a pie. The wind was light. Several sailboats slipped through the darkening waves, tacking toward home.

Home. He thought of holing up at Pine Cone Cottage, alone, and the concept was no longer as appealing as it once had been. But that didn't mean he was ready to risk a relationship with Connie, who needed more than he could give. If he was going to play the hero, he'd start with his own son.

The cocktail hour had wound down, with guests heading toward the staircase. Connie hung back with Sean. "Dinner must have been called." She smoothed her windblown hair. "We'd better go in."

"Do we have to?"

"You're a bad influence." She gave him a shrug. "But you're in luck—Kay mentioned that it's a buffet. We might even get away before the sun has fully set."

"Good. I've had enough of these people."

Connie stuck out her chin as they walked past a couple of the waiters standing at attention with half-empty trays. "You didn't even try. Some of them are very nice."

"Like the guy who thought a 10-49 was a tax form?"

"What *is* a 10-49?"

"The code for wrong-way traffic."

"Heavens. I think I need to give you a lesson on proper cocktail party conversation."

"I've got to warn you," Sean said. "I'm not the

fancy-party type." And never would be, if that was what she wanted.

She only laughed as they descended the enclosed spiral staircase. "You have no idea of the irony of me teaching any kind of etiquette. I used to have absolutely no sense of propriety. My husband always said I'd talk doctrine with a ditchdigger and earthworms with the Pope."

"Is there something wrong with that?"

"Not really." She'd stopped to glance down a long hallway to the landing, which opened to the vast foyer with whitewashed beams and an oversize blackened iron chandelier. The other dinner guests had all vanished, but their chatter rose like the squabble of the gulls in the harbor.

"But it proves that I've come a long way," Connie added, without much enthusiasm.

Sean stepped up beside her and took her arm. "To dinner," he said. "Unless you're willing to commit a 10-49 with me."

CHAPTER SEVEN

THE BUFFET WAS NOT LIKE the noodle casserole, ham roll and Jell-O salad spreads that Connie had grown up with. The silver and crystal were elegant. The food was almost too beautiful to eat. But she was grateful they weren't having an interminable and pretentious six-course meal.

A waiter appeared to whisk away her plate as soon as she finished a portion of an obscure fish in an even more obscure sauce. Connie checked her borrowed silk dress for spots, then looked around the room for Sean, more interested in talking to him than any of the guests, aside from one older man who'd spouted Latin plant names at her and had tucked her business card inside his cigarette case.

She walked from room to room, sipping wine, feeling lucky to enjoy such a magnificent home. There were brick fireplaces with old master oil paintings over the mantels and tall windows that boasted stunning ocean views. Wide-plank wood floors were waxed and buffed to a honey glow and covered with muted Oriental rugs. The furnishings were solid antiques, with large comfy couches and chairs upholstered in white cotton duck or faded chintz. Plaster walls had been painted the softest hues she'd ever seen—mottled cream, the silvery green of moss, a soft seashell-pink—and hung with sepia photographs of Edwardian picnics and three-masted schooners.

Yet for all the home's beauty, it made her appreciate her own humble house even more. Hers had that lived-in feel. The patterns on the carpet were old stains; her fresh flowers were cheap and cheerful bouquets plucked from a bucket at the local florist. It was a comfortable place, where anyone would feel at home.

Including Sean, who'd seemingly disappeared.

Connie was returning to the sideboard for dessert when she came across Kay, who waved grandly at the traditional dining room. "Next summer, all of this will go. Now that the garden is finished, I can concentrate on the interior. Every surface will be modern—granite, stainless steel, marble for the fireplaces. It's my mission to drag Peregrine House into the twenty-first century."

"Oh, don't do that," Connie blurted. "It's lovely as it is. Historic, even. The house must have been this way for ages."

"Historic?" Kay laughed disdainfully. "Don't you mean old and stodgy?"

"Old is beautiful."

"I must say," put in Kay's companion, "the antiques are invaluable." She was an older woman without an ounce of fat on her bones. Beneath her blond bob was the leathery, windburned face of a New England sailor. She looked like she'd been soaked, put through a wringer and drip-dried. "It would be a travesty to replace them."

"Well, of course I wouldn't touch the antiques." Kay's smile was overbright. "Only, you know, freshen them up a bit."

"Ah." The other woman nodded.

"New paint, new accessories. Maybe get rid of some

of those moldy old pillows, and there are so many fussy knickknacks. Anders has commissioned an artist to paint my portrait, and it will be hung over the main fireplace...." With a sour glance over her shoulder at Connie, Kay moved with her companion toward the next room, gesturing with less confidence.

"Fiddlehead." Connie frowned down at her dessert, a floating island so light she half expected it to take flight. "Stepped in it again."

Sean approached, hands in pockets. He looked around the room with a dubious air. "Stepped in what?"

"Manure," she muttered. "I'm always tracking it inside."

"I doubt it, but who cares? That's what they hired you for."

She laughed. "Not exactly. Turns out that designing gardens for the social elite is a lot more complicated than digging a vegetable patch for my uncle's neighbor."

"Just a bigger scale. With better food."

"And homes. And views." She stared longingly toward the French doors that opened onto a wide stone terrace overlooking the ocean.

Sean nodded toward them. "Ready to slip away? It's not dark yet. We can take a walk along the cliffside and enjoy your client's million-dollar view for free."

"Is that where you were hiding, out on the terrace?"

He looked sheepish. "Just perfecting my hermit act."

Was it an act? Connie wondered. Perhaps. He'd agreed to be her escort readily enough.

She set aside the uneaten dessert. "You can be the hermit while I play the serf with delusions of grandeur. And we've both put in enough of an appearance for one night." She reached for his hand, but only to push up his sleeve and check his watch. "I've got the sitter for another hour." The housekeeper's daughter had come to stay with Pippa, much to her daughter's displeasure at being treated like a baby.

"Then let's not waste any time."

"The other way," she said, when he started for the French doors. "Through the kitchen. So no one will see me ditching early except the caterers."

She led him to a swinging door at the other end of the room, which opened into a through-room that was called the butler's pantry, then to the kitchen proper. She'd used the space as a temporary potting shed. The last thing she expected to come across was Anders Sheffield with a pretty young maid backed up onto one of the zinc countertops.

Connie stopped so abruptly that Sean clipped her heels.

"Oopsie. We've got company." The maid giggled, blushed and tried to squirm away.

Anders coolly released her. He gave a tug at his tie and looked at Connie with one upraised eyebrow, only his disheveled thin silver hair betraying his usual bespoke formality. "Lose your way, then?"

"No." Her face had turned hot. "Just going to the kitchen." She burst through to the next room, shot a warning look at Sean and quickly made her way past the catering employees and household staff to the exit.

The cool air felt wonderful. "Pretend you didn't see that," she said flatly, although her stomach felt queasy.

"Naturally," Sean replied.

She sighed. "Stepped in it *again*. It's a damn lucky thing this job is almost over."

"I'm starting to understand what you meant about the complications."

"Yeah. You'd be amazed by the dirt that the Sheffields' staff and employees are privy to. Until I started this job, I thought *Upstairs, Downstairs* was just a TV show." She brushed her hair off her neck and hiked up her knotted sweater sleeves. "I've learned the value of discretion."

Sean regarded her steadily, an expressionless expression that was becoming familiar.

"You have no worries for my part," he said, but his coolness made her suspect he held little respect for the Sheffields and their ilk. "As long as no crime is involved, I won't talk."

"Good." She looked down at her borrowed dress, aware that although she'd joked about being a serf, she really was playing a role, from her borrowed finery to her careful handling of the Sheffields. But that was how it had to be.

She glanced at Sean apologetically. "I don't have to like them, you know. I'm here to do a job."

With a shrug, he offered his elbow. She took it and they strolled along the low stone wall that overlooked the sea cliffs. Other guests had also wandered outside, but they stayed clustered on the terrace.

Connie and Sean continued walking along the peninsula until they stood at the edge of the cliff. The jagged rocks and crashing surf were dramatic. Behind them, the stately home was accentuated by a cinematographer's dream backdrop of tall trees and the faded remnants of a gorgeous sunset.

She felt as though they'd been plunked into a Technicolor Alfred Hitchcock movie. Only a murder was missing.

The thought made her shiver.

"Here." Sean loosened her sweater from around her shoulders and held it out for her.

"Thanks." His hands splayed across her shoulders, staying there even after she'd slid her arms into the sleeves. He moved a step closer. She sensed his body heat, and yearned to press back against him and luxuriate in it.

She shoved her sweater sleeves up past her elbows, felt the tingle of her skin responding even to her own touch. She'd been that quickly aroused.

She leaned forward to stare down at the dizzying drop. The dark sea swelled, crashed, foamed.

Her stomach lurched. They were so near the edge. One push was all it would take.

She swayed, although her feet remained firmly planted. *I'm falling.*

But not off the cliff. One small push and she'd be tumbling headlong into love, regardless of its dangers.

"Careful." Sean caught hold of her, both hands locked firmly around her upper arms. "Too much wine?"

She spun around, almost collapsing against his chest in the heady rush of everything she was feeling. Sensations she'd forgotten had resurfaced, reminders of what it was like not to fall apart but to fall into. Into wondrously unfamiliar depths. A swan dive toward a turbulent sea.

He rocked back a little but held on. "Why is danger so enticing even when you're scared?" she asked, catching her breath.

His grip steadied her. "Is it?"

"Sometimes. I was looking over the edge, thinking what it would be like to fall—" She broke off with a shudder. "Or to be pushed."

"Not by me, I hope."

"Not really."

"Not really? But maybe?"

She produced a light laugh. "Well, you are the mysterious stranger in this scenario."

After a glance toward the terrace where the party guests were silhouetted against the house, busy with their own dramas, Sean put his face near hers. Their noses bumped. A spark leaped in Connie's veins.

"Solitary and unknown I'll admit to, but not strange." For a moment, his palms flattened as they stroked down her arms. Then his fingers curled around her elbows. He drew her closer. A low moan came from deep in his throat and his thumbs tightened on the softer flesh of her inner arms.

"Not strange," she agreed. Closing her eyes, welcoming the pressure.

She had the fleeting sensation of their breath combining, then felt the warm velvet touch of his lips. New lips. Strange lips. But lovely ones, Connie thought with a sigh as he withdrew, ending the kiss much too soon.

"I didn't come here for this," he said in a guttural voice.

She gave her head a little shake to clear it. What did he mean? *This* was their kiss, but what was *here?* The walk? The party? The island?

Did it matter, when she was going at a hundred miles an hour, and he was putting on the brakes?

"That's all right." She took a step back, leaving his chest with a light pat. It took her a couple of seconds to grab hold of herself, recognize that the wine had gone to her head. "Neither did I," she added.

I didn't come for this, but I'd stay for it.

"I'm not in a place..." He cleared his throat. "I'm not looking to meet anyone right now."

"Yes. Bad timing all around."

"Well. You're agreeable."

She raised her eyebrows. "I should argue?"

She almost laughed. Because she knew that as much as he wanted to retreat, and she'd wanted to avoid the temptation altogether, they'd started something that would be extremely difficult to ignore. If she was falling, he'd have to admit to taking a pretty big stumble, at the very least.

Sean shook his head, but now there was a grin plucking at his mouth. "Can't you even act disappointed, just a little, as a salve to my ego?"

"*Pffft.* I don't cater to men's egos."

"Well," he said once more, considering. "I like that."

She took a different sort of leap. "I like *you.*"

His eyes got dark, his expression serious again. But his regard wasn't cool this time, unless she counted a cold so cold it burned.

"I like you, too." Gingerly, he reached for her hand. "And that's why I'm taking you home. Straight home."

"Home?" she said, unable to resist teasing him as he pulled her along beside him. "Would you be referring to Pine Cone Cottage?"

He glowered in the direction of the dark forest. "You know what I meant."

Let him plunk me on the doorstep, she thought as they cut past the gardens and the maze and the pale curve of driveway. The pink-ribboned sky had turned to a rosy dusk.

This time.

"IT'S NOT ONLY ABOUT SEEING," Sean said. "You have to train your other senses, too."

"Like feeling," Pippa said. "Touch." She stooped and picked up a pinecone. "It's sharp and dry. But this part is sticky."

They stood at the edge of the forest on the Sheffield estate, in sight of Connie, who was up at the garden overseeing the final preparations for the party tomorrow. After sticking close to her mother the entire morning, Pippa had needed distraction. Connie had waylaid Sean near the front gate as he completed his morning walk around the island. After lunch in the guesthouse, she'd begged him to stick around and amuse her daughter for an hour or two.

Despite all his talk of preferring isolation, he hadn't been able to think of a good reason to say no.

Pippa dropped the cone and rubbed her fingers on her shorts. "We feel stuff all the time. How does that help to solve crimes?"

"A detective could be examining a crime scene and miss a clue if he or she didn't feel, for instance, that the floor was gritty with sand. Which might mean that the perpetrator had come off the beach."

Pippa dropped to one knee and scribbled in her notebook. He saw that she'd written *Use all your senses!* and had underlined it.

"What else?" she asked.

"Hearing. You want to be able to identify all types of sounds and learn how far they carry, given the conditions."

"What do you mean?"

"Sound carries farther at night. Rain or wind will obscure it. Fog distorts it."

Frowning, Pippa tilted her face toward him. The dappled sunshine glanced off her eyeglasses. "I don't like fog. It's creepy."

"That's only because you're not familiar with it, and it makes you more aware of sounds you usually miss."

"Like footsteps!"

"Right. Did you know that the sound of footsteps carries farther on a paved road than a dirt one?"

"Pffft." The sound Pippa made reminded him of Connie the previous night, when she'd been trying to convince him she was detached and levelheaded despite the preternaturally vivid color in her eyes and cheeks. Her arousal had been alluring...nearly disarming. He'd spent the remainder of the night reminding himself why he was better off alone.

"Tell me something that's not obvious." Pippa stood, the notebook folded open and tucked against her arm.

"Depending on the situation, voices in a normal conversation might carry about three hundred yards, while solo footsteps carry only forty. A scream—" He stopped. Better not to get into screams and gunshots.

Pippa took the eraser end of her pencil out of her mouth. "Double?"

"More like sixteen hundred yards. If you're ever in trouble, scream as loud as you can."

"Ob-vee-ous," she said, but made a note.

"Sound carries well on water. You might hear someone rowing from as far as two thousand yards." He smiled. "But that's only if you're not surrounded by the crashing waves at Whitlock's Arrow at the time."

Pippa nodded, too absorbed in writing to respond. "What else?"

"Let me think." He gave a wave to Connie and walked with her daughter along the edge of the forest until they reached a dirt path that led them toward the water. "Vehicle headlights, two to five miles, depending on the terrain. A small bonfire, four miles. Flash-lights can be seen at just over a mile."

Pippa looked up when she stumbled over a tree root that had buckled the path. "How come you know all this?"

"I trained." The thicket of spruce and pine thinned out, giving way to the wild blue vista of ocean and sky.

They stopped at a clearing where pink rocks thrust out of the earth, interspersed with patches of nodding daisies and buttercups. "Like I'm training right now?"

"Not quite. You're getting an early start. I didn't do it on my own." He walked to the sloping edge of the clearing, thinking of his father and brothers, his sister, Jannie. The standards they'd set were a double-edged sword.

"After I graduated from college, I enrolled in the MSP academy in Framingham. MSP—that's Massachusetts State Police. But the academy's in New Braintree now."

"New Braintree." She giggled, reminding him that she was just a kid. "A tree with a brain. That sounds kinda funny."

"Massachusetts has lots of funny names. Uxbridge, Assonet, Chicopee," he recited. As a trooper who'd been assigned to several posts over the years, he knew the state backward and forward. "There's even a small town called Florida. And another called Orange."

Sean gazed over the ocean. The color of the water reminded him of Connie. Her clear, sparkling eyes. He didn't know whether it was her or the sun or the island as a whole, but... The world didn't seem as dark and dismal as he'd believed.

Behind him, Pippa plopped onto a rock. She turned a page in her notebook. "Keep telling me."

She was worse with the curiosity than Josh had been as a little boy, when he'd barraged Sean with questions about why the grass was green and birds had feathers. Later, the questions were even more impossible. *Why are you getting a divorce? Don't you want me?*

At least he knew how to answer Pippa.

"How about you tell me?" He swung around. "Which do you think could be seen from farther away—a lit match or cigarette?"

She poked her tongue into her cheek. "A match."

"Why?"

"Um, I guess because it burns hotter. And it's, like, a bigger flame." Pippa eyed him almost belligerently. "Do you smoke?"

"Never."

"My mom used to." She ducked her head down and scratched at the rock with her pencil. The change in her demeanor was marked. "When…when my dad was sick."

"She was probably stressed."

Pippa sucked her lips inward. Her glistening eyes lifted to Sean's. "I made her quit."

"Good for you."

"But she used to cheat. After he died. She tried to keep it a secret, but I could smell the smoke on her."

"There you go," Sean said. "You used your sense of smell and drew a reasonable conclusion."

The thunderclouds in Pippa's expression parted.

"But what if your conclusion had been wrong?" he asked. "What if she was meeting every day with someone who smoked and that was what you smelled?"

"Phooey. I didn't think of that."

"Observation is only one part of being a good investigator. You also have to analyze your facts and apply critical thinking to the why and where and how of them. Never jump to conclusions."

"Ho-kay," Pippa said with a little sigh. She yanked up a daisy by the roots and began to peel off its petals, asking after a while, "Do you think that if I don't become a private detective like Trixie that I could be a police officer instead?"

"You sure could." He paused, uncertain whether Connie wanted him to encourage Pippa quite that much. "But, you know, you've got a lot of time to decide."

There'd been no question that he would follow his family's trooper tradition, but young girls were probably different. His brother Bobby's oldest daughter was only in junior high and she'd already gone from wanting to be a NASA physicist to a fashion designer.

And then life threw its own curves at you, such as the one Connie had taken when she'd lost her husband.

Or the one he'd faced. So far he'd only had vague thoughts of actually quitting his job, but he had little enthusiasm remaining for it, either. His father had said that would return, but then the old man had never been involved in a shooting, not in thirty-some years of active duty.

"Can we go down to the shore?" Pippa closed the cover and folded her abused notebook into a tube, which she wedged into the deep pocket of her khaki shorts. "I want to see what sounds carry best on the water. I bet cracking rocks together would make a good Morse code."

Sean agreed. He followed Pippa down a narrow path to the pebble-strewn shore. A line of kelp marked the high tide. The smell of it was strong in his nose. Boats from the nearby harbor speckled the indigo sea, a rainbow of spinnakers bellied by the wind. He took it all in—the knife-edge glance of sunshine, the breeze on his face, the child happily splashing in the shallows with her sneakers tossed over her shoulder.

Babysitting a ten-year-old hadn't been in his vacation plan. But he was gradually gaining the clarity to see that Pippa—and Connie—might fit well into his recovery.

THE FULL DAY of vigorous exercise, sun and salt wind had worked its tonic on Sean. By evening, he was sapped, and his leg was stiff and feeling the strain of too much walking. A quiet night was what he needed.

Quiet…and, finally, *alone*.

Avoiding all thoughts of red-haired gardeners and how they kissed, he got a beer from Alice Potter's fridge and a thriller from her bookshelf.

With nightfall, a chill had crept into the cottage. After a moment of debate, he got back up and started a small blaze in the fireplace with short lengths of logs from a woodpile out back. The fire didn't give off much heat, but it was enough to warm the room.

He settled down. It wasn't so bad, being alone.

Spending the afternoon with Pippa had made him think more than ever about his son, Josh, living so far away in California. A few shared holidays and one month in the summer wasn't enough time together.

But August was coming. He'd have fully recovered by then. This time he'd find a way to break down the barrier of the boy's hurt and resentment.

Maybe he'd even say, "What the hell," quit the job and move to California to be with his son. But what would they have, then? Weekends? Shuttling Josh back and forth between homes?

Was that any better?

Sean threw the book across the room. It hit the wall and dropped with a *thunk.*

He was instantly sorry. He had better control than to

pitch a fit like a thirteen-year-old. Josh had been angry last summer, and Sean hadn't known how to handle the boy. He'd even kicked a hole in the wall of their Cape Cod beach house when Sean had said he couldn't go motor biking with some kids he'd met in town. The rent had been expensive, but the house had been cheap, with walls made of thin plasterboard and the smell of rot in the air.

And yet it had been the best Sean could do, something he'd waited for all year. Just the two of them. He'd ended up cutting the beach visit short and taking Josh to his parents' house instead. They knew how to soothe a savage teenager.

Sean stretched out on the couch. A pain shot through his leg, but he ignored it. Was that what this time alone was about? The chance to beat himself up without distraction? That seemed like a waste. Maybe this was actually his chance to make a decision to commit himself fully to his son.

A few minutes later, his cell phone went off. He had no use for it here and hadn't been carrying it, but his mother was bound and determined to check in every few days.

Feeling as creaky as an old-timer, he got off the couch and found the phone in the pocket of a discarded jacket. Flipping it open, he saw that the number of the caller was unfamiliar.

Connie answered his hello. Tension in her voice. "Is Pippa there with you?" she asked, without preamble, then gave an awkward chuckle. "By chance?"

"Of course not. It's almost nine."

"I didn't think so." She let out a breath. "But there was no one else to call."

"Pippa's missing? What about Peregrine House?"

"I tried there. Got one of the staff, and they haven't seen her since this morning."

"She wouldn't go to the shore. Not after…"

"I don't—I don't think so." Connie's voice trembled. "Oh, Sean. I just don't know! She was in her room, reading before getting ready for bed. I didn't go up right away, so I can't say exactly how long she's been gone. Why would she go out at night? She doesn't even like the dark. And it's getting dark out there. Very dark."

Sean thought of their conversation that day, about sounds on the water and voices carrying at night. Matches and flashlights in the dark.

Pippa might have gotten it into her head to test a few theories.

Damn his big mouth.

"Listen," he said. "Sit tight. I'm on my way."

CHAPTER EIGHT

Pippa Bradford's Book of Curious Observations

LEARN MORSE CODE and sign language. Mr. Rafferty says three short, three long, three short is SOS. We practiced on the beach and stones worked lots better than sticks. But I wish I had a secret code like Trixie. I wish I had a friend like Honey to share it. Mr. R. is cool and I don't think he's a criminal anymore, but he still doesn't count.

Practice skills of observation. If I get good enough I could even be a supersecret spy. I will remember everything. Everything.

Practice using my senses.

1. Sight. I hate my stupid glasses. I wonder if Mom will let me get contacts? Do they do that operation for seeing on little kids?

2. Taste. I guess I'm pretty good at that, but I don't want to taste anything yucky for sure. I don't think detectives go around tasting stuff at crime scenes. LOL!!

3. Touch. I don't touch people exsept my Mom because she is huggy and kissy. I like to pet animals but I will never, ever touch the worms in our garden. They are gross.

4. Smell. This house smells like mothballs and pine

trees and wet things. My house at home smells good
like warm cookies and that spicy stuff Mom puts in
bowls. My dad's TV room smelled like him and books
and the Skittles he hid from Mom so she didn't yell
at me for getting decays. I remember all of that.

5. Hearing. My mom is singing to herself downstairs. The window is open but I only hear birds and
things in the trees. But I think I see some of the lights
from the big house through the branches. It's getting
dark so if I use my binockulars maybe I could see a
cigaret or a lit match like Mr. R. said.

"You don't have to read it *all*." Sean looked down at
Connie, sitting on Pippa's bed with the creased notebook
in her lap. She was hesitating to even open the cover.

"It's like a diary. Would you read your— Okay, you
don't have a child, but if you did, you'd understand."

"I do," he said. "I have a son."

Her head snapped back. "You do?"

"Joshua. He's thirteen. Lives in California with his
mother and her new family."

"I didn't— Well, of course I didn't know. You didn't
tell me." Connie blinked. "So. Wow. I guess you were
married, too."

"Yes. And divorced."

She was getting that sympathetic look again.

"Go on, read the notebook," he said gruffly. "Just the
last entry, in case it gives us a clue where she went."
Pippa had likely been gone for no more than twenty
minutes. When he'd arrived after a quick run through
the woods with a flashlight, Connie had called him
upstairs to the bedroom.

"Yes," she said, opening the book. She flipped

through pages filled with notes and doodles to the last entry. "Hmm. There's something about you, and learning Morse code."

"Then she wrote it later than this afternoon."

Connie scanned. "Observation skills. She lists..." She stopped, biting her lip. "Oh, Pippa."

"What is it?"

"Just something about her father." Connie cleared her throat. "Okay. What about this? She mentions seeing the lights up at Peregrine House. Matches and cigarettes? Does that make any sense?"

"That's something we talked about, yeah. You said you already called the Sheffields?"

"I spoke to the housekeeper. She knows Pippa and she hasn't seen her."

"But she'd be outdoors, don't you think?"

Connie slapped the book shut and stood, so agitated her hair seemed to be made of live wires. She ran a hand through it, and he was surprised it didn't crackle. "Maybe. I know she didn't go to the water."

She'd spoken as if she was trying to convince herself. Sean wished she could convince him, too. "Let me see exactly what she wrote." He took the notebook and read the last few sentences. "We should go up to the house."

Connie had opened a bureau drawer and was rifling through her daughter's things. Sean glanced through a pile of books, all with a sassy blond girl on the cover.

"The binoculars aren't here." Connie frowned. "If she managed to sneak past me, she'd have taken the binoculars. But would she go out at all, in the dark?" Connie appealed to Sean. "She used to be terribly scared of the dark when she was small, and the old fear came back after Phil."

Sean tapped the open notebook. "It was only starting to get dark when she wrote this entry."

"Right. And if she saw something intriguing through the binoculars, she might have tried to get closer. We need to go and look for her."

They headed for the stairs.

"Don't worry, we'll find her." Outside, Sean clicked on his flashlight. "Take this. You go up the driveway and I'll use the shortcut through the woods. We'll meet at the house."

She pushed the light back at him. "You need it more than I do. There are lights along the drive."

He swung it in an arc, flashing the trees. "Pippa! Pippa Bradford!"

"I called for her," Connie said.

He gave her a gentle push. "Go. I'll bet we find Pippa somewhere between here and the main house, too scared to go on and too afraid of a scolding to return."

"Yes," Connie said, still trying to convince herself.

He hurried off through the woods, adding his voice to Connie's as they shouted for her daughter. In minutes, they reunited at the edge of the circular portion of the driveway.

Connie panted. Her cheeks and lips were ruddy in the cold ocean air. "Any sign of her?"

He surveyed the grounds. "What's that?"

"Where?"

"The light near the maze."

She strained to see farther in the dark. The half-moon was out and that helped, but the lamps placed throughout the garden still left too many pockets of deep shadow. "I don't see a light."

"Something flickered. Maybe a flashlight."

Connie opened her mouth to shout, but Sean put a

hand on her arm. "We should get closer first." *And listen.* A certain uneasiness had crept over him.

They walked silently through the cool grass. "Was the light *in* the maze?" she whispered.

"I couldn't tell." He indicated the tall hedge. "Let's circle."

They came to the far side, where it was darker. Connie made a small sound. "I want to call for her."

"Go ahead." There was nothing to hear except the susurration of the wind and sea. "Softly."

"Pippa?" Connie's voice wobbled in vibrato. *"Pippa."* Silence.

Connie whispered, "I hate this maze."

Not far away, past the next angle of hedge, a weak light near the ground blinked on and off. On and off.

SOS.

"That's her," Sean said, and Connie let out a joyful yelp that split the silence. She took off, and he was left standing flat-footed. He marveled at how completely she'd trusted him.

"Here she is!" Connie cried.

Pippa's voice rose above the hedge. "Jeez, Mom. You're spoiling my surveillance."

"I SAW THE LIGHT from a cigarette," Pippa said ten minutes later. She was tucked into bed with extra covers.

Connie sat beside her daughter. Sean stood at the footboard, his head grazing the slanted ceiling striped with strange shadows cast from the lone bedside lamp. The moment felt odd to her. Like a tableau from Norman Rockwell, except that Sean shouldn't have belonged quite so well.

"Huh." Connie weighed the binoculars and flashlight

she'd confiscated, then laid the light on the bedside table, atop her daughter's Book of Curious Observations.

Sean bent to peer out the window toward Peregrine House. "Not from here, you didn't."

Pippa made her guilty face. "Well, no. I went outside first."

"You put on clothes," Connie said. A jacket, jeans over her pajama bottoms, running shoes. "You sneaked past me."

"That wasn't hard. You were all hunched over your garden drawings."

Connie pushed that aside for now. "All the same. You sneaked past me because you knew I wouldn't allow you to go out. And then…" She stared Pippa in the eye. "What happened then?"

Pippa's chin puckered. "There were lights at Peregrine House. I wanted to look through my binoculars to see if I could identify what kind of lights, so I took the trail through the woods to get closer. It wasn't too dark yet, Mom."

"Dark enough. But go on."

"Well, that's when I saw the match and the cigarette burning." Pippa glanced at Sean. "Just like you said."

"A guest went outside for a smoke," Connie replied, exasperated. "Why would that rouse your curiosity?"

"I heard voices, too."

"Voices? That's nothing."

"It's my fault," Sean offered. "I was telling her about using all of your senses in surveillance work, and I mentioned how far voices carry, and the distance that—"

Connie cut him off. "Fine. But it was my darling daughter who chose to go skulking around the garden in the dark without telling me." She tucked the covers in even tighter. "Pippa, I've had enough of your spying and inventing wild scenarios. Did you ever consider what I would think when I found you gone?"

"I'm sorry, Mom. I just wanted to see if I could hear the men talking." Pippa's small voice gained volume. "And it wasn't my imagination. They were *plotting*."

"I doubt they were plotting," said Connie.

Sean wasn't as dismissive. "What did they say?"

"Don't encourage her." Connie blushed, realizing that she'd previously told him the exact opposite.

"I didn't hear much," Pippa admitted, looking vastly disappointed. "They were both whispering, and then they walked into the maze before I got there. So that's why I was being superquiet and going around it, to get closer, y'know? But all I heard was something about a rock. I *think* they said they were going to meet there and split the money."

Sean thrust his hands into the back pockets of his jeans. "Hmm."

"Pip, you misunderstood." Connie kept a firm voice. She did feel leery of the overheard conversation, but she wasn't dealing with this now. Pippa shouldn't be any more involved than she already was.

"What did they sound like?" Sean asked, and Connie shot him a glare. "Did you recognize either of them?"

He lifted his shoulders, made big puppy-dog eyes at her. Couldn't help himself.

She wished she had a rolled-up newspaper.

Pippa was thinking so hard she'd squeezed her eyes shut. "I don't know for sure. One of them was real quiet. The other guy had a husky kind of voice and an accent. Like the man in the general store who says 'ayuh.'"

"At least one of them might have been a local, then," Sean said.

"Never mind," Connie said. "We're not thinking about this right now. It's time for bed for you, Miss Snoop, and Mr. Snoop is going home. Tomorrow is the garden party and we all need a good night's sleep. At least I do."

She stood and gestured Sean out of the room, putting her hands on his back and prodding him along to keep him moving. All she needed was for her daughter to have a coconspirator in her obsession.

"Good night, Pippa," he called.

"G'night." Pippa sniffed. "What about my binoculars, Mom?"

"I'm keeping them." Connie's stern expression softened. "Lights out, Pippa. Sweet dreams."

No nightmares, my little one.

She sighed when they reached the bottom of the stairs. "There was no sign of anyone in the maze. Or the garden."

"If they hadn't already gone before we got there," Sean said, "after the noise you made, they were probably smart enough to keep quiet and wait for us to go."

Connie was uneasy about the whole thing, even though Pippa hadn't seemed particularly frightened. She'd barely seemed to notice how dark the sky had grown.

"Assuming they were up to no good in the first place," Sean added. A shiver prickled Connie's skin.

With her finger on her lips, she nodded up the staircase. "Outside," she mouthed.

"Sorry," he said as soon as the door was shut behind them. "This was my fault. And maybe I shouldn't have asked questions, either, but you have to admit the conversation that she overheard seems suspicious."

"*If* she heard what she says she heard. I told you about the so-called stolen goods in my neighbor's shed, right?"

"Right."

Connie scraped her hair off her face, feeling jittery. She'd tried to stay calm with Pippa, but thank God for Sean's solid presence.

"Okay," she said. "Maybe Pippa's not so wrong this time. Maybe there was something odd going on up there. But I don't care. I want to finish my work here and not get into any unnecessary complications. I definitely don't want my daughter involved. For a timid girl, she's gotten awfully adventurous since we came to the island."

Sean was doing his taciturn thing again. She looked up at the sky, at the sharp glitter of stars that seemed so much closer on Osprey Island. Everything did. Her emotions, old dreams and new longings—all rising to the surface and demanding to be satisfied.

She'd called Sean for help. And it had seemed natural, when she'd felt so alone since losing Philip. Proud, independent, stubborn...but alone.

And lonely.

Sean stamped his feet and rubbed his arms, which were bare. He'd come running in just a short-sleeved T-shirt and jeans, she realized. Her heart filled with a warmth that she wished she could give to him by the handful.

"Isn't that what you wanted—Pippa being more, uh, outgoing?"

"Yes," she said. "But preferably not demonstrating that by creeping around in the dark or drowning in the ocean."

"Of course." He nodded. "If I told you about the scrapes I got into as a kid..."

She smiled, a little. "And me."

"Don't be too hard on her."

"I don't want to be. It's just that I'm at the end of my rope, trying to deal with her and the party. I'm already worrying about what on earth she'll get into tomorrow, because I won't be able to keep an eye on her every single moment."

"I'll talk to her. I'll explain about inappropriate risks."

"Thank you."

They had walked to the edge of the clearing around the guesthouse. The house had no yard to speak of, only a skirting thick with rust-colored pine needles. A border at the front of the house was sadly choked with weeds. Connie would have filled it with shade-loving plants— coleus and hosta and great clouds of impatiens.

Sean folded his arms. "I'll keep an eye on her tomorrow, too."

"You will? That would be such a relief. Except I thought you weren't attending the party."

"I hadn't planned to, but now I'm curious."

"Not another one!" Connie's laugh was a bit too loud. There was a sudden flapping in one of the trees. One dark shape winged away, then two more. "Don't turn my daughter into your junior detective, please."

"'Course not. But I will keep my eyes open." Sean turned his head, following the birds' flight. "She would have recognized Sheffield's voice, don't you think?"

"Stop," Connie commanded. "I can't go there right now."

He nodded. "I'll come by early," he said, "so you can get up to the house before the party."

"Thank you. Thank you so much." She laid her hands on his crossed forearms and gave him a squeeze.

"For racing over. For rescuing us again. For everything." His arms felt like cold marble. "Go home. Get warmed up."

His expression was already warm, hinting at a desire that neither of them would voice—not yet.

Suddenly Connie's heart was in her throat, beating wildly.

A long time had passed since she'd been with a man, or even wanted to be. It had been even longer since she hadn't felt the weight of the world on her shoulders. The allure of casting everything aside and losing herself in Sean's kisses and a long night of loving was a temptation almost impossible to resist.

"Good night, Mr. Snoop."

His smile transformed his face. "Not the nickname I'd hoped for, but I like it better than Mr. Limpet."

CHAPTER NINE

THE CELL PHONE was chirping again when Sean let himself into the cottage. He grabbed it and went to stand by the fire, which had almost gone out. Better that than burning down the place.

He opened the phone and said, "Hello," distractedly moving aside the fireplace screen. Beneath the white ash, the coals of the fire glowed red. He tossed on one of the remaining logs.

"Finally!" His former wife was the last caller he'd expected. They e-mailed logistics of their son's life, he mailed child-support checks, but they rarely talked unless there was trouble.

"I've been calling all day," she said.

Uh-oh.

"Hello, Jen. I've been out. I'm on vacation."

"Oh, you're calling it vacation now? I thought it was exile."

"It's vacation."

"How's the leg?"

"Healing."

"Must not be too bad if you're going out. Don't you ever check your messages?"

"Not often."

"Same guy I married. Why communicate verbally

when smoke signals will do?" Jen chuckled, but there was no humor in it. She'd once liked his self-control, but later had called him passionless. Just as she'd first thought that his job was impressive, but had soon grown disillusioned by the long hours and stagnant paychecks.

Sean waved at the acrid wisps rising from the sputtering coals. He replaced the screen and sat down right there, on the brick hearth. His arms were covered in goose bumps. "Is it Josh?"

"Of course it's Josh."

"Trouble?"

"That's his middle name." Jen had never been easy to get along with. She was a bossy, brassy Bostonian, accustomed to shooting off her mouth. They'd shared an attraction but no real foundation for a lasting relationship, and would have broken up before marriage if it hadn't been for the unplanned pregnancy. Even aside from giving them Josh, Sean still couldn't say their years together had been a waste. He'd learned a lot about himself and what he did and did not want.

Yes to spirit and ambition like Connie's. No to Jen's upwardly mobile demands.

"I'm sending Josh to you early," Jen said. "I've had enough of the kid for this summer."

"What?"

"You're always saying you don't get to see him. Consider this my gift to you."

"But I'm in Maine. On an island."

"That'll be a challenge." Jen was breezy now that she believed the issue was decided. "Bruce and I are going to a cooking class in Paris for ten days. The girls have tennis camp."

"Cooking class," Sean repeated. Jen had changed.

The woman he remembered wouldn't let a chef's knife near her manicure.

"Bruce's idea. All of a sudden he's a French chef. I'll be shopping while he's chopping."

"But what about Josh?"

"Keep up. Josh will be with you."

Sean closed his eyes. The fire had warmed him through. "When?"

"As soon as I can book a flight. What's the nearest airport? After your son's latest escapade, the sooner he's out of my sight the better."

"What did he do now?" Sean asked, trying to keep the smile from his voice. For once, he almost didn't care what the bad behavior had been. It was getting him what he wanted.

AFTER MAKING CERTAIN that Pippa was asleep, Connie got into her pajamas and went downstairs to make a cup of tea. She carried the cup and one of Suzy Q's coconut cupcakes over to the corner chair.

No sweater. She still felt flushed.

The tea was too hot to drink. She checked her cell phone for reception and dialed Lena in Boston. They hadn't talked in a couple of weeks.

"Connie!" Lena squealed.

The bite of cupcake she'd just taken went down the wrong way. She wasn't used to such girlish enthusiasm from Lena, who spoke and traveled at the same clip—swift and low-key.

"*Mmph.* Lena. I expected voice mail."

"What are you eating?"

"Coconut cupcake."

"Lucky. I have a packet of water crackers and a shriveled-up piece of Stilton. My cupboards are bare."

"Aren't they always?"

"No matter. I had dinner with a client at L'Espalier."

"A client? Too bad." Lena's love life was only slightly more active than Connie's.

"What about you?"

"Wall-to-wall clients. Yesterday I walked in on Sheffield making out with one of the maids."

"I'd heard that about him. Has he gone for you yet?"

"No. Thank God."

"You're probably being all widowish."

"In buttoned collars and sensible shoes?" Connie smiled. "You'll be pleased to know there was a cocktail party last night and I wore that silk dress of yours."

"Sexy." Lena whistled. "Aren't you glad I talked you into taking it along?"

"I suppose, but I also wore a sweater. It was chilly."

"Then not so sexy. Did anyone notice? Were there any single male guests that aren't the kind to diddle the maids?"

"Well…"

Lena was clearly surprised that she took a beat to respond. "You met someone?"

"I met someone."

"Tell me."

"Divorced. One child. Tall, dark and handsome."

"Excellent. Any drawbacks?"

"There is the bullet hole in his leg."

"What?"

"A bullet hole. He's a statie."

Lena hooted. "Leave it to you to find a wounded

state trooper in the wilds of Maine. Where's he stationed—in the city?"

"No, he said but I can't remember. Somewhere in the middle of the state. Pippa's practically in love with him."

"She is? That's a surprise." Lena knew how attached Pippa had been to her father. "But what about you?"

"I'm…interested. But it's only been a few days. Seems like more, though. You know how it is when you meet someone you click with and it's a natural attraction, hardly awkward at all?"

"I've heard stories." Connie could hear Lena shaking her head. "Are you *serious?*"

"I don't know. There's the bullet hole to consider. And the fact that he claims to be a hermit."

"Most men fancy themselves hermits, as long as hermits get ESPN. You can overcome that easy enough."

"Not so easy in this case, but…" Connie considered. "Maybe. He's showing signs of life."

"Wow. I am stunned." Lena bit into a cracker. "Here's the test. Have you kissed him?"

"Yes."

"Now I'm *really* stunned."

"And I didn't even think about Philip when it happened." Connie bit her lip. Her gut churned. Everyone had told her she had to move on with her life, but kissing another man without qualms over her husband's memory was moving faster than she'd expected. "That's supposed to be good for me, right?"

"After three years? Hell, yes."

"I wish I had your certainty."

"What does Pippa think, aside from being in love with him?" Lena asked gently.

"That part is tricky. She loves him for his occupational skills. I don't know how she'd be if we were dating."

"Then you're going to be dating. It's not just a vacation fling."

"I don't know. I'm probably not even capable of a fling."

"Everyone's capable. Remember what I did when I went to Round Hill two Christmases ago?"

"Ah, yes—the sailboat charter guy. But you knew that you'd never see him again."

"Until he showed up at my office in Ray-Bans and Bermuda shorts."

"I forgot about that." She took a big bite of the cupcake. "I am never having a fling."

"Maybe that's what you need. I like staties as much as the next girl, but I'd rather have one out of uniform than in."

More cupcake. She'd forgotten how direct Lena could be, always sure that she knew what to do and how to do it. She was usually correct, but then her emotions weren't nearly as mercurial as Connie's could be. Lena didn't need impulse control; she had no impulses, only directives. Even the sailboat guy had been planned before she'd left on vacation: golf, sand, sun, sex.

Connie scraped the cupcake paper with her teeth. Her lists featured aphid poison and fertilizer. "Well. I haven't actually seen him *in* uniform."

Lena exhaled. "Look, Con, don't take offense. You know I'm thrilled down to my pinkie toes that you've finally found a guy you're interested in. But cops have dangerous jobs. They get *shot* at. Yours already has a bullet wound."

"People die without being shot at."

"Okay."

"Pippa's not *that* attached."

"I shouldn't have said anything."

"No, I wanted you to. I'm not— This is strange for me." Connie pressed her face against her knees. "I needed your clear head."

"I had half a bottle of Bordeaux with dinner."

They laughed, but Connie's heart wasn't in it. She wanted that feeling back, the flying sensation of being one inch away from falling in love. Instead, she had a realistic list of why she should keep away from Sean: his job, her job, his far-away son, her needy daughter. The lingering memory of Phil.

Moving on didn't mean leaving their old lives behind. The baggage would have to come with them.

Maybe there was simply too much of it.

THE GARDEN PARTY AND MAZE unveiling was less exclusive than the cocktail party. Two large striped tents had been set up on the lawn. Caterers had arrived by ferry that morning with truckloads of equipment and preprepared food. In the second tent, a dance floor had been laid.

By the time Connie returned to Peregrine House after changing out of her work clothes, a small orchestra was playing lively music. Guests had already begun trickling in on foot from all over the island, gawking over the garden and maze.

Connie let herself through the back door into the kitchen. She'd spent the morning grooming the grounds until they were impeccable—unnecessary fussbudgetry, really—with Pippa as her assistant to tote the hedge clippers and whisk broom. They'd strung up the wide satin ribbon Kay had wanted for the ribbon-cutting. Pippa had retied the bow four times before she was satisfied.

Back at the guesthouse, Sean had arrived as Connie was climbing out of the tiny shower stall. She'd sent Pippa to entertain him until she'd emerged in a pair of good pants and a lightweight cashmere sweater that he'd claimed was the color of the Connemara hills. She had said that clearly he'd kissed the Blarney Stone one time too many, which led to Pippa's needing an explanation of what that meant. With only a twinge over the spiky memory of Lena's words and her own doubts the night before, Connie had left the pair of them in close cahoots.

"Don't you look nice, Mrs. Bradford," said Rachel Wells, the housekeeper, a village widow. She was only in her midforties, a slender woman with upswept hair and a sedate demeanor. In her mouth, the familiar Maine accent was as rich and sweet as jam made from the island's wild berries. "Mrs. Sheffield, now. *She's* wearing silk and pearls, with a pair of those shoes my daughter claims cost six hundred dollars."

Rachel looked at Connie. "I can't imagine. The ways these people waste money."

Connie smiled noncommittally. She'd never spent more than a hundred bucks on a single pair of shoes, but Lena certainly had. That didn't make her a bad person though.

"La-di-dah," sniped one of the maids, passing through the kitchen with a handful of tableware. Connie recognized her as the young woman from the butler's pantry. Jealous.

"Hush, Kitty," Rachel said. The housekeeper returned her gaze to Connie. "Mrs. Sheffield's stiletto heels should do a fine job aerating the sod."

Connie dodged one of the caterers, passing by with

a platter of lobster rolls. "Then I take it Kay won't be running the maze."

"I expect she'll be sticking close to Mr. Sheffield's side," Rachel said with a glance at the young maid's twitching hips. Kitty was an islander, with heavily made-up eyes and an insolent mouth. "Are you ready for the ribbon-cutting ceremony, Mrs. Bradford?"

Although they had chatted several times over tea and shared stories—Rachel having lost her lobsterman husband to the sea some years before—Connie had given up on getting the woman to call her by her first name. The locals kept a distance between themselves and the summer people, while Connie had to straddle both worlds.

"Just about ready," she said.

"The island children are certainly looking forward to your maze," Rachel replied. "Even my sullen teenagers are out to win the prize. They're expecting something lavish, like a sports car, no matter what I say about how miserly rich people can be." It was the housekeeper's daughter Molly who'd sat with Pippa the other night.

"They're sure to be disappointed," Connie said. "I've been told there will be one prize for the children and another for the adults. Which reminds me, I came to see if you have a pair of scissors for the ribbon-cutting."

"Certainly." Rachel slid open a drawer. "My kitchen scissors. Don't misplace them."

"I'm surprised the lady of the manor didn't buy a special golden-handled pair," sniffed Kitty, returning from the butler's pantry. "With diamond studs."

"That'll be enough, Kitty," Rachel snapped. "Take that tray of extra wineglasses to the caterer's tent." She closed the door behind the maid and the departing catering assistants before shaking her head. "That girl is riding for a fall."

Connie ran her thumb along the blade of the scissor. "Then you know."

"It's no secret, even to Mrs. Sheffield."

Which explained the increased petulance, Connie supposed. The Sheffields had been at odds all week.

"Not that she admits it," Rachel said. She pressed her lips into a straight line while she polished the countertops and chrome faucet. "Neither should I."

"I'll keep it zipped," Connie promised, although she had to wonder if there might be a connection between the pair's squabbles and the suspicious conversation Pippa had overheard in the maze. Unlikely, she decided. Even absurd.

But she would like to place the two men...before Pippa did.

A thought occurred to her. "You were here late last night."

"Yes," Rachel said. "Mrs. Sheffield asked me to stay to help serve dinner. The cook went home early to start her day off. The guests were wearing on her nerves."

"I see. Then the houseguests were also here?"

"As far as I know."

That didn't help much, as Connie had no way to identify which of them might have been in the maze. "What about rest of the staff?"

"Kitty and Mary-Rose were here." Both maids.

"No one else?" Connie was trying to remember if the Sheffields employed any other men besides Graves and the local boy who helped him with the heavier grounds-keeping. Both lived in the village and should not have been on the estate after dark.

"None that I can think of." Rachel eyed Connie. "Why do you ask? Was that why you called? I suppose Pippa got into something she shouldn't have. That girl is some snoop."

Connie wasn't sure how Rachel meant that, but she hadn't known the woman to be snide. She gave her the benefit of the doubt. "Turns out that was a false alarm. Pippa's perfectly fine."

Rachel raised her eyebrows even higher; Connie felt she had to elaborate. "We— I found her right away. She'd only gone for a walk, without realizing how quickly night would fall. I was asking who was here because apparently there were also a couple of men somewhere on the grounds last night. Pippa heard them."

"Oh. Two men, was it? According to Pippa…" The housekeeper laughed.

"I know." Connie didn't smile. "Probably her imagination." She held up the scissors, preparing to leave. "Thanks for these."

"Wait," Rachel said. "There *was* a mechanic. He'd been working on the convertible, and Mr. Sheffield wanted it delivered to the house before morning."

"When was the mechanic here?"

"I couldn't say precisely, except that dinner was over. I offered him a cup of coffee and a slice of cake while I finished wiping down the counters." Rachel seemed bemused by all the questions. "It was Wink Kennedy. He's been the island mechanic for thirty-odd years."

Sheffield and an ancient mechanic? An unlikely pair. But if so, Connie recalled something they'd said, *according to Pippa.* "Is there a local meeting spot, possibly scenic, some sort of rock?"

"A rock?" Rachel laughed again. "Really, Mrs. Bradford. There are rocks all over the island."

"Of course. But maybe this is a special place, known particularly to the islanders?"

"Are you planning an outing?"

"After today's over, I'll be on vacation," Connie said, evading her question. "Pippa wants to explore."

"There's Whitlock's Arrow and Cutter Head. They're on all the maps. And that large, mossy rock near the yacht club is something of a landmark."

"Hmm. Yes, I know it."

"Speaking of the yacht club, you should bring Pippa to the regatta on Sunday. We take our own picnics and chairs, but we have just as good a time as the club members."

"I may do that," Connie said, distracted by the rising volume of music and conversation outside. She'd wasted enough time.

"Bring your man, too," Rachel said with a little wink.

Connie twisted the scissors in her hand. She clenched her fist around the cool metal. "I don't have a man."

"No?" Rachel's smile was aggravatingly serene. Almost smug. "Perhaps I'm mistaken, then, and that handsome fellow from Pine Cone Cottage wasn't with you last night."

CHAPTER TEN

Pippa Bradford's Book of Curious Observations

CLUES FOUND at the garden party:

1. Mr. Sheffield flirts a lot. He even put his hand on one lady's rear end, when Mrs. S. was standing by him. Yuck.

2. The old man gardener who doesn't like my mom has dirty fingernails. He was hanging out at the fountain in the maze until Mr. S. made him leave.

3. I saw one of the man guests and the blond lady who looks like Mrs. S. pour extra alcohall into the punch. It already had alcohall because I tasted some by accident on purpose. It was disgusting.

4. The maid Kitty was crying in the kitchen (she has red hair like me and is beautiful when she's not crying). Mrs. S. thinks she stole a diamond ring but she didn't. The other maid said she should quit and take the Sheffields to court for slander and win a million dollars. Mrs. Wells told them to be quiet or they would both be fired. Then she caught me eavesdropping and she made me go. So I don't know what else happened.

5. Molly Wells kissed a boy behind one of the tents. I don't like her very much because she is only fifteen and she thinks she's the boss of me!

6. Some people were talking about how much money the Sheffields have. They said the paintings should be in a museum and Mrs. S.'s jewelry was worth a fortune. They said that anybody could walk in to steal stuff, but that Mrs. S. probably just lost her diamond.

P.S. from before the party: Mr. Rafferty has a SON named JOSHUA!!! He used to be married to Jen, I think. I heard him on his cell phone and he sounded kind of mad at her, but then he was happy because his son is coming here. Oh, boy.

MIDWAY THROUGH THE afternoon, Anders Sheffield called for the guests to gather around for the ribbon-cutting. He waved them over with the hand that wasn't holding a scotch and, looking rather bored with the entire event, surrendered the floor to his wife.

In her silk and pearls with a sun hat so large it could have sheltered a small family, Kay might have been fresh in from a day at Ascot. After a brief welcoming speech and a self-congratulatory discourse on the importance of preserving Osprey Island history for future generations, she introduced Connie. "Kudos to our brilliant garden designer, Connemara Bradford."

The guests applauded. Connie nodded and waved. As planned, she put her hand on the ribbon while Anders pretended to hold the other end. In the middle, Kay smiled brilliantly for a photographer from the local newspaper. She brandished the scissors, then snipped cleanly through the ribbon. Her husband pronounced the maze open.

A group of children crowded near the entrance, ready to race pell-mell to the center. Connie made them wait while Kay and Anders—sharing not a word—worked their way through the twisting path. They would award prizes to the first arrivals.

At their call, Connie brought down her arm. "Go!" She stepped aside to avoid the stampede. Several adults were almost as eager as the kids.

When the crowd thinned, she spotted her daughter and Sean nearby. "I'm sorry you can't compete, Pip. You know it wouldn't be fair."

Pippa tried to look mature. "I know."

"Why don't you go in now? You can still have fun. Some of the little ones might need your help getting to the center."

"Yeah, they might." Pippa beamed. "Will you hold my notebook for me?" She thrust it at Connie and darted off, calling, "Don't look inside!" over her shoulder.

Connie tucked the book under her arm. "Didn't I tell her to leave this at home?"

"She insisted," Sean said. "And she's done lots of spying and note-taking. I've been following her from afar."

"Oh, dear." Connie smiled, not particularly perturbed. "That can't have been much fun for you. I didn't intend for you to stick to her so tightly that you couldn't enjoy the party yourself."

"I'm seeing it from Pippa's perspective. She really gets around."

"I hope she's not getting into too much mischief."

Connie heard herself speak, but she wasn't really paying attention to the conversation. Sean was distracting. He'd dressed casually in jeans with the navy blue sports coat he'd worn to the cocktail party. The collar of his pale blue button-down shirt was open, drawing her gaze down the column of his throat to a few stray strands of soft, dark hair.

She forced her eyes upward, scarcely aware of the guests entering and exiting the maze. His temples were lightly peppered with gray. There was a small scar near his top lip. And he'd been *married*. He had a thirteen-year-old son. Perhaps that explained his gentle treatment of Pippa. She was amending her perception of him every day.

She still thought that he was handsome, which wouldn't ever change, no matter how gray or wrinkled he got.

Her throat tightened. Once, she'd felt the same way about Phil.

That's right, you did. And you can handle remembering that without letting it crush you. No matter how ready she was to move on, there was going to be regret for what she'd lost.

"Just kid stuff, like tasting the hard punch," Sean said. Connie wondered what he saw when he looked at her. "I did lose sight of her a couple of times."

She licked her lips. *Pippa. We're talking about Pippa. The daughter you've promised all your attention to, after today.* "I'm sure she was fine. My worries about her seem much less urgent in the light of day."

"Hmm." He smiled, his eyes crinkling. Today they were the color of the sky. Again she looked at the tiny white scar by his lip. One day soon she'd ask him about that.

She tore her gaze away. Party guests were strolling in and out of the maze. There was a lot of laughter and noise coming from inside the tall green walls. Several people came up and complimented her on the fine job. She thanked them, even handed out a few of the business cards she'd tucked into her pocket. And none of it seemed as real or important as the man standing beside her.

"I've done some observing myself," he said at one point. "Watching for suspicious characters."

"Discover anything alarming?" she asked lightly, keeping her eyes on the maze. Anders had emerged and walked briskly toward the house. A minute or two later, the curvaceous wife of one of his business associates followed, looking ruffled around the edges.

"There's talk among the guests about the Sheffields. They've been fighting a lot. I guess she lost a diamond."

"I heard that Anders gave one to another woman." Connie shook her head. "Gossip."

"I'm keeping my ears open."

She gave Sean an arch look. "You're serious?"

"Let's just say that my curiosity is piqued."

"Let's don't." She seized his hand. "Let's dance instead."

IT WAS COOLER under the tent, out of the dazzling sun. The orchestra played popular dance songs. Connie felt very good in his arms. Her cheek rested on his shoulder while they danced, but every now and then she would lift her head and ask him something.

"When were you married?"

"June first. I was twenty-six. Josh is going on fourteen, so you do the math."

"Have you ever sailed? Do you own a pair of Ray-Bans and Bermuda shorts?"

"Toy boats. And no, but I'll buy 'em if you like 'em."

"What's your favorite color?"

Though he said, "Blue," he was thinking red. The burnished red-gold of an Irish setter's coat, of the trees in the fall, of Connie's head nestled near his as they danced.

"Do I get to ask any questions?" he ventured when

she'd been quiet for a long while and he'd become too aware of the soft pressure of her breasts against his ribs and the curve of her hip under his palm.

She raised her head. "No."

"Why not?"

"Because I'm an open book. I've told you lots more about my life than you have about yours."

"It's important for you to know that I sailed toy boats in the bathtub?"

"Might be. These little details can be important, you never know."

"The name of my first crush? The date of my wedding?"

"All part of the puzzle."

"Now I'm a puzzle."

"Everyone's a puzzle when you first meet them. But you—you're also a mystery wrapped in an enigma."

He tightened his embrace. "Right now, I prefer being wrapped in you."

"Mmm." She returned her cheek to his shoulder, stroked his chest. "Five more minutes. Then I really have to get back to the party. There might be someone stranded in the maze."

"I've lost all sight of Pippa."

"I'm hoping that she's playing with the other kids instead of making Curious Observations," Connie murmured, her voice an indolent purr. An instant later she pulled out of his arms. "The notebook. What did I do with it?"

He looked around. There were very few dancers. Most of the guests were still milling around the garden and maze. "I don't know."

Connie flapped her arms and shimmied a little, as if

she expected the notebook to drop out of her clothes. "Pippa will kill me if I've lost it."

He shoved his fists into his pockets. That shimmy had been damn sexy. "Where did you put it down?"

She rolled her eyes.

"I mean, where might you have put it down?"

"The refreshment table. We stopped for glasses of punch, remember?"

He remembered. She'd drunk hers straight down and turned very red in the face. Five minutes later, she'd been draped all over him while the orchestra played "My Funny Valentine."

They hurried to the table, where the once-pristine linen now sported pink stains under a plethora of sticky punch cups. The crystal bowls had been drained to puddles. Waterlogged slices of fruit stuck to the sides.

"Here it is." Connie snapped up the notebook. "Thank heaven."

Sean reached for it. "We should see what Pippa's latest observations are. As keen as she is, I wouldn't put it past her to have discovered an interesting rumor or three."

She batted him away. "Not a chance. Last night was an emergency, or at least I thought it might be. I won't betray Pippa's trust again. Ask her, if you want to know. She might tell you, as her mentor of all things curi—"

Pippa was standing beside them, her face blanched. "Mom?" she quavered. "You read my notebook?"

"No," Connie croaked. "That is, I took a glance. Just the last page. So we knew where to look."

"You read my notebook."

"It was my fault, Pippa." Sean took a step toward her. "I did it."

The girl snatched it out of Connie's hands and

whirled away with her ponytail flying. "I'll never trust either of you ever again," she yelled, and ran sobbing from the tent.

"SHE'S IN THE BUTLER'S PANTRY," Rachel Wells said. "That's the second time I've found her there."

"The second time?" Connie asked distractedly. After she'd regained her composure—like mother, like daughter—they'd followed Pippa into the house.

"The first time, she was having a high old time listening to the kitchen gossip, just some nonsense between the maids. This time, I heard her crying. I gave her a glass of cold milk and a plateful of cookies and left her alone."

Rachel, wiping her hands on her apron, glanced doubtfully at Sean. "You're the one that's staying in Alice Potter's cottage. It's not like Alice to rent Pine Cone to a stranger."

"But she did."

"Ayuh. I reckon if Mrs. Bradford trusts you, I can, too."

"Well, you should. He's a Massachusetts state troo—"

"Let *me* talk to Pippa," Sean interrupted. He hushed her when she started to protest. "I'll appeal to her rational intellect."

Connie stepped aside, but she was skeptical. "Be my guest."

"You trust me." He nodded at the housekeeper. "She told me so."

That pulled a wry smile out of Connie. "Housekeepers know best." She gestured at Rachel. "Maybe we should send *you* in."

"Not me. Pippa says I remind her of some woman called Miss Trask. I haven't decided whether she means that as a compliment."

Sean left the two of them as Connie began an explanation about Trixie Belden's fictional world. He nudged open the swinging door and peered in at Pippa. She sat slumped on top of the counter, sniffling into a glass of milk. There were cookie crumbs on her chin and purple T-shirt.

"Can I come in?" he asked.

"No," she said, like her mother.

"You sure?"

She swung her plump legs, not looking at him as she thudded her heels on the lower cabinets. "I guess you can if you want."

He hoisted himself onto the opposite cabinet. If someone came through unannounced, he'd take a door in his kneecaps. "It's sort of nice in here," he observed, considering the deep crown molding and vintage zinc countertops. On one side was a stainless steel sink with a shallow bowl, on the other a deep farm sink. Rows of barware neatly lined the open shelves above Pippa's head. "Nearly as big as the kitchen in my condo."

Pippa didn't respond.

"What about yours?"

She gripped the glass tighter, making fingerprints in the condensation. "We have a house."

"Big like this one?"

"It's small."

"But nice, I'll bet."

She drank, then licked away a milk mustache. Her eyes flicked to Sean. "Just so you know, I'm never gonna move."

Josh had been only six when Jen had moved out, seven when she'd packed up and hauled him to California. How had Sean forgotten—or deliberately put out of his mind—the sad look on his little boy's face when they'd said goodbye?

He coughed to clear his throat. "I'm sorry about the notebook," he said. She had it wedged under her thigh. "Your mom didn't want to read it, even when I told her that we should."

"How come?" she said softly. "How come you wanted to read it?"

"I guess I was thinking of my job. The troopers share their information. We write incident reports for public record." He made a quick calculation, betting on Pippa's fighting spirit. "But I forgot that you're just a little girl."

"I'm ten. That's not little."

"Right. Still, I shouldn't be reading your diary."

"It's not a diary! It's my Book of Curious Observations." Pippa's mouth had taken on a stubborn set. "Diaries are stupid."

"I wish I'd thought to keep a Book of Curious Observations when I was a boy." He shrugged. "So do you forgive me?"

"S'pose."

"And your mother?"

"Well, she's not a state trooper. She didn't have any reason to read it."

He bit the inside of his cheek. Boxed in by a ten-year-old. "But she's your mom, and she was just worried about you. I think you should cut her some slack."

"Maybe."

"And you might think about sharing some of your observations with us."

"Like…putting our brain power together to solve the crime?"

"Yes, just like that." He reconsidered. "If there was actually a crime, that is."

"There was, or else there's gonna be," Pippa said with surprising vehemence.

He heard a floorboard creak on the other side of the door and casually put his foot against it. "Why do you say that?"

"'Cause of all the expensive stuff up here. I heard people talking. *And* somebody already stole a diamond ring."

"Whoa." Sean laughed. "Slow down, Pippa."

"You said we could co—collab—"

"Collaborate? I may have spoken too soon. What I meant was that I didn't want you getting into a dangerous situation on your own."

"Oh. Like I'm a *baby* who has to have a *babysitter.*" She glared at him. "I bet my mom made you say that."

He heard a snort from the other side of the door and stifled his laugh. "Could be."

PUZZLES, MAZES AND JUMBLES weren't Sean's bag. He was a straightforward guy, a linear thinker, and even when roadblocks had thrown him off course—the divorce, the shooting—he kept on going. The two weeks on Osprey Island weren't supposed to be a detour. They were meant as a breather, a time to lick his wounds. After the stay here was over and his leg was fully healed, he'd expected to continue much as before.

He hadn't expected the impending arrival of his son.

And he hadn't expected Connemara Bradford.

He came to a juncture and stopped, looking down the green corridors, considering his choice. Normally he went with his first instinct, which was usually right, but Connie's presence was throwing him off.

"Give me a clue here," he said.

She wagged her head no.

Right, he thought, but went left. The next turn brought him to a dead end. Glancing back, he caught Connie's mouth twitching. "You think this is funny?"

"I expected more from a big, strong state trooper," she teased. "Do you get lost on the highways and byways of Massachusetts?"

"I follow maps." He grunted and retraced his steps.

"Jeez, you guys," Pippa called from a distance. "Hurry up."

Sean took the other path. Several turns and another dead end later, he stopped again and mopped his forehead with his sleeve. He took off his sports coat and slung it over his shoulder. "Hot in here."

"Without the sea breezes, these high hedges really hold the heat." Connie smirked. "Then again, frustration makes you sweat." She stooped to retrieve a crinkled candy bar wrapper from beneath the hedge.

He clenched his thigh muscles and felt the tightening of the fresh scar. The walks he'd been taking every morning had gotten him into better shape, but it had been a long day. Connie had said he couldn't go home without trying the maze first.

He glanced at her. "You're a little pink around the edges yourself."

She pushed her hair out of the way with the back of one wrist. "I've been busy."

"Meaning?"

"Well, I asked around about who all was on the Sheffield estate last night."

"What did you learn?"

"That there's no proof of anything." In a low voice, she told him about her conversation with the house-keeper, naming the dearth of local suspects with the accent Pippa had indicated, and the surplus of rock for-mations on the island.

"After applying my own keen abilities, I came to the same conclusion," he admitted. "But there's still the talk about the missing diamond."

"We'd better just forget it," she said. "And encour-age Pippa to do the same."

He agreed, with some misgiving. He might not be a creative thinker, but he sure as hell knew when one and one were making eleven instead of two. He wasn't ready to dismiss Pippa's "curious observations."

"Almost there," Connie said a few minutes later, when Sean was ready to give up ever finding the center of the maze.

"You're a fiend," he grumbled.

"Ha." She brushed one hand along the hedge as they walked, almost like petting an animal.

"In ancient times," she said, "it was believed that demons could only travel in straight lines. Thus the maze, to baffle the evil spirits."

He smiled. "Then how come it's me who's baffled?"

"Perhaps because you haven't figured out your life goal yet." She caught his frown and quickly elaborated. "It's also been said that mazes are symbolic of life and death. The entrance is birth, the center represents death. In between, we become lost, we are blinded, we face temptation and confront danger and change at every twist and turn. Finally, we reach our goal and we are redeemed."

"By the symbolic death?"

"Salvation, I presume." She made a face. "Never mind me. At the start of this project, I did a lot of reading on the history of mazes and labyrinths."

They had reached the center. Pippa sat on the ground near the splashing fountain, paging through her notebook. Sean greeted her with spread arms. "You are a sight for sore feet."

"Such a complainer," Connie said with a laugh. "The kids ran the maze in no time flat. Even Graves seems to know his way around it pretty well, and he grumbles more than you."

Sean passed his jacket from hand to hand. "I'm a grouch?"

"That tends to go with being a hermit. But don't worry. Pippa seems to have cured you."

Of course she was right. He'd come to the island to stew in his own juices, and what a waste of time and energy that had been. Would have been, if they hadn't made him a part of their lives. At least for the short time that they were on the island together. There was no saying what would come tomorrow.

He looked at Connie and said quietly, "You, too. You helped."

She patted his shoulder, then pulled back her hand when Pippa glanced up. "I'm glad that we were able to get to know you, Sean. Pippa and I have been alone…" Her eyes went to her daughter. "Alone on the island, even with my job. It was good to make a friend."

A friend. Was she trying to tell him to forget about the kiss? That since he'd stopped it, the kiss was no big deal to her, either?

He went over to the fountain and dipped a hand into the water in the wide stone basin, then patted inside his collar and along his hairline. The sun was no longer high overhead, but he couldn't stop sweating.

Maybe because Connie appeared to be saying *so long, goodbye, it's been nice to know you.*

Hell.

"What are you going to do," he asked, "now that the party's over?"

"I thought we'd stay a few more days, spend some girl time together." Connie's eyes shadowed for a moment when she looked at Pippa, who remained absorbed in her notebook, and he supposed that she was leery about the girl delving into the goings-on at the Sheffield estate. "Tomorrow I thought we'd go on a hike and a picnic, then there's a regatta in the afternoon. How does that sound, Pip?"

"Can Mr. Rafferty come?"

Connie opened her mouth. "Uh…"

"Not this time, Pippa." He forked a damp hand through his hair. "Your mom wants you to yourself."

"But you said you'd teach me more about investigations." Pippa climbed to her feet. "I've been practicing. I made lots of new observations and I wrote them all down."

Connie shook her head. "Maybe we'll see Mr. Rafferty at the regatta. There'll be lots of new things to observe there."

"Actually," Sean said, "I may be off the island."

Connie's eyes widened. "You're not going home so soon?"

That was more gratifying. "No. But I'll be having a guest. My son. He's flying out from California."

Pippa caught her lower lip between her teeth. "Joshua."

"That's right. I don't remember telling you his name."

"I *observed.*"

"You eavesdropped." Connie dropped a heavy hand on her daughter's shoulder. "Pippa, really. What have I told you? It's not a nice habit."

The girl pushed her smudged glasses up her nose. "Sorry."

Connie let the matter slide. "Well, this is unexpected, but we look forward to meeting your son." She blinked. "I mean, if we happen to run into you two."

"We'll see about that." He smiled grimly. "Apparently Josh got into some trouble out west and threatened to run away. His mother called his bluff by sending him to me early. I usually get him for most of August, but now she's had enough of his behavior and wants him out of the house."

"Could be a good opportunity for you two," Connie said.

"Or it might be very bad. He's angry with me, too. I can't get anything out of him on the phone."

Connie gave Pippa a loose-armed hug. "Osprey Island will bring you together. Wait and see."

Sean wasn't so sure. "Josh is bound to be dis—"

He broke off at the sound of stamping feet as someone made their way through the maze. He'd thought all the other guests had departed. The Sheffields and their entourage had returned to the house. Even the caterers and orchestra had packed up and gone.

Connie put a finger to her lips. "A straggler," she whispered. "Don't give away our location."

They waited in silence, grinning at each other with cozy coconspiracy as the maze walker made a wrong turn. "Goddamn friggin' maze," said a male voice. "The last thing I need…"

Connie sobered. "I know who that is."

"So do I," said Pippa. Her eyes were big.

The footsteps stopped. In one of hedge doorways stood an older man, his bulk wizened by age. He wore dark work clothes and a sullen, sunken-eyed expression. His spade dropped to the ground with a pebbly crunch. "What the— What are you folks doing here?"

"Walking the maze," Connie said pleasantly. "Why are you here, Graves?"

The gardener grunted. "Maintenance. This place ain't nothin' but a whole lot of extra work for me."

"Hmm. If you're doing maintenance, you should have a rake, not a spade. And a waste bag." Connie pointed to the small pile of trash she'd collected, mainly candy wrappings, as she'd trailed Sean through the maze. The older children hadn't been as pleased as the younger ones that the Sheffields had awarded only goody bags at the completion of their race. "Since you're here, you can clear the trash away. Thank you."

Graves scowled, not moving.

Connie smiled, equally determined.

The gardener gave up. He scooped up the refuse and walked away muttering, one weathered brown hand locked on the neck of the spade.

Connie had a funny look on her face. "Graves has come around. He never wanted a part of the maze until the past few days. Lucky me—I get to give him instruction on hedge trimming before I leave the island." She put her hands on her hips. "And did you see that he was carrying one of *my* spades? I believe that man has light fingers."

Over on the bench, Pippa opened her notebook.

CHAPTER ELEVEN

SLEEPING LATE wasn't a luxury Connie had indulged in for a very long time. The experience was so unfamiliar that when she slowly came awake the next morning, she mistook the less-than-comfortable bed for her own at home. She tugged the sheet up to her neck and rolled over against a solid shape. She reached for Phil's shoulder, but when he turned the face she saw was Sean's.

She bolted upright. No, the sailboat-patterned walls were not hers, but there *was* an extra body in her bed.

She licked her dry lips. "Pippa?"

"I fell asleep." Pippa rubbed her eyes. She was on top of the covers and already dressed in boxy white capri pants and a sleeveless top. "You wouldn't wake up."

"I was dreaming."

"I know. You said Dad's name."

Connie blew out a breath. At least she hadn't said Sean. Pippa sat up. "I still dream about Daddy, too."

"Aw, sweetie. I hope we always do."

"But sometimes I don't remember his face. Or, like, he's Dad but he's different. And sometimes I just hear his voice and he's not there at all. Then I wake up sad."

Connie hugged her. "You should come and talk to me when that happens."

"You're always up already and running around the house yelling at me to hurry up."

"Not today. We're officially on vacation. We have days and days together, to do anything we want to do."

"Anything?"

"Whatever your heart desires."

"I want to see Cutter Head."

"Fine." Connie got out of bed and into a robe. "After I take a shower, I'm going to make blueberry pancakes for breakfast. Then I think I'll do tabbouleh for our picnic lunch. Except that needs to sit awhile, so maybe we should go on our hike first and take the picnic to the regatta."

She babbled on, through a lick-and-a-spit shower. That's what her dad used to call it when she was racing at full speed as usual, on her way to cheerleader practice or her summer job lifeguarding at the community pool. She pulled on her skinny jeans and the striped boat-neck top she'd bought for the island because it looked so nautical. Not until Pippa and she were sitting at the table in front of stacked pancakes and a bottle of blue-berry-infused syrup did she ask the question she'd wanted to from the start.

"Where did you hear about Cutter Head?" Her voice wasn't as casual as she'd meant to make it.

"I asked some of the kids."

"Asked them what?"

Pippa concentrated on slicing into her pancakes.

Connie sighed. "I guess I already know." She could hardly expect Pippa to open up without going first. "I did the same thing. There's a rock in the harbor, too, near the yacht club. I think that one's more likely as a meeting place.

"But, Pippa, you have to listen to me now, and I

mean it. Just because you overheard a suspicious conversation is no reason for you to get involved. You're not Trixie Belden. She's fictional. Nothing bad will ever happen to her, even when she gets into a fix. Real life doesn't necessarily go that way."

"Yes, Mom."

Connie almost regretted the lecture. If any kid knew that life could be harsh and hurtful, it was Pippa.

But that didn't change the present situation. "You are *not* to go off on your own. Under no circumstances, let alone ones that might be dangerous. Do you understand?"

Pippa's chin jutted a little, but she nodded. "Yes, Mom."

"Good. Because our primary object is to have fun. If we happen to overturn some...uh..."

"Clue?"

"All right," Connie said with a laugh. "Have it your way. If we happen to find a clue that actually means something, we'll tell the authorities. All right?"

"Yeah."

"Trixie should always do the same."

"Usually she does. And then she solves the case anyway." Pippa squinted one eye. "Mr. Rafferty is an authority, isn't he?"

"Technically, but he's not on duty. This isn't even his state."

"How far is Massachusetts from us?"

"Not very far. Depends on the traffic, but at most a couple of hours by car. Why do you ask?"

"I just wondered." Pippa brought her empty plate to the sink. "I kinda wish he was coming with us today, but not if his son has to be there. I bet he's a mean boy. He'll tease me."

"I doubt Mr. Rafferty would let that happen, but if it did, you'd just have to tell me and we'd come up with some good comebacks for you."

Pippa giggled. "Uncle Ray told me about the names you used to call him."

"He deserved every one of them, too. Sez Spud."

THE HIKE TO CUTTER HEAD was uneventful, although they had a wonderful time picking shells on the beach and scaling a hillside starred with daisies and buttercups. The tenacity of the small but sturdy pines that clung to the rock with gnarled roots summoned up an overwhelming thankfulness in Connie, as did the sheer, wild beauty of the place. She was glad to be alive.

They returned to their cottage at noon, rested for a few minutes, then packed up their lunch and headed downhill to the regatta. Pippa swore she'd never been to a regatta, but Connie told her how they used to take her every Fourth of July to see the fireworks and the boats sail by with their colorful flags. Her heart ached as she watched her daughter absorb that detail to add to her small store of memories of her father.

When they reached the village, Pippa was complaining about all the walking. So they decided to rent bikes for the remainder of their stay. They coasted the short way to the harbor, the old-fashioned wicker picnic basket Connie had found in the guesthouse strapped perilously to her handlebars.

The races had already begun. Sloops dotted the water. Connie looked hopelessly for an empty patch of grass or rock among the crowd of spectators until Jilly Crosby caught her attention. She called them up to join her and Kay on the deck of the yacht club. Most of her

VIPs had departed on the morning ferry, so there was plenty of room.

Anders was nowhere in sight. When Connie asked, Kay shrugged and retreated behind a pair of big round sunglasses and a hat with a floppy brim that covered most of her face. Jilly kept up a steady stream of chatter to fill the silence, until her voice began to sound like the squabbling ducks. Connie tuned her out.

The seemingly random comings and goings of the boats was confusing, but she and Pippa enjoyed the spectacle. Now and then they would hear the flat pop of a starter's gun across the water, and another small fleet of boats would glide out to sea.

Pippa went to the deck railing with her binoculars and her notebook, turning to burble to Connie whenever she made an especially exciting discovery: a sailor clinging to the line of a racing boat; a striped spinnaker; two boys winging pebbles off a row of mailboxes; and a fuzzy black dog who stole a hot dog out of a little girl's hand.

The afternoon grew long and Connie felt the flush of too much sun on her cheeks. She called to Pippa to come and help her pack up the hamper. Kay and Jilly had grown bored with the boat races and had disappeared into the club. They'd been laughing over martinis with several male admirers, but now even they were gone. Connie had thought of Sean on and off, and had searched again for him among the colorful crowd. But the only person she'd recognized was Rachel Wells, who'd been watching her from a plastic lawn chair parked along the side of the road. They had exchanged waves.

The ferry bleated its arrival. Rumpled day-trippers gathered at the wharf to board for the return trip to the mainland.

"Pippa, time to go. We've got a long trek up the hill with the bikes." When there was no response, Connie realized that her daughter had vanished.

She shoved her sunglasses up, anchoring them in her hair. The vivid, distorted colors of the harbor scene hurt her eyes. She squinted. "Pippa, where'd you go?"

Connie found her around the corner of the wrap-around deck, leaning perilously over the railing with both hands locked on her binoculars. She had them pointed at *Siren Song,* the Sheffield yacht. The couple was out on the deck. Even from a distance, Connie could hear their angry shouts.

Connie grabbed the back of Pippa's waistband and hauled her down. "Give me those."

"But, Mom, the Sheffields are fighting."

Connie bent to speak in Pippa's ear. "That's none of our business."

"Mrs. S. said she was going to throw her diamond ring into the bay," Pippa persisted. "I wanted to watch where it landed. What if a seagull swooped in and grabbed the ring before it reached the water?"

Connie hustled Pippa away. "Nonsense. They're having a fight. Grown-ups do that. I'm certain no diamonds are ending up in the bay." She looped the binoculars around her neck. "Go and get the picnic basket."

Pippa went, dragging her feet on the wooden deck. Connie lifted the glasses to her eyes, spun the knob to focus on the yacht. *Just a quick look.*

Kay's arm swung wide and her palm cracked across her husband's face. Infuriated, he yanked her toward him, knocking her hat off as he got in her face.

Connie dropped the glasses. She didn't want to see any more. Ashamed that she'd looked at all, she moved swiftly to get herself and Pippa away from the club and its prime vantage point. But she half expected to hear the splash of a body hitting the bay.

They were wheeling their cycles out of the bike stand when Sean called out. "Connie! Pippa!" He was just leaving the wharf with a teenage boy at his side. "Wait up."

Pippa moaned under her breath.

"Hey," Sean said when he reached them. His eyes creased. There was something different about him, beyond the boy at his side. He seemed…happier. "I'm glad we caught you."

Connie yanked a strap taut around the picnic hamper. "This must be your son."

"Joshua Rafferty." Sean put a hand between the boy's shoulder blades, bringing him forward. "Josh, these are the Bradfords, Connie and her daughter, Pippa. They're the ones I mentioned, staying in a cottage across the island from ours."

Connie nodded. "Nice to meet you, Josh."

"Yeah, you, too," he said without quite meeting her eyes. He was tall for a thirteen-year-old, rangy like Sean but with a rounder face and a mop of wavy dark hair that brushed his eyebrows and neck. He wore a backward baseball cap, a baggy T-shirt and shorts that reached past his knees. He carried a backpack in one hand and a skateboard under the other arm.

Connie smiled, relieved that Josh seemed like a typical teenager. "Welcome to Osprey Island."

He kicked a stone across the pavement.

Pippa pushed her bike toward the road. She was usually shy around new kids, but she cocked her head at Josh and said, "You know you can't use a skateboard here."

He tilted his head and sneered at her, pulling an I'm-older-and-cooler attitude. "Says you."

"I'm afraid I said it, too, son." Sean set down the duffel bag he'd been carrying. "There's no pavement except right around here. The rest of the island is all dirt roads."

Josh looked at the barren track of the steep road that led up into the forest. "What a stupid place."

"No, it isn't," Pippa said. "It's the best place in the world."

Josh scoffed and turned his back. Pippa's down-turned face was flushed, and she stabbed at the pedal of her bike with her foot, making it spin.

Sean's expression was apologetic, but Connie shook her head. "You two should rent bikes. We just did. It's going to be a haul to get up the hill, but I'm looking forward to the next ride into town. All downhill."

"What do you think, Josh? The skateboard for a bike?"

"I don't care." Josh put the board down and slung his backpack over his shoulder. "Do they have mountain bikes?"

"We can check."

Connie and Pippa accompanied them to the bike-rental shop but stayed outside while the two males went inside. "I don't like him," Pippa said, but she had the same look on her face that she got with Molly Wells, the teenage babysitter. Guarded fascination.

"Give him time. This is all new to him and he's bound to be a touch defensive."

Pippa's shoulders hunched over the handlebars of her bike. "Mr. Rafferty won't want to spend any more time with me."

"We're going to be busy, anyway," Connie said, although she'd had her own hopes for the next few days.

Sean and Josh came out of the shop with the owner and chose their bikes from the lineup beneath the store-front window. Without a backward glance, Josh climbed on his off-road cycle and sped away, standing on the pedals and pushing hard as Shore Road steepened.

Not to be outdone, Pippa followed at a much slower pace. Partway up the road, her bike slowed to a crawl and she finally had to get off and push.

"Looks like I'm pushing the whole way." Sean piled his son's skateboard and duffel into the bike's basket, making a precarious load.

"I'll join you," Connie said. "We've been watching the sailboat races and the sun has sapped most of my energy. I wondered if you'd show up."

"I got the confirmation from my ex last night and took the morning ferry to meet Josh in Bangor. He's not exactly happy about being here. I considered cutting my stay on the island short and taking him back home. At least he knows the town, and has a few friends from previous visits."

"But you didn't." It might have been easier on her if he had, but that didn't mean she wanted him gone.

Sean winced as he stretched over the unwieldy bike, pushing past the steep section of the road. "I don't like to leave my affairs unfinished."

Connie put her head down and pushed.

He glanced sidelong at her as they rolled to a stop at the top of the hill, where the road forked toward the opposite sides of the island. "Not that you're an affair, exactly…"

She pulled at the shirt sticking to her skin. "Uh, well, this is where we part ways." He looked startled until she indicated the road sign—two quaint old wooden paddles with the words *Shore* and *Cliff* carved into the blades. They pointed in opposite directions.

Choose one, Connie thought. *Dead end ahead.*

"I'd say Pippa's got another idea." Sean pointed down the west-side road, where Connie's daughter was peddling as fast as she could after Josh.

Connie smiled, ridiculously relieved that the choice had already been made. "So we'll go the long way around."

They continued toward Pine Cone Cottage, still walking the bikes. "Want to stay for supper?" Sean asked when they were within sight of the cottage. Pippa waited by the mailbox.

"We shouldn't. You probably want to spend the time alone with Josh."

"He hardly said two words to me on the ferry. He's always been slow to warm up when we first get together, but this time he's worse than ever. I guess he considers this trip his punishment for getting into trouble at home, so he's going to make sure I'm punished, too." They arrived at the Potter mailbox. "Wait'll he finds out there's no Xbox, PlayStation or cable. Then I'll really be in for it. Having you and Pippa around would be a relief."

"Gee, given all that, I'm not so sure we *want* to stay." Connie laughed before turning to her wary daughter. "Mr. Rafferty has asked us to supper. What do you think?"

Pippa scrunched her face. "Okay."

"Nothing fancy," he said. "Hot dogs and hamburgers on the barbecue. I noticed there's an old charcoal grill out back." He looked toward the house. "Where's Josh?"

"I told him this was the place, but he kept going," Pippa answered. "He said he was taking a ride."

Sean frowned. "That should be okay. There's no way to get lost on an island the size of Osprey."

"He'll be back." Connie was determined to be cheerful. "What a pretty little cottage! It's like something out of a storybook."

"That's right, you haven't been here." Sean left the bike by the curved willow gate, grabbing his son's luggage. "Come and see."

Connie took in the lavishly haphazard flower garden and the whitewashed cottage with gingerbread trim. Window boxes spilled with begonias and English ivy. At one corner, a mossy barrel collected rainwater from the downspout. Tucked under the wide eaves near the door was an old-fashioned porch swing suspended on rusty chains.

"It's absolutely perfect—a true enchanted cottage. The Peregrine guesthouse is nice, but we're closed in by all those trees. You've got both the pines *and* a seaside view."

"I'm not sure about the enchanted part."

"Oh, it's enchanted. It's got to be." She inhaled. "I can't seem to get enough of the air here. All that clean pine and sharp salt and hot sun. I want to swallow big gulps of it. Suck it straight up through my pores."

"I know what you mean. It's bracing."

Connie nodded. "Yes. I keep thinking that a person's troubles would be scoured right away in a place like this." She chuckled. "But that's probably not the case."

"We can wish." Sean opened the door. "Come inside."

She was dying to see the interior but held back. "We should give you two time to settle in before dinner. I'd like to go home and freshen up and drop off our things, anyway."

Sean leaned against the doorjamb. "All right. I'll see you in about an hour?"

His handsomeness hurt her eyes. Every time he came

near, her body reacted instinctively. She swayed toward him, yearning to feel his arms around her, his lips, his breath, his beating heart.

Pippa watched from the gate.

Connie reined herself in. "Yes, we'll see you then," she said, sounding quite prim.

He smiled at her with scalawag eyes, and she got the distinct idea that he suspected what she was feeling even if she couldn't say it right then.

CHAPTER TWELVE

Pippa Bradford's Book of Curious Observations

CLUES FOUND at the Osprey Island Yacht Club:

1. Mr. and Mrs. Sheffield. They fight a lot. I think he has a girlfriend. This is called extramartial sex. My mom doesn't know I know that SO SHE BETTER NOT BE READING THIS!!!

2. The lady named Jilly is nicer than Mrs. S. even if they look alike. She talked to me about dancing in shows in Las Vegas and said that it's not too late for me to start dance class. I tripped on a chair leg and almost dropped my binoculars into the water, so she was just trying to be nice and help me from being clumsy.

3. There was nothing suspicious about Cutter Head. But I found out there is a place called The Rock in the harbor. People here say, "Meet me at The Rock." It's actually in the water, but they just mean to meet nearby. My mom doesn't know about The Rock yet.

4.

(I had more clues but now I can't remember them. That boy is here in the backyard with me and my mom. Mr. R. is starting the barbecue grill. That boy is just sitting in a lawn chair, but he saw me looking at him and made a face at me. I hate to say it to Mr. R., but I think his son is a big mean turd.*)

*His name is Josh. He's kind of cute if you like big mean turds.

"WHO WANTS TO HELP with the salad?" Connie called from the kitchen of Pine Cone Cottage. When there was no answer, she stuck her head out the back door. "Don't everyone volunteer at once."

"Josh," said Sean. He lifted a bag of charcoal briquettes and motioned with his head. "You go and help Mrs. Bradford."

"Why me?"

"Because Pippa is my assistant." The charcoal rattled in the bottom of the kettle grill. "Matches?"

"I got 'em." Pippa flung aside her notebook and scrambled up from the grass.

Josh glowered.

"Come on," Connie said. "You can chop the tomatoes and cucumber while I make the hamburger patties. It'll take five minutes."

Reluctantly, the teen abandoned the chair he'd slung himself into when he'd returned from his bike ride.

"You'll like Osprey Island." She handed Josh a knife. "Even though there are no skateboard ramps and video games. It's more of a natural experience."

"That's for sure." He turned his hat around, using the band to lift the hair out of his eyes. Without instruction, he rinsed the vegetables and got out the cutting board.

"Have you ever rock-climbed?" Obliquely, she watched him slice tomatoes. Satisfied that he knew his way around a kitchen, she turned back to the pile of ground meat.

"Only in a gym."

"There are some steep cliffs on the east side of the island. I'm sure you can find gear and an instructor in Jonesport." He didn't respond. "You can try sea kayaking and sailing, too. Pippa and I might give the kayaks a go, but we're rank beginners. She may not dare. She's already had one ocean dunking."

"Huh."

"Your dad fished her out. He was a real hero. The water here is ice-cold and can cause hypothermia in a matter of minutes."

Josh continued chopping.

The cucumber was down to a nub. She became a little desperate. "You must be used to warm water, being from California. Are you a surfer?"

"Not that much. We don't live near the ocean."

"You have a step-siblings, is that right?"

"Nope." He had Sean's bluish-gray, approaching-thunderstorm eyes. "They're halves. Two half sisters."

"Oh, well, that's just as good as the real thing, isn't it?"

"Just as bad, too."

Connie laughed and went to wash her hands. "Pippa's an only child. She claims she prefers it that way, but I think she'd be better off with some brothers and sisters to fight with."

"So, like, that means you're hunting for a husband?"

Connie's voice strangled in her throat. She swallowed and reached for a dish towel. "Er, not in particular. I was an only child, and I turned out okay."

"My dad is from a big family, but that doesn't mean he likes kids."

"Oh? Why do you say that?"

Josh just gave a sneering "huh" and clomped out of the kitchen. The back door swung shut with a bang.

Connie replaced the towel. She scraped the heap of neatly chopped vegetables into the salad bowl, where they added a contrast of color to the purple and green organic salad greens. "At least *that* went well," she said to herself.

Making friends with Josh was going to take a while.

THE MEAL WAS AWKWARD. Neither of the children cooperated with Connie's attempts to include them. She and Sean ended up talking to each other, but even their conversations dwindled and died from trying too hard.

She started to wish she'd stayed at the guesthouse with Pippa. After Phil, they had learned to make a comfortable and self-contained party of two. Why change now? She was *not* husband-hunting. She'd started out thinking that a few dates might be nice. The strength of her attraction to Sean was something she hadn't prepared for. Certainly she hadn't envisioned getting seriously involved with a single parent who had plenty of issues of his own.

On the other hand, it bothered her that she'd let Josh's discouragement get to her.

"Ketchup," Josh said abruptly.

From across the table, Sean leveled a stern look at his son.

Josh twisted his mouth to one side. "Please."

Connie passed him the bottle.

He lifted off the top of his half-eaten burger and squeezed more ketchup onto it. The bottle let out a loud burp and the condiment erupted, splattering the plate and table.

"That sounded like a—a—" Pippa gave way to a fit of giggles.

Ruddy color suffused in Josh's face. Then he wrapped both hands around the ketchup bottle and squeezed hard, making it blurt even more rudely.

"Enough." Sean's jaw bulged with an unswallowed bite of burger. "You're making a mess."

Connie grabbed a paper napkin to mop up, but she caught Pippa's eye and began to giggle. Suddenly they were all laughing, including Josh. He looked like a baby-faced kid when he laughed—almost innocent. Connie remembered that he was only three years older than Pippa. Just a boy.

After that, their awkwardness with each other wasn't so bad. They weren't one big happy family, either, but at least they were able to speak almost naturally and swallow the meal without lumps in their throats.

They discussed the history of Osprey Island, which Josh was disappointed to find included more whaling and fishing boats than pirate skullduggery. He was mildly intrigued by the stories of boats lost at sea. Connie explained about widow's walks, like the one at Peregrine House. She invited Josh to visit the maze.

Pippa remained quiet. Connie smiled when she saw her daughter sneaking admiring looks at Josh from beneath her lashes while he talked with his dad about home. Apparently he played baseball in a summer league but had been kicked off the team after the recent trouble. The admission came out grudgingly after careful questioning by Sean.

"So what?" Josh inclined his shaggy head. "Who cares?"

"I do, I'm sure your mother does, and I believe you

do, too." Sean set his fists on either side of his plate, obviously struggling to keep his cool. "We'll discuss this later." He apologized to Connie with a grim nod. "Not in front of our guests."

"They aren't *my* guests." Kicking back his chair, Josh stood. He acted defiant, but as he ran into the house, his face was scrunched with a kind of desperate fury that went straight to Connie's heart. She recognized his need to rage.

"Please excuse my son's rudeness," Sean said, tight-lipped.

"Don't worry on our account." Connie wasn't bothered until she saw the hurt reflected in Pippa's eyes. "We know that Josh isn't angry with us. Right, Pip?"

"I guess."

"He's mad at me," Sean said bleakly.

"Why don't you go inside and talk to him in private for a few minutes? Pippa and I will clean up out here."

"Thanks," Sean said, clearly relieved.

"Maybe we should go home?"

"No, stick around." He rolled his eyes. "Buffer zone, you know?"

Connie glanced doubtfully at Pippa, her thin-skinned child, but she agreed to stay.

"WHAT KIND OF TROUBLE did Josh get into?" Connie asked once the storm had passed and their children were safely ensconced in front of the TV with a movie to watch.

In the interest of togetherness, Sean had pushed for a puzzle or a board game out of Alice Potter's games closet—she truly had one, right there in her living room—but Josh hadn't been interested. Not surprising, since he'd never heard of Parcheesi and none of them could work up the enthusiasm for a two-thousand-piece puzzle of the Swiss Alps. The TV had only a couple of snowy channels. The kids had settled on a DVD of *Pirates of the Caribbean,* with *The Legend of Sleepy Hollow* as backup. The absent Miss Potter seemed to be a Johnny Depp fan.

"If you don't mind me asking," Connie added. She put a toe to the ground and pushed, setting the swing swaying. They had come outside to watch the sunset, but the sound of sword fighting from inside was taking away from the experience.

Sean got up, went inside and closed the double-hung window with a loud screech of the warped wood. Josh sat glumly in one corner of the sofa, his chin on his chest and his hat pulled down to his eyes. Pippa sat in the other corner, staring fixedly at the TV with pink cheeks and her arms crossed over her middle. They didn't look happy, to say the least.

"How are the kids doing?" Connie asked when he'd settled back down beside her.

"Thrilled with each other's company."

"Uh-huh."

Feeling something like a teenager on his first movie date, Sean shifted and put his arm along the back of the double swing. "To answer your question…"

Connie angled her head and smiled his way, as though she'd forgotten all about any question. The ends of her hair tickled his arm.

"He was caught vandalizing cars, with a couple of other guys. Nothing too terrible, but bad enough— letting the air out of tires, stealing license plates, stunts like that. The worst of it was a broken window."

"Were charges pressed?"

"Nope, but he's making full restitution. He'll have to find a way to earn extra cash when he goes back home."

"Then he is going home? I wondered if he might live with you."

A look of stark longing crossed Sean's face before he frowned. "Jen wouldn't hear of it. My ex-wife."

"But being with his dad might be what he needs."

"I don't know. Sometimes I think I've forgotten how to be his father. He moved away when he was six. I've missed out on so much of his life." Sean closed his eyes, tilted his head back. The sounds of the sea washed through him; he wished it was that easy to sweep away his regrets. "If I could do it over, knowing how hard it is to be a part-time dad, I'd have followed him to California and shared custody."

"What stopped you at the time?"

That answer was simple. "My job. I couldn't imagine not being a state trooper. My father was rewarded for heroism and bravery, my brothers and sister both joined up straight out of college and are still on the job. I never once thought of doing anything else with my life."

Connie pursed her lips. "Has that changed?"

"Maybe."

"Because of the shooting?"

He grunted.

"I'm sorry. I'm being nosy." She put her knees together and pushed off with her toes, several times, until the swing was going steadily with a *screek screek* of the rusty chains. "I forget my boundaries."

"What are your boundaries?" he asked.

"My boundaries," Connie mused. "Phil would have said I have none. Back then, there weren't that many.

But now..." She shrugged. "I've got a few. Life seems riskier than it used to."

Sean glanced inside at Pippa and Josh. "Can't disagree with that."

Connie sighed.

They lapsed into silence, watching as the setting sun lit up the clouds with bright golds and deep, glowing blues. Birds hopped around the hedges at the roadside. He stroked his thumb across Connie's shoulder, finding the inch of skin that showed between the armhole of her top and the lightweight scarf she'd pulled around her bare arms.

"Tell me about your marriage," she said abruptly, then laughed. "There I go again. You don't have to answer if you don't want."

Surprisingly, he wanted to. They didn't have much time left to get to know each other.

"Well, it happened too fast," he said after considering how to start. "We met and married within eight months, with Josh already on the way. By then Jen was already realizing that she wasn't so thrilled with my job, especially when I was reassigned and we moved from Boston to a small town. Five years later, we were done. Straightaway, she found another guy who was a lot more successful than me, and was going to do even better with his new job in California."

"Ouch. Ego blow."

Sean shook his head. "I knew going in that my career would never make me rich. I didn't care. There are other rewards."

"You're preaching to the choir. Not that I don't like success and the things that money can buy, but I've been sticking to a budget for as long as I can remember.

It's practically second nature by now." Connie turned her head and kissed his knuckles. The gesture of acceptance was more meaningful to Sean than he'd expected.

"I've always thought that a good home life is most important," she said. "The little, everyday kind of stuff, I mean. Like they say, life is what happens when you're not paying attention. So if you're not enjoying the small daily moments—a sunset or a laugh over dinner, for instance—what's the point?"

"But you can enjoy a sunset from a mansion as easily as a humble cottage."

"Of course. Either way you look at it, the trappings aren't what makes you happy. I learned that real fast when Phil got sick and we had to put every penny toward the medical bills that our insurance didn't cover."

Sean squinted into the sun, ablaze on the horizon. "So it's your turn. Tell me about your husband."

"We met in college, at U Conn. I had about half a dozen boyfriends at the time, and Phil was just a friend at first. He was the nicest guy. Incredibly funny and smart. He made me laugh every day, and after a while I realized that I'd rather spend my time with him than any of the others. He, of course, said that was the plan all along."

"Then it's true that women go for a sense of humor above looks?" Sean made a face. "Damn. I was counting on my classic profile and toned physique to dazzle you."

"Don't discount those yet." She tipped her head forward to run her gaze over him. Her eyes twinkled like fairy lights. "Besides, for a man who says he's the serious type, you've got a pretty keen sense of humor."

"Get back to you and Phil."

"Well, let's see." Her hesitation was awkward, as if

she didn't know whether reminiscing with him was the right thing to do. "We eloped midway through our junior year," she began in an even tone. "Money was tight, so I dropped out to make ends meet while Phil finished his degree. We had Pippa when I was twenty-three, one of life's little surprises. By then, Phil had a good job and his parents had helped us out with a downpayment so we could buy a house. Then, just when everything was set for happy-ever-after, he was diagnosed with leukemia."

Sean's hand on her shoulder suddenly felt heavy and wooden. "I'm sorry."

Connie nodded, and he knew that any sympathy he could offer would be inadequate.

Eventually she took a deep breath and kept going. He admired the way she faced up to her hurt. "Phil was determined to beat it. And he did. He went into remission. I had started a vegetable garden to help with the food budget and gradually that turned into a part-time business. Then Phil got sick again." She stopped, biting her lip and blinking to keep the tears back. "He couldn't work. I took a monotonous office job and went to master gardener classes at night, keeping up with my gardening clients on the weekends."

"I knew you were tough."

"Phil was tougher. But in the end, still not tough enough." She dabbed at her eyes. "The past few years have been a struggle, but at least my business has thrived."

"You should be proud of yourself."

"I am, for the most part." She let out a long breath, and he felt the tension drain out of her. "I worry about Pippa and how losing her dad has affected her. But I guess you know that already."

"It seems to me now that my parents made raising a family look so easy, but here I am, struggling to get it right with just one."

"Yeah." Her mouth puckered into a tight smile. "Why can't our kids just cooperate the way we did?"

"Okay, maybe it wasn't easy for our parents, either."

She sighed and leaned back in the swing, turning her face toward his. "Teaming up helps."

Her expression was remarkably unguarded for a woman who'd seen such hard times. He glanced toward the window, wishing he could be half so open. "Those two in there might not agree."

"Pippa's trying not to show how much she wants Josh to like her."

"Josh doesn't want to show that he likes *anything*."

"Were you ever like that?"

"Still am."

"Ah, yes." Her lids drifted lower, almost closing. "It's a good thing adults know how to show their affection even when they don't want to say it out loud."

He clasped the back of her neck, his fingers tunneled through the fine silk of her hair. "How would that be?"

"See if you can figure it out."

He settled his mouth on hers with a quiet deliberation, despite the turmoil inside that said kissing her right now, right there, wasn't a good idea. He simply wasn't able to resist, especially when she shifted against him, put her hand on his chest and parted her lips the slightest bit. His desire became as fluid and hot as the sunset. Arousal prickled in his bloodstream.

He wrapped her in his arms to deepen the kiss. Her lips tasted salty, but her tongue was soft and sweet when he touched it with his.

"Did I do that right?" he whispered after a while.

The answer simmered between them. She pressed closer, rubbed her nose and cheek over his jaw. "I haven't decided yet. We should try again."

"Good idea."

They kissed, sharing light caresses. Gradually, his concerns became less important. Funny how sex did that to a guy, he thought, still distantly recognizing that he was playing with fire. Except even that warning was too easy to disregard when Connie felt so right in his arms.

"We shouldn't be doing this," he whispered against her mouth.

Her tongue licked across his lip. "I know."

Reluctantly, he pulled away, but only far enough to put an inch or two between them. He kissed her forehead, breathed in the scent of her, told himself to savor every moment, remember every detail, in case…

Instinctively, he opened his eyes.

Josh stood on the other side of the door, glaring.

CHAPTER THIRTEEN

JUST WHEN CONNIE HAD RELAXED and rested her head on Sean's shoulder, expecting the emotional roller coaster she'd been on for most of the evening to cruise to a stop, the ride took a hairpin turn.

Sean pulled away. "I can't do this. Not now."

She sat up and pressed her fingertips to her mouth. Hard.

"You can't do what?"

He didn't look at her, only stared at the window before answering as if he'd swallowed a truckload of gravel. "Start a relationship. Fall—fall for you."

Connie wanted to whip out a sassy comment about how she didn't know that was what they'd been doing. But her lips quivered. She did know. She'd known all along, even when she'd been telling herself they were simply passing their vacation time together.

She dropped her hands to her lap. "I wasn't aware it involved a decision."

"Right," he said heavily. "It should just happen."

"Um, I don't know. I don't..." She was no more prepared for their unexpected romance than he was, but having it withdrawn had opened a sucking whirlpool in her gut.

She put a tentative hand on Sean's leg, trying to get him to turn and look at her. "Why are you doing this?"

He turned, but it was to glance toward the window once more. "Josh. He saw us."

"Oh, no." She spun around. "Where is he?"

"He took off. Out the back door, I think."

"What about Pippa?"

"It's okay. She's inside, watching TV. She doesn't know."

"She probably wouldn't be as surprised as Josh, even if she had seen." Connie had already faced the fact that, by necessity, Pippa would have to be a part of any relationship she began. Would have to approve. That had been an easier theory to accept when it hadn't been put to the test.

"Why is it so bad that Josh saw us together?" she asked. "He must know that you're not a monk."

"It's not that, exactly." Sean groaned, obviously disgusted with himself, but in a way that singed Connie's pride. That he avoided looking at her didn't help.

"Then what is it?" she asked, seething.

"It's about letting him down. His mother remarried so fast. Objectively, he can handle that I've dated other women in the past seven years, even if I haven't paraded any of them in front of him. And I suppose he knows that I might marry again in the future." Sean gestured. "But piling that on him right *now*? It's a critical time for us. I can't afford to be distracted."

"*Distracted?* Is that what you call it?" Connie leaped to her feet, wishing she could also escape the telltale flush that had flooded her face. She looked down at Sean, her eyes narrowed. She should never have let herself get so vulnerable, so fast.

"Tell me," she said. "Did you decide our relationship

was ill-timed—practically doomed—before or after you kissed me?"

He pulled back as if jolted. "What?"

"You couldn't figure it out before, huh? Not when there was a chance to have a little amusement first." Somewhere at the bottom of the hot whirl of emotion, Connie knew she wasn't being fair. Sean had never struck her as a player. Then again, what did she know? She'd also believed that he was solid and dependable.

"It wasn't like that, Connie."

She chuffed.

"Try to understand. I have to concentrate on Josh. No distractions. He deserves that. Hell, he's pleading for it."

"Yes." Connie nodded stiffly. "I'm a parent, too. I get it."

She certainly did. And she also got that for Sean, she wasn't a woman with needs of her own. She was a *distraction.*

Fuming over her all-too-ready acceptance of his kisses when she'd *known* they would only complicate matters, she pushed through the screen door into the cottage. "Time to go, Pippa. Get your things."

Pippa's head popped up over the back of the sofa. "But the movie's not over yet."

"Doesn't matter. You've seen it before, anyway. Quickly, now. The Raffertys need their privacy."

"Connie…" Sean pleaded.

She looped her arm through Pippa's and said, "It's perfectly all right, Sean. Pippa and I have plans of our own, and only a few short days to fit everything in. I'm sure we'll run across each other before it's time to go."

The back door banged and Josh reappeared. His cheeks were mottled, but he lounged in the kitchen doorway, staring first at his father, then at Connie with coolness bordering on disdain.

She schooled her face into composure and squeezed her daughter's arm as if nothing had happened to upset any of them. "Say goodbye to Josh, honey."

The air was so tense it prickled. Pippa blinked. "Bye, Josh."

He flicked the hair out of his eyes. "Yeah. Bye."

Sean stood ramrod straight, as rigid and unrevealing as he'd been on the first day they'd met. "I'll see you, Pippa." Connie felt his gaze on her as he added, "Connie."

She nodded. Managed to form a smile with her mouth.

But she couldn't make herself say goodbye.

The instant Connie and Pippa were gone, Sean turned to confront his son. But Josh had disappeared into the kitchen. He kept his back to his dad, searching the cupboards for something to eat. He knocked a box of instant oatmeal off the counter, spilling the packets. Tore into a package of cookies and jammed two into his mouth at once. Crumbs fell.

Disorder bugged Sean, but he said nothing. *Let the kid cool off.*

Josh shot a glance at his dad. As he stepped to the refrigerator, he ground one of the packets beneath his shoe, splitting it open. "What are you looking at?" he said thickly.

"I've missed you."

Josh's head dove into the fridge. "There's nothing to drink in here. Can I have a beer?"

"You know the answer to that."

He emerged, chugging milk straight from the container.

Sean got the whisk broom and dust pan that hung on the kitchen wall. He handed them to Josh. "I'm sorry about inviting Mrs. Bradford and Pippa over. I shouldn't have done that on your first day. I was— I guess I was nervous about having you here."

Josh shook his head so the unruly hair fell into his eyes. "I don't care."

"Obviously you do." Sean winced, thinking of the way he'd dismissed Connie. She'd understand his need to put Josh first, but that didn't forgive his abrupt change of mind. "It bothered you, to see me kissing her."

Josh looked down at the dangling dust pan. "Do what you want."

"I want…" Connie's face appeared to Sean. A change of mind didn't equal a change of heart.

He brushed her aside. "I want to spend time with you, Josh. I want us to be father and son again."

Josh knelt to sweep up the oatmeal, muttering, "It's not like we have a choice."

Sean squatted beside him. "I did once. About a year after your mom moved you to California, your stepdad wanted to adopt you. They said it would be better if you had their name. That you'd feel more like one of the family."

"Shi— Sheesh." The broom dropped out of Josh's limp fingers.

"They made a good argument, but I couldn't do it."

Josh raised his head to stare challengingly. "Why not?"

Their eyes locked. "The biggest mistake of my life was letting you go in the first place. Losing you completely would have killed me."

"I doubt it," Josh said, but he had to blink and look away.

Despite Josh's stiff-shouldered resistance, Sean gave

his son a brief, hard hug. "It's the truth." He cleared his throat. Picked up the whisk broom. "Now, let's get this mess cleaned up."

"WHY CAN'T WE ASK MR. R. and Josh?" Pippa whined, late the next afternoon. It had been a dreary, boring day. The fog they'd awakened to that morning had never completely dissipated.

It was, in fact, returning now that the weak drizzle had died. Connie stepped away from the window. Dejection and an unnamed dread lodged in her stomach like bricks.

Depressing weather. Anyone would feel anxious being stranded in a tiny cottage on a fog-bound island, with a long evening looming ahead.

"We can't invite the Raffertys to go kayaking because we're giving them space," Connie explained patiently, even though it had to be the sixth joint outing that Pippa had suggested. Apparently she'd warmed up to the idea of having Josh around.

Was a small island enough space? Connie wondered. In spite of the previous evening's abrupt end, she felt the pull of Pine Cone Cottage like a magnet. Maybe Pippa did, too, and that's why she'd been so fractious all day.

"How come they need space?"

"The same reason we do. To spend time together."

"Sometimes it's funner doing things with other people along," Pippa said hopefully.

Connie couldn't disagree. But she shook her head.

Pippa slapped her book shut and dropped it carelessly on the coffee table. Her gaze caught on her notebook. She frowned. "I think you're just mad at Mr. Rafferty. But I have to see him again!"

"Why are you so adamant?"

Pippa's lower lip stuck out. "I don't know what that means."

"Dogged. Unyielding."

"Like stubborn?"

"Yes."

"Stubborn like you not letting us go see Mr. R. and Josh?"

Connie sighed. "Yes, I suppose you could say that." She walked around the living room, picking a fleck of lint off the chair, straightening a framed painting of a sailboat at sea. The contrast between the paint-by-number and the old master works at the main house was vaguely amusing.

Connie looked down at her daughter. "Why are you so intent on seeing Mr. Rafferty?"

Pippa hugged the notebook to her chest. "I have stuff to tell him."

"Can't you tell me?"

"I'd rather tell Mr. R. *He's* a professional."

Still with the "curious observations." Connie had hoped that, with the completion of the maze project and the distraction of their vacation, her daughter had put all that aside. No such luck.

"I'm sure you'll see Mr. Rafferty again before we leave the island. Just not today."

Pippa brooded. "At least can I go for a walk?"

"If you stay close by. Put on your rubber boots and windbreaker. It's damp out there."

After Pippa was gone, Connie sat on the couch and picked up her daughter's discarded book. *Trixie Belden and the Mystery of the Emeralds*. The copyright was 1965, and on the cover Trixie was looking fearfully over her shoulder. She paged through, reading a paragraph here and there, looking at the old-fashioned illustrations. Trixie was on the trail of emeralds hidden at a Virginia plantation. The story was sprinkled with lessons learned and wholesome exclamations like "Jeepers!"

Connie set the book aside and shut her heavy eyes. She hadn't slept much the night before. Sean's rejection still stung.

Was it as easy to fall out of love as it was to fall in…? She didn't think so.

Suddenly her head jerked and her lids sprang open. It took her a second to realize that she'd fallen asleep. For how long? She wasn't wearing a watch, but she couldn't have been out for more than five or ten minutes.

She sat forward, yawning. The house was quiet except for the drip of rain off the eaves. No sign of Pippa.

Pippa.

Connie walked from room to room, checking out the windows. The fog had thickened. Beyond the clearing around the house, the pine trees had become black sentinels rising from a primordial mist.

Unsettled, she grabbed her garden wellies from near the door. "If that girl has gone calling on Sean…"

Outside, everything was gray and bleak and silent. Connie took one look and returned to the house for the flashlight. She switched it on, although it didn't do much good at piercing the pea-soup fog. She shut it off again once she reached the main driveway. There, the fog drifted slowly in diaphanous clumps. She could see beyond it to open space and that helped her keep her bearings. The gate was to her right, the gardens and house to the left.

"Who's there?" A shape appeared out of the fog.

"Pippa!" Connie rushed forward. "It's me."

"Mom." Pippa wrenched out of her mother's crushing hug. "Y-you have to c-come. I think I saw a *murder*."

"Oh, no, Pippa. Not a murder, not now."

"*Maybe* it was a murder. I was up at th-the b-big house, and I heard a scream."

Connie's skin crawled. She managed to keep her voice remarkably steady. "Pippa, no. You didn't hear a scream. It must have been the gulls."

"Wasn't the g-gulls."

"Your teeth are chattering and you're wet through. I'm taking you inside to warm up."

Pippa tugged at her sweater. "But, Mom. We have to go investigate."

"No, we don't. Look at the fog. We'd get lost." Connie turned slowly. Even the high iron gates had disappeared from view. She tightened her arm around Pippa, circling once again. Which direction was the path?

She kept talking to keep the fear at bay. "This fog is so bad I can't even tell where we are, and we haven't moved a step. How could you possibly know what you might have seen or heard in it?"

"I *do* know. The fog wasn't so bad then."

"Well, it is now. We're going back to the guest-house. You can tell me everything once we're inside." Connie took a tentative step on the wet pebbles. "I think it's this way."

She heard a soft crunching from somewhere nearby, although it was difficult to be sure from which direction.

"Mom?" Pippa quailed. "What was that?"

"I'm not sure." Connie raised her voice. "Anyone there?"

There was no answer, only a scraping sound.

Pippa moved closer. "I'm scared," she whispered.

I am, too. Connie would have normally laughed at herself for being such a coward, but the creepy weather had taken the bravado out of her. "It's nothing, honey. Even ordinary sounds get distorted in a thick fog." She gripped Pippa's hand. "Stay with me."

They took several careful steps and stopped. Connie stared into the drifting fog, trying to discern their path among the shadows of looming trees.

Behind them, there was a loud *screeeek,* followed by a metallic *clunk.*

Connie ducked down. "The gate," she said into Pippa's ear. "Someone's at the gate. Don't make a sound."

Pippa nodded. Pearls of mist had collected on her rat-tailed hair and bleached cheeks. She shivered with clenched teeth.

The state of her frightened little girl raised Connie's temper. The pebbles crunched. A footfall? She hefted the flashlight, ready to swing it to defend herself and Pippa.

"Connie?" A man.

Sean? But his voice seemed different. *It's just the fog playing tricks with you.* She took a breath nipped short by the fright she'd had. "Sean?"

"Where are you?"

"Here." She flicked on the flashlight. "Pippa's with me."

"I thought I heard your voices." His tall, broad-shouldered shape stepped in front of her. "What are you doing out here?"

"What are you?" she croaked, although she was glad to see him.

He wiped a hand across his damp face. "Josh ran out of DVDs and snacks. I made a run to the general store."

He raised a limp paper bag. "The fog wasn't this bad when I set out, but I just kept following the road. I wasn't sure how far I'd gotten until I saw the gates of Peregrine House."

"You gave us a scare, coming through the gate like that," Connie said, feeling slightly ridiculous now that they were safe.

"I didn't mean to. Like I said, I heard voices and I wondered what was up." He turned as if to go. "If you're all right…"

"We're fine. I came out to find Pippa, but we're going directly back to the guesthouse." Connie thrust out the flashlight. "You should take this. You have a longer way to go."

"Mr. Rafferty can't go!" her daughter piped up. "What about the murder?"

"Pippa…hush."

"What murder?" Sean said, waving off the flashlight.

"Nothing but my daughter's overactive imagination at play."

"I heard a scream," Pippa insisted. "It came from Peregrine House."

"Must have been a seagull," Connie said, emphasizing the words even though she wasn't sure what to believe.

"Huh." Sean pondered. "That would make sense, except that the gulls seem to be hunkered down until the fog lifts, like everything else. I didn't even hear them down by the harbor."

Pippa pulled on Connie's hand. "See, Mom?"

"Even if there was a scream," she said, "and I'm not conceding that, you're making a giant jump to conclusions with talk of a murder. I will grant you that the fog is enough to get anyone's imagination going, especially yours." Connie took Pippa by the shoulders and turned her toward what she hoped was the path. "You're marching back to the house. No more argument."

"But it *could* have been a murder."

"Go."

Pippa shuffled forward. "Is this the path?"

"Let me see." Connie felt Sean press up against her. He reached over her frozen form and took the flashlight from her hand. The light searched through the fog. "Right there. Is that it?"

"Yes," Pippa said.

Sean gave her the light. "You lead the way."

They walked three in a line toward the cottage, splattered by drooping, wet branches as they went.

When they reached the door, Connie shook out her hair and picked a V of pine needles off her cheek. She scooted Pippa into the house and told her to go upstairs to change into dry clothes.

"But, Mo-om…"

"Even Trixie obeys her parents. Go."

Pippa kicked off her boots and stomped up the steps. "Tell Mr. R. not to leave until I get back."

Sean was hovering on the doorstep. "Come inside," she offered.

He stepped in. "Tell me about this 'murder.'"

Connie shook her head. "There's no more to the story than what we've already said. I don't know what she heard, but I seriously doubt it was a murder."

"Could have been a real scream, though."

"Perhaps."

"There might be trouble at Peregrine House." He reached for the flashlight Pippa had parked on a side table by the door. "Mind if I take this? I'm going up to see if everything's all right."

"You believe Pippa."

"I don't discount her."

Connie looked down. "It's not that I do, either. Not entirely. But I've seen how her mind can work, and I know how eager she is to impress you. Chances are that you're going on a wild-goose chase."

"If that's so, no harm done." He gave her the package from Lattimer's. "Hold on to this. I'll be back shortly with a full report."

Connie reached for him, then withdrew her hand. The dread was back; she was shaking with it. She didn't want him to go, but there seemed no way to make him stay. "What if there really is something going on up there and you don't come back? What'll I do then?"

"That won't happen. I will return." He stared evenly at her until her stomach dropped down around her knees. "We'll talk," he said, and she knew he meant they'd talk about more than this mystery.

"What about Josh? He'll be wondering what happened to you."

"Josh is fine. For all he knows, I'm kicking back in the village, waiting for the fog to lift." Sean switched on the flashlight. It only pierced a few yards of the cottony mist, picking out the path they'd just followed.

"What if…" Connie's voice dried up in her throat. She wanted to ask him what if there really was a dangerous situation at Peregrine House and he landed in the middle of it because he was playing the hero for them. But he was a lawman. Who better to handle the situation?

"You might get lost," she rasped. "You could wander off the edge of the cliff."

Sean smiled. "That definitely won't happen. I'm sure the lights are on at the house." With a jaunty wave, he moved away, vanishing before her eyes. His voice drifted back to her. "Keep Pippa occupied until I return."

Connie stood holding on to the door for a few seconds before she could get her tongue to work. "Be safe," she said. "Come back soon…or I'll kill you myself." That didn't come out as humorously as she'd thought it would.

THE FOG NOT ONLY distorted sound, it distorted shape. Pine trees became haggard witches. Rocks were hulking beasts. Sean soon gave up swinging the beam of the flashlight back and forth and focused on the road ahead. There was no reason he couldn't follow it right up to the house's front porch.

He plodded onward, thinking about Connie. Her attempts to stop him hadn't been about making up after a fight. She'd been seriously spooked, regardless of her insistence that Pippa had misheard.

He jumped at the long, low bleat of a fog horn, then had to laugh at himself. The spooky ambience had worked its spell on him, too.

The road curved up the slope. The diffused lights from the house hung disembodied in the fog. He could hear the water now, lapping at the rocks, but the rest of the seaside world was strangely silent, with only the sound of his footsteps to break the quiet.

Suddenly the maze loomed out of the fog. A slow examination with the flashlight revealed one of the entrances. Strange—the lanterns were out. Perhaps they weren't always switched on, but something about that altered detail made him veer off the road. He paused near the entrance to listen, taken by the eerie Gothic ghost-story feel of the place. A haunted moan or the scrape of a shovel would have seemed quite fitting.

But there was only silence.

Sean moved on, up the lawn to the porch. The house was really lit up. With the shutters open and no draperies drawn, he could see inside many of the rooms as he crossed to the front door. There was no sound, no movement.

He rang the doorbell. Then, when no one answered, he knocked loudly.

"Coming!" a voice sang out.

He tucked the flashlight under an arm, slicked back his dampened hair.

The door was opened by the housekeeper he'd met at the garden party. She was startled, then amused, to see him. "Good Lord," she said heartily. "Sean Rafferty, isn't it? What are you doing out in this weather?"

"I was at the guesthouse with the Bradfords," he said to cut short the explanation. "We heard, uh, some loud sounds that seemed to come from this direction. I walked up to see if everything's okay."

The housekeeper dropped her gaze. "I thank you for the concern, but we're quite all right…now."

Reflex had him reaching for his sidearm. Of course, there was no weapon at hand. He'd brought his official weapon with him on his vacation, a Sig Sauer 9mm, but it was stowed in its carrying case in the closet at Pine Cone Cottage, safely unloaded.

He widened the door and stepped inside to look around. "What happened here?"

One of the maids glanced out from the end of the long hallway that led to the kitchen.

"I believe it's called a domestic disturbance." Rachel

Wells kept her hands folded in front of her body. "My folks would call it a plain old knockdown, drag-out fight."

"Mr. and Mrs. Sheffield?"

She nodded. "Ayuh. Just a loud fight, no more."

"No physical violence?"

"She may have thrown something at him. Upstairs." Mrs. Wells glanced upward. "Here's Mr. Sheffield now."

The silver-haired businessman trotted down the wide staircase, his joints apparently well oiled by years of physical fitness. For once, he wasn't in a suit, only a pair of soft woolen pants and a quilted robe that Sean believed was called a smoking jacket. He'd thought no one but Hugh Hefner wore those.

"Mr. Sheffield, this is Sean Rafferty, a visitor to the island. He came to check up on us." After making the introduction, Rachel Wells murmured a discreet "Pardon" and slipped away.

"How neighborly." Anders Sheffield's smile was as well oiled as his joints. He even crinkled his eyes so that the smile came across as warm and genuine. "Rafferty, was it she said? I remember you from the other day, but I don't recall where you're staying."

"Pine Cone Cottage. It's on the other side of the island."

Sheffield chuckled. "And you came all this way in the fog to call on us?"

Sean felt certain the man knew full well where he'd come from, as well as every other word he'd spoken to Mrs. Wells. "You were having a problem?"

"My wife." Sheffield made a dismissive gesture. "She's high-strung."

"I see." Sean angled his head to look up to the second-floor landing. "I wonder if I could speak to her?"

Sheffield stiffened. His expression became haughty.

"Excuse me. Do you have some jurisdiction here I'm not aware of?"

Sean gazed steadily at the man. "Why would I need jurisdiction?"

Sheffield's gaze narrowed. Seconds passed. Without averting his eyes from Sean's, he cocked his head and called, "Darling? Kay? Our kind neighbor would like to say hello."

Moments later, Kay Sheffield appeared at the balcony railing, her blond hair ruffled around her face and her hand at the throat of a silk dressing gown. She leaned over the railing. "Hello."

"Ma'am." He stared, trying to discern whether she was obscuring a black eye or bruised throat. "Everything okay?"

"Just fine and dandy," she said faintly. "You've caught me in a state of undress, I'm afraid. The weather is so dreary, I'd planned to retire early. We weren't expecting callers."

Sean held up a hand. "No problem, Mrs. Sheffield. I'm not staying." He stared at Sheffield again. "So your houseguests have left?"

"All but the Crosbys." Sheffield smiled, not bothering to disguise the chill of it this time. "Did you also wish to speak to them?"

"That won't be necessary." Sean stepped out onto the porch. "Did you know the lights by the maze are out?"

"Really. I'll have to get my little red-haired gardener right on that."

Without a word of reply, Sean slammed the flashlight into the palm of his right hand and switched it on. He walked away, clenching his jaw tightly, his spine like steel.

Only when he was well down the drive did he turn

to look back at Peregrine House. Sheffield had known exactly what he was saying, and had, in fact, said it to get Sean's goat. For no good reason that he could determine, except that the man did not like being called to question.

Sean's father had taught him that a man should never do anything he wasn't willing to own up to. A lesson, it seemed, that Anders Sheffield had never learned.

Pippa Bradford's Book of Curious Observations

MOM DOESN'T BELIEVE ME about the scream or the maybe-murder.

She NEVER believes me.

So I'm not even going to tell her about the man with the shovel. I only saw him from far away, but I'm pretty sure it was Graves. (Note: he was in the maze with a shovel, too, remember?) If it was him, I'll bet a zillion bucks that he was coming back from burying something, or else he was going to bury something. I thought it would be money or jewels, but what if it's a BODY!!!

CHAPTER FOURTEEN

"IT WAS A FAMILY FIGHT," Sean said to the Bradfords, five minutes later. "No more, no less." He lifted a hand, signaling *caution* to Connie before focusing on Pippa.

Her face had crumpled with disappointment. "But what about the scream?"

"Mrs. Sheffield was probably pretty angry with her husband."

Pippa slumped back on the couch. She crossed her arms over her middle. "How come?"

Connie passed a coffee cup to Sean before patting her daughter's knee. "That, my little investigator, is grownup stuff. None of your business."

"Humph." Pippa roused herself to take a mug of hot chocolate from her mother. "You never screamed at Dad like that."

"And certainly not in a mansion in the middle of a fog storm on a remote Maine island," Connie replied lightly. "We were thinking of starting a game of Monopoly, Sean. Clue might be more appropriate. Would you like to stay and play?"

"I guess I shouldn't. Josh, you know."

"You could get Josh and bring him here." Pippa brightened. "Or we could go to your house. I wouldn't even be afraid in the fog, not this time."

"Pippa, I don't think so." Connie looked away from Sean. "You know what we talked about."

"Ugh, yeah. *Space.*"

"Space?" Sean gulped the steaming coffee. He had taken off his jacket at the door and swiped at the fog droplets clinging to his hair and face, but he still felt rather damp.

"Mom says you need space," Pippa explained. "Away from *us.*"

"That's not what I…" Connie's protest died. She shrugged.

"Your mom's right." Sean was watching Connie; he caught the wounded look she quickly shuttered. His backing out had hurt her, even though he'd told himself it was better to do it sooner than later. A serious relationship required forethought, not just proximity.

Proximity? Who was he kidding?

They had incredible electricity. Plus, they genuinely *liked* each other. They'd connected, regardless of his reluctance.

But he was throwing that away, and why? Out of his fear of taking on responsibility for another person when he'd already failed so badly. On the job, and with Josh.

Sean put down his coffee. "You see, Pippa, I don't get to spend a lot of time with Josh, and just now, it's especially important that I do. That doesn't mean that I never want to see you two again." Connie moved to the window. She had her arms wrapped around herself, as she stared at the condensation beading the leaded glass. "Only that we take it slow."

Pippa licked the rim of her mug. "I don't get what you mean. I don't go fast, except on my bike."

Connie came to life. She stood. She laughed, too brightly. "You'll understand someday, kiddo."

Sean walked to the door. "Thanks for the coffee."

"Thanks for checking things out. I wouldn't have slept if you hadn't." She dropped her voice. "It was like you said?"

"Yes. Domestic disturbance."

"Bad?"

"Par for the course, according to the housekeeper." Sean glanced at Pippa, who was watching them over the back of the sofa. "Nothing for your girl to get involved in."

"I'll try to explain the situation to her."

Sean opened the door and looked outside. The fog had lifted enough that he'd be able to see his way back to Pine Cone Cottage. But he didn't want to leave without making some kind of overture. "I wanted to say—"

"Don't forget this." Connie handed him the bag from the general store.

He didn't know if she'd interrupted him on purpose. "I wanted to say—"

"You don't have to. I understand."

"They why won't you look at me?"

Her head snapped back and she stared at him, eyes blazing out of her white face. "There. Happy?"

"Not until you are."

A slow shake of her head. "Sean. We had bad timing. That's all. I can handle it. I might not be happy at the moment, but I'm not angry."

He started to protest and she stopped him. "I *get* it. I have a child of my own who needs my attention." She put her fingertips against his chest and gave him a push. "Your instincts were right. I sincerely thank you for easing Pippa's mind, but do us all a favor and go on back to Josh."

IN THE MIDDLE of a *Fantastic Four* ass-kicking, Sean reached over to the popcorn bowl balanced on Josh's chest and took a handful. "You like this movie?"

"Eh. It's okay. I've seen it before."

"You should have told me."

Josh shrugged. "I can watch it again."

"Would you prefer *Reign of Fire?* There was a limited selection at Lattimer's."

"Fire-breathing dragons." Josh made a gesture that seemed to indicate approval. "Let's save it for later."

Sean munched. Minutes passed before he spoke again. "I stopped at the Bradfords' place."

Silence.

He gauged the nonresponse as relatively normal. Josh's first, intense reaction to seeing his dad in a compromising position had eased into wariness. "The fog had spooked them."

"Girls," Josh scoffed.

"Pippa was out in it. Curious as a cat, that one."

"Yeah, tell me about it. During *Pirates,* she was going on and on about some stupid made-up buried treasure. I had to tune her out."

Buried treasure? Sean stopped, his hand halfway to his mouth, losing a piece of popcorn between the cushions of the couch. How did buried treasure fit in with the voices at the maze and the scream in the fog?

In Pippa's mind, he supposed it might. "She believes she's onto a mystery."

Josh tossed a kernel at the TV screen. "Dumb kid."

After a while, Sean said, "She's actually pretty smart for a ten-year-old."

Josh put the popcorn bowl and his feet on the coffee table. "Yeah?"

"I've gotten to know her fairly well in the past week. Mrs. Bradford, too."

"Huh."

Sean waited, but that was his son's only reply. "About last night…" he started.

Josh screwed up his face. "Gross, Dad. I don't want to hear it."

"You seemed upset."

"Yeah, well, I wasn't."

"I'm not abandoning you for her, if that's what you think."

"Whatever." Josh scowled. Color flared in his cheeks, and Sean remembered how mortifying any reference to his own parents' love life had been.

"I just wanted you to know that."

Josh's knees jounced. "She's your girlfriend, then?"

"Not really." Sean hesitated. Connie deserved more than that; he hadn't forgotten her reaction to being called a distraction. "But I'm interested in her. Maybe something will develop, down the road. After we've got you sorted out. Would you hate that?"

"You said—" Josh shook his head. "On the ferry, you said you wanted me to stay. But I'm just in the way."

"You're never in the way. Never."

Josh scoffed. "I am at home. No big deal."

"I've always wanted you." Sean took the risk and draped an arm around his son's bony shoulders. "Sometimes I nearly forgot how much, but that was a mistake. A bad one. It won't happen again, even if there is a woman in my life."

Josh's shoulders tensed. He shifted on the couch, but he didn't withdraw. "Yeah, well, I guess that maze thing sounds kind of cool," he eventually said. "I'd check that out. For, like, five minutes."

Sean leaped at the chance to get them all together. "I'll see if Connie—Mrs. Bradford—will give us that tour she mentioned."

"Connie," Josh echoed with a smirk. "You really like her, huh?"

"Yes." Sean eyed his son obliquely. "What did you think of her, aside from that one embarrassing moment I won't mention again?"

The nervous twitch had moved to Josh's toes. His feet seemed to have grown inches since their last visit. "I s'pose she's okay."

"Just okay?"

"Kinda cute. For a mom."

"Uh, yeah." Not an area he'd explore with his son.

"But you could be dating a hot young chick," Josh blurted. "I mean, if you have to. I see gnarly old dudes doing that all the time where I live."

Sean blinked. He'd thought *Connie* was a hot young chick. "In case you forgot, I'm forty. That may be triple your age, but I'm not ready for gnarly old dude status yet." He chuckled. "And I wouldn't be looking for hot young chicks either way."

Josh stared at the movie. A hot young chick was shooting fire from her fingertips.

Sean waited a few minutes for the extinguishers to be brought in. "So, about Mrs. Bradford. Are you okay with it?"

Josh's feet waggled. "What does it matter?" He buried his chin in his chest and glowered at the screen. "I'll only be here for a month."

Sean winced. "Your opinion is important to me, even when you're not here."

"Yeah, sure." Josh shifted position. "Really?"

"Really."

"Even though you had a good thing going until I showed up and wrecked it?"

Sean tensed and immediately felt it in his thigh, like a needle pricking his conscience. *Dammit.*

"That is *not* what I was trying to say, Josh. You're top priority. Always. In case you didn't get it the first time, I'm not looking to dump you in favor of a woman. All I wanted to know was if you had a problem with me seeing someone. Not hot and heavy, but, you know, once in a while."

Josh seemed to give the question actual thought. But he said flatly, "Do what you want."

"No. I don't let *you* do whatever you want, do I? I'm the adult here, but I still want your…" *not permission, not even consent* "…your approval, I guess."

Josh looked askance. "So if I said no, you'd stop seeing her?"

"Possibly. If you had good reason and weren't just being bratty."

The boy grinned. "Like when I tried to get Mom to stop from going out with Bruce by setting off a stink bomb in his car?"

"I'd forgotten that story." Sean laughed. "Well, you were only six. I hope you've matured since then." He put his feet up on the coffee table. "But, yeah, like that."

They settled back into the movie. Five minutes later, Josh nudged his father's foot. "If you hafta hook up, give me a warning first. And don't ditch me with that Pippa."

"Be nice to her."

Josh sighed. "Okay. Maybe once in a while, I can make the sacrifice."

"Very kind of you."

Josh made a bashful face. "It's nothing."

Emotion had closed Sean's throat. "But, you know, even without a woman, I'm not alone. I have a son." He thought again of the little boy whose father had died at his hand, and how that had haunted him, in the hospital and beyond. No wonder. "You're not alone, either, as long as you have me."

Josh ducked his head. When he raised it, there were two spots of color high on his cheekbones. He squinted at the TV. "Sheesh, you're getting corny. Grandpa warned me that you've been all introspective and mushy since you got shot."

"Being shot tends to make a person reevaluate." Sean slung his arm higher around Josh's neck and knuckled his head. "I'm glad you approve of Connie. And I'm really glad to have you here early, even if I'm not too happy about the reason. Just remember what I said—the biggest mistake of my life was not always being there for you. I'm going to do better about that." Sean breathed deeply, easing the tightness in his chest. "How's that for mushy?"

"Get off me." Josh pulled away, laughing unevenly. His eyes were bright. He took off his baseball cap, brushed his hair down over his forehead and put the cap back on, tugging it low. "Boy, wait'll Mom hears about this."

"What?"

"All these years, I never met any of your girlfriends. I didn't think you even had any. Mom always asks when I come back from a visit if there's one yet." Josh considered. "She might be kind of disappointed this time when I have to say yes."

CHAPTER FIFTEEN

CONNIE SQUELCHED ASHORE in her water shoes and wet suit. She and Pippa, similarly attired, looked at each other ruefully and turned in unison to haul their kayaks onto the beach.

Their morning had not been completely successful. In an effort to keep her daughter's mind off Peregrine House, Connie had roused Pippa for an early clamming expedition. With rakes and buckets, they'd padded around the shore at low tide, digging countless holes until they were wet, muddy, stinking of seaweed and the proud owners of a truly meager collection of clams. Once Pippa had learned they were expected to cook and eat the slimy sea creatures, she'd pulled the Greenpeace card and had insisted they must set the clams free.

After a large, hot breakfast served in the dining room of the Whitecap Inn, they'd returned to the harbor for a kayak lesson. Thus the wet suits. And Pippa's dunking, when she'd leaned too far over the side to look for sea turtles. Luckily, she'd been only yards offshore and the instructor had immediately pulled her out of the cold water. But after that, Pippa would go no farther than a halfhearted paddle around the bay, shrieking with every wave that lapped at the kayak.

"Maybe we should try sailing next." Connie handed

their paddles to the instructor. The honk of the late-morning ferry announced the arrival of a new group of tourists.

Pippa's teeth chattered. "Sure, Mom, but only if it's *warm* water."

"On our next trip to the Bahamas," Connie said with a laugh as they trudged toward the changing room. "Thanks for being a good sport, Pip. We've had a few exciting adventures on this trip, haven't we? I'm actually sorry we leave tomorrow. It's so soon."

Or not soon enough. Sometimes a woman had to go while the getting was good.

Pippa squinted at the sun, which had made a welcome appearance, turning the morning sky from drab-gray to crystal-blue. "Couldn't we stay longer?"

Connie smoothed her daughter's hair, which was springing into haphazard corkscrews as it dried. "Nope. It's time to go."

"But Trixie never leaves until the mystery is solved."

"Then it's good that we have no mystery to solve," Connie said lightly. "Look, there's Mr. Rafferty. And Josh." She waved. "Ahoy, mateys!"

"Gleeps," Pippa muttered.

The Raffertys were on wheels. They'd paused at the harbor road to watch the ferry passengers disembark. At Connie's call, they pedaled over to the edge of the bank that rimmed the beach.

The dazzling dance of sunshine on the water was electric. Although sunglasses hung around his neck, Sean shaded his eyes with his hand as he angled to look down toward Connie and Pippa. "What are you two up to?"

"Kayaking." Connie pointed to the brightly colored

sea kayaks lined up in front of the water sports store-front. "*Attempted* kayaking."

Sean was looking her up and down. She became hot inside the skintight rubber suit. "Mrs. Limpet," he said with a grin.

She snorted. The description was, unfortunately, all too accurate. There might not be fins or scales, but she had a smoothly fishlike body and a human head erupting in a mop of out-of-control curls. "Gee, thanks. You couldn't call me Ariel instead?"

He dropped his gaze, too intent to reveal whether or not he got her Disney mermaid reference. "The porpoise suit looks good on you."

Suddenly Connie didn't know where to put her hands. The wet suit was pretty revealing, and Sean wasn't a man who missed much. "Um, what's your plan for the day?" she blurted out, although she'd sworn to maintain the space between them.

Sean glanced at his son. "Got any plans, Josh?"

The boy was leaning low over his handlebars. "Nope."

"Lunch. Soon, I guess," Sean said. "Then we'll play it by ear. We're hanging loose."

"Have a good day." Connie turned away before she said too much. "Gotta go change."

Pippa motioned to her from her outpost at the shop, where she was half-hidden by the open changing room door. "Pssst."

"What?" Connie mouthed as she walked over.

"The *maze*. You gotta invite them to the maze."

"I'm not—" Connie stopped. She *had* promised, sort of.

Sean and Josh were getting ready to pedal away. "Hey, guys, wait a minute." She crossed the pebbled flats and clambered up the rock-strewn bank. "Pippa wants me to invite you to visit the maze."

Hiding behind her daughter. *Real adult, Mrs. Limpet.*

Sean's eyebrows went up. "What do you think, Josh?"

"Yeah, okay."

"How about this afternoon?" Sean took a drink from a sports bottle that had been attached to the bike, then handed it to Connie. "I was hoping to get the chance to talk to you anyway."

She avoided responding by taking a big swallow of water.

"Talk," said Josh out of the corner of his mouth. "Jeeeez." He got back on his bike and pedaled past the row of stump posts that marked the drop-off to the beach.

Connie felt herself blushing. She lowered the bottle and dabbed her mouth with the back of one hand. "What was that about?"

Sean slid on his sunglasses. Either his color was high from physical exertion or he was blushing, too. "Josh and I had a little talk about us getting involved."

"Us?" Clearly, the water hadn't washed away the frog in Connie's throat. She coughed and tried again. "I mean, you and me? We're not involved."

"Oh. I thought we were."

She was getting even more confused. "Not as of the other night." The clammy wet suit clung to her skin. She inched the zipper down. "Usually when I'm involved with a guy and he kisses me, he doesn't follow up with an announcement that I'm only a distraction."

Sean clenched his jaw. "I said that? Ouch."

"Imagine how I felt."

"I didn't mean it to sound so cold."

"I'm over it," she insisted, too breezily. "Anyway, like

I said, it's okay. Or at least it's understandable." She glanced back to find Pippa, but she'd disappeared inside the shop. "Remember, my child needs me, too."

Connie handed Sean the water bottle. "Bad timing, that's all this is. Really lousy timing." She was working awfully hard to convince them both.

His fingers brushed hers. "What if Josh gave us his approval? What if Pippa did?"

"Approval for what?"

"To see each other."

To fall in love. Despite the rising heat, Connie shivered. "Does approval really matter? We're going home tomorrow, and you and Josh are staying here."

"Only until next Sunday. After that, we'll be back in Holden. You and I don't live that far apart. You even said that your clients are starting to come from all over the region, like the Sheffields."

"But I…"

I'm busy enough as it is. Already spending too much time away from Pippa. It's not the right moment for a serious relationship, and even if it was, I might not be smart to choose a man who plays hero for a living.

Excuses, Connie thought. *Only excuses.*

She remembered what Philip had said when they'd learned they were having a baby. They were strapped. He'd just been diagnosed, and was going to get worse before—*if*—he got better. She hadn't dared speak it, but down deep she'd also been afraid that eventually she'd be raising their child on her own. She'd wanted his baby but had also felt certain that she was too young, too unprepared, too frightened to handle the reality of taking such a big step.

Philip had said there were always reasons not to try

something new and scary. But what would the world be if no one had the courage—and faith—to go ahead anyway?

Connie squinted at Sean. "Josh gave his approval, huh?"

A nod. "Also, I realized I was being a jerk."

"That's right. You were. It's not like I haven't had my doubts, too. I can't tell you how many times I've gone back and forth over this in my head. For a while, I even had myself convinced that we could have an island fling and walk away with smiles on our faces."

Sean slipped his sunglasses down his nose to give her a wicked wink and a broad smile that carved brackets around his mouth.

"Don't look at me that way." She laughed. "I quickly realized that flings don't happen with an über-observant ten-year-old hanging around."

"Hmm. That's why we meet for a date halfway between your place and mine."

Connie couldn't keep still. She brushed at the sea salt clinging to her arms, her throat, her chest. Sean's gaze followed every movement. She licked her lips and tasted salt there, too.

"I'll think about it," she blurted, then spun and descended the bank at an ungainly pace. She had to get out of the wet suit before she melted. "After we're back in the real world."

"What about the maze?" he called when she hit the beach.

"Come over this afternoon."

"Will the Sheffields mind?" After last night, Sean figured he was no longer on the invitation list.

Connie lifted her hands. "Doesn't matter. When we were kayaking, Pippa and I saw the Sheffields boarding their yacht. They'll probably be gone the rest of the day." She waved and hurried off toward the shop.

Josh rode up to Sean as he snapped the water bottle back into place. "What's with the Limpet stuff?"

"I don't know. It's from some old movie. Lattimer's didn't have it." Sean looked out over the ocean. He felt expansive. Optimistic for the future, even, for the first time since the shooting.

"So we're doing that maze thing?" Josh asked.

"Do you mind?"

The boy shook his head. "As long as Pippa doesn't think she can boss me around."

"She might try. She's a little fighter like her mother. Why don't you give her some leeway? Listen to her instead of tuning her out. She's only trying to impress you."

Josh shrugged his all-right-but-don't-expect-me-to-act-happy-about-it shrug.

"Ready for lunch?" Sean asked as they biked along the road. Traffic from the ferry arrivals was beginning to clear. "We have a couple of choices. Deli sandwiches from the general store, if the tourists haven't snapped them all up, or we can dust off the road grime and head over to the Whitecap Inn for a real meal."

A Mercedes convertible roared by, spitting gravel. Sean threw up an arm, trying to shield Josh from the spray. He yelled a sharp "Hey!" at the driver, catching sight of the man's profile and thinning silver hair as the vehicle sped away up the hill.

Anders Sheffield.

Alone.

Sean removed his sunglasses and scanned the harbor. The *Siren Song* was nowhere in sight. He wondered why Kay Sheffield had left the island on her own. Or if it had been by her choice.

CONNIE WALKED DOWN to the garden shed while Josh and Pippa were touring the maze. "Wait up," Sean called, but she was in a hurry to finish. She wanted to gather any of her belongings that had been left on the estate grounds, leave a checklist for Graves regarding future maintenance and get her butt off the island.

Sean arrived as she was tacking her list to the inside of the shed door. "Didn't you hear me?"

"I'm in a hurry."

"Afraid Sheffield will see us?"

"Of course not. He's a civilized man."

"I wonder."

"What are you suggesting?" Connie looked around, distracted. She found her hedge clippers and the spade with her business logo on them. Good old Graves. She had her doubts about his capabilities, but the Sheffields hadn't wanted to hire the landscape maintenance crew she'd recommended. A foolish decision, in her opinion, but she had to learn to let go of her projects once the job was over.

"I'm suggesting that your client is a real creep." Sean took the garden tools but stopped her when she moved to close the door. "Spare me a minute, will you? I didn't want to say this in front of Pippa, but I've got a few doubts about what went on in Peregrine House the other night."

"Doubts or suspicions?"

"You mentioned that you saw Mrs. Sheffield board the yacht this morning."

"Yes."

"How did she look?"

"Normal, I suppose. We were at a distance. She wore a hat."

"Could she have been hiding a black eye?"

Connie gasped. "You think he abuses her?"

"That's a possibility." He read her doubt. "You disagree?"

"There's been no hint of that kind of thing. I know he's not the nicest man. Obviously a philanderer. And they fight. But Kay seems to give as good as she gets. I think they're the sort of couple who thrive on their mutual wretchedness. There'll always be more diamonds or girlfriends on the side to fight over."

"Maybe. Was anyone else aboard the yacht, other than the crew? Like the Crosbys?"

"They weren't in the launch. I can't say for sure who was on board. Come to think of it, I haven't seen Jilly or her husband since the garden party."

"Sheffield claims they're still here."

"He *claims*? You don't believe that, either? Why would he lie?"

"I don't know. The whole thing seems a little strange."

Connie frowned. "You're worse than Pippa."

She wasn't prepared for what happened next.

Safely out of sight behind the shed door, Sean took her into his arms and kissed her. Deeply. Soundly. Thoroughly. The oxygen went out of her body as if she'd been slammed to the ground.

When she got her breath back, her brain clicked back in. She immediately wrapped her arms around his neck and returned the kiss tenfold.

They broke apart. She stood and stared, panting. "Wow." The kisses had left a burning imprint. She had to resist the urge to lick the taste of him off her lips. "What was that for?"

"Can't you tell? I wanted to kiss you." He brushed his mouth across her lips again. "I always want to kiss you."

She stepped back. "That's all?"

"You can also take me to the house," he said urgently.

"The guesthouse?"

"Peregrine. I want to see if Jillian Crosby is there."

Connie blinked several times, trying to wrap her mind around the twists and turns he'd been taking when all she really wanted was to keep kissing him.

"You *are* worse than Pippa," she finally cried. "I can't imagine what convoluted scenario you're inventing, but do you really want to go looking for trouble?" She clenched her hands. "Let's just take the kids and get away from here. Leave the Sheffields to work out their own problems."

Sean took a step back. He lifted his face toward the sky just as the shadow of a passing cloud cleared. Sunlight swept along the lawn like an ocean wave. "You're right. I don't know what I was thinking. We should stay out of it."

She exhaled. "Thank you."

They collected her gardening tools and walked toward the maze. "Here's the thing," Sean said as they reached the hedge walls. They continued around the maze to the back entrance, which was closer. "There are a number of inconsistencies and unanswered questions from the past several days. Who did Pippa overhear making a deal to split money? What happened to Kay Sheffield's supposedly stolen diamond? Why did she and her husband argue so violently? And was it really her on the yacht today?"

"Who else?" Connie asked faintly.

"Jilly," he said. "They look alike, especially from a distance."

"But why would she... Oh God. Sean. You're not saying that you think Kay was *murdered?* That Anders is masterminding a plot to make it seem as if Kay left the island on the yacht when really she's..." Connie couldn't finish.

"No, I'm not saying that." Sean's eyes were hard; his voice fell flat. "When you put it that way, it sounds absurd. Straight out of a Hitchcock film."

Connie shuddered, remembering how she'd conjured up her own Hitchcock scene the night of the cocktail party, when they'd stood at the cliffside with the sunset dying above the ink-black forest.

"I don't have any answers," she told Sean. "But you've convinced me of one thing. We need to get away from here right now."

"Did you hear that?" Pippa whispered to Josh on the other side of the hedge. "I told you so."

"You said there was a buried treasure in the maze."

"So what? There could be a murder, too."

"You're nuts."

She puffed up her chest. "I'm going to be a private investigator."

"Yeah, well, I'm going to be an astronaut on Mars."

"You don't have to be so mean."

"You don't have to be so—" Josh made a scoffing sound. "Never mind."

"No one ever believes me." Pippa pouted. "But just wait and see. I still have until tomorrow to solve the mystery. I don't know how, but I swear I'm going to, even if I have to do it all by myself."

CHAPTER SIXTEEN

BY TACIT AGREEMENT, the Bradfords and Raffertys returned to the guesthouse to have dinner together. Connie immediately began pulling food out of the cupboards and the refrigerator, assembling her remaining groceries to cobble together a final evening meal.

"This is going to be a hodgepodge," she warned. "I can make one of my amazing clean-out-the-fridge casseroles, and there's half a carton of ice cream for dessert. The salad greens are gone, but we can fill in the cracks with hot dogs wrapped in Pillsbury biscuits. This won't be my most nutritious meal."

"Sounds fine, right, Josh? Rafferty men will eat anything." Sean picked up a fuzzy brown fruit. "Except fuzzy brown fruits."

"You don't like kiwi?" Connie made a face. "I'm shocked." They were trying hard to keep things light, aware of the kids watching them closely.

"Where did you find a kiwi on Osprey Island? All I saw in Lattimer's were bananas with brown spots and a few hundred pints of blueberries."

"I came prepared."

Pippa chimed in. "She brought *six* bags of groceries. Graves didn't like it because he had to use his pickup to haul all our stuff from the ferry."

Connie shrugged. "What can I say? I like to cook." She noticed Josh watching her. "Don't you ever cook? I thought you did."

"Me? Heck, no. Nobody in my family cooks. We get takeout."

"What about Bruce?" Sean saw Connie's questioning look. "His stepdad. I heard he's into French food."

"Oh, yeah." Josh shrugged. "I've never seen him actually cook anything. They mostly just leave us home and go to restaurants. So, you know, when we get tired of ordering pizza, I might make my sisters something."

Connie nodded. "I noticed you knew how to handle a knife."

"Your Grandma Mo cooks, and she sure counts as your family." Sean was at the sink filling a pot with water. "And I make a damn good omelet, if I say so myself."

Connie gave him a private smile. "Something to look forward to," she murmured. She looked away before their chemistry ignited. "Okay, enough talk. Who wants to help?"

"Not me," Pippa said. "*Hannah Montana* is on TV, if I can get the channel to come in." She went to the living room and switched on the small portable television set.

Sean motioned to Josh. "Go keep her company."

He groaned about watching a stupid girl's show but got up to follow. Seconds later, they heard him instructing Pippa on how to position the antenna for best reception.

Almost like brother and sister. Connie shook the notion off. She'd given Sean the big spiel about having faith and taking risks, but how far was *she* willing to go?

Time will tell.

They worked in sync, as naturally as if they'd been doing it for years. Only after the casserole was in the oven was she ready to broach the subject that was on both of their minds. "Can I ask you a question?"

"Sure."

"What was that kiss about, really?"

He pulled back his head. "I thought you were going to bring up the Sheffields."

She stretched over the countertop to see into the living room. Josh watched the snowy TV with a look of disgust, while Pippa was paging through her notebook. Connie dropped back on her heels. "The less said about that, the better."

Sean wasn't willing. "It's my job, in a way."

"Not on the island, it isn't." She cracked open the can of biscuits. "Speaking of that, you'll be going back to work soon. Do you feel ready?"

"We'll see."

"Don't go all taciturn on me." She noticed that his hand had strayed to his thigh. "How's the leg?"

"Better."

She sighed.

"Look, what should I say? That I'm really looking forward to my psych evaluation? Count how many times I still wake up in a sweat from reliving the shooting? That I've considered chucking the job and going to California to learn how to surf?"

Connie stuck out her chin. "Why are you being sarcastic with me?"

"I apologize." His mouth turned down. "I've been living alone for too long. I'm not used to this."

"Talking?" She waggled a frankfurter at him. "If you're serious about getting together off the island, you'd better get used to it. The Joe Friday act is fine in a TV show, but in real life I need to know what's on your mind."

Sean moved up behind her, his hands on her waist. "I'm serious."

"Then *talk* to me."

"I'll have to put some distance between us. When you're within reach, I'm not thinking about talking." He went to sit at the table. "All right. You wanted to know about my job." He took a breath and launched into a description of his work. In minutes, she was entranced by his passion and dedication, and how obviously he relished the chance to do good for the communities he patrolled.

"You're not going to California," she said with a smile.

His gaze drifted to Josh in the other room. "I guess not."

"I suppose joint custody wouldn't work, considering the distance, but have you ever suggested that he spend the whole summer with you?"

"Jen has always said she would miss him too much."

"Like you don't?"

Anyone could see how much his son meant to him, Connie thought. Except perhaps Josh. She wished she had the solution that would magically take away the tension and misunderstanding between them, just as she wished she could take away Pippa's fears and her own struggle to figure out the right thing to do for herself as well as her daughter.

Impossible. They all had to find their own way.

But maybe they could do that together.

CONNIE MANAGED TO KEEP SEAN talking throughout the meal. She even got Josh going. They had a rousing debate over favorite college baseball teams and the designated hitter rule, then united as members of the BoSox nation. Only Pippa remained silent, but every time Sean checked she was listening with rapt attention, taking in everything he and Josh said with a hunger that made him ache for her loss.

He understood where she was coming from. Looking around the table, he saw the shadow of the family he'd had but lost forever. And the new one that might be forming to fill the gaping hole in his life.

He volunteered the kids to do the cleanup, then announced that he and Connie would go for a stroll. She protested, but he promised they wouldn't go far.

Sean gave his son a man-to-man look. "Josh, you're in charge."

Pippa looked up from scraping the last spoonful from her ice cream dish. "He is not!"

"Yeah, I am." Josh swaggered to the kitchen with a couple of dishes. "I boss my little sisters around all the time. I'm used to it."

Sean snared Connie's hand and pulled her outside. "I don't want to leave—" she started to say, but he hushed her with a quick kiss.

"We're only going far enough to be out of sight." A glance over his shoulder told the tale. Two faces peered at them from different window panes. "Beyond the sight of nosy children."

"Why do we have to be out of sight?"

He could tell by her small smile that she knew. "I have a question to answer."

"Oh? Which one?"

"Something about a kiss."

"Kisses, I believe."

"That's right."

They'd come as far as the main driveway, where the light was growing long as dusk approached. They reached for each other, and their attenuated shadows did the same.

"We shouldn't be doing this," Connie said softly.

He cupped her cheeks. Kissed the end of her nose. "We can't be dull and responsible parents *all* the time."

Her eyes flashed. "Hey, who are you calling dull?"

He dropped his hands. This wasn't going the way he'd planned. "I meant dull as in *safe*. Wasn't that what you wanted? You know, up at Peregrine House?"

"Because I made us come back here instead of putting my child in danger?"

"But you don't believe in my Hitchcock theory."

"Even you admitted it was absurd."

"Right." He slid his hands around her waist, bringing her snugly against his body. Her gaze lifted to his face and her teasing half smile made his heart turn over in his chest. "I didn't bring you out here to rehash that. There was something else… Something about… What was it again?"

She tapped his chest with her fists. "Quit fooling around and kiss me. You have five minutes before I call time and go back to the house."

He bent his head to hers. "Then I'd better get started with the explanation."

He used the five minutes well. By the end, Connie was pink and soft and breathing almost as hard as he was. Her hair was tousled from his running his hands through it. He'd had those hands on her body, too, but she'd backed away with a warning look in her eyes when he reached for her again.

She refastened a couple of buttons. "Making out by the side of the road like teenagers," she said. "And I *still* don't have my answer."

Gotta cool down. He dragged his gaze away from her sweet lips, the fullness of her breasts. Her skin had been smooth. Warm. Supple.

"We can try again," he offered. "You're buttoned wrong, anyway."

She looked down at her rumpled shirt. "Thanks."

As she redid the buttons, he caught a glimpse of her bra cupping the ripe curve of one freckled breast, and felt as if he'd swallowed fire. He was supposed to be cooling down, using his logic. He conjured up baseball statistics, ten-page crime reports, insurance forms, but none of them had any effect.

Connie had pulled herself together. "Why *did* you kiss me that way, in the shed?"

"I was— I don't know. Trying to get you back."

Her eyes darkened. "I didn't go anywhere, Sean."

"No, I know. It was me. I pushed you away."

His convictions were in tumult. *The hell.*

He was never like this—running hot and cold, letting his imagination run away from him, changing his mind from one day to the next. That was why, once Jen had persuaded him that he should put his son's best interests first, he'd never reneged on the agreement. Even when he'd gotten over feeling rejected by the divorce and had realized he'd made a mistake in listening to her talk of the golden life Josh would have in California.

But, no. He held steady. He did not give way.

But you did with Josh. You let him go.

And you hesitated that night on the roadway because of the child, even though his father was pulling a gun on you. That one second of doubt might have taken your life instead of the other man's.

Costing Josh *his father.*

"Listen, Connie." Sean's voice shook. He stopped, reached for the solid ground of what he *could* do— forgive himself. "That made sense, when I said we should slow down." He didn't want to waffle back and forth, but he didn't want to make a mistake, either.

"True," she admitted. "Still, it's wasn't an easy thing to hear. I'm a passionate person." She pushed back her hair, looking rosy and glowing in the dusky light.

Sean's head whipped around. "Car coming."

Lights flashed among the trees. He and Connie retreated to the path just as the sound of tires signaled the car's approach.

The convertible again. Sean straightened, no longer caring if they were seen, but Connie held him back with her hand on his arm. "It's just Anders," she said.

"I suppose he's going back to the marina for his wife." There was nothing suspicious in that. Sean couldn't figure out why his cop instincts were so aroused.

He remembered Pippa's talk of "The Rock." Connie's mention of a meeting place at the harbor. Was Sheffield being blackmailed, perhaps by a townie like Graves who knew about the man's infidelity? That might fit, except that Kay Sheffield already seemed to know about her husband's betrayals. In fact, they were common knowledge.

Connie was thinking, too. "With Anders gone, that means the house should be empty," she said. "Except for staff."

Sean eyed her warily. He gestured toward the driveway. "Want to…?"

"Check it out?" She was torn. "I admit I'm curious. But we shouldn't leave the kids."

"They have no idea of my latest suspicions."

"Pippa has enough of her own."

"We'll look in on them first. I'll give Josh orders not

to let Pippa out of his sight. Then we'll stroll up to the house, knock on the door and ask for Mrs. Sheffield. What could possibly go wrong?"

THE DOOR WAS ANSWERED by Kitty, the pretty young maid previously seen locked in her boss's embrace in the butler's pantry. She was out of uniform, to put it mildly, in bare feet, short-shorts and a clingy tank top with spaghetti straps that wouldn't stay up.

The redhead's smile faded when she recognized them. "What are you two doing here?"

"Is Mrs. Sheffield available?" Sean asked.

Connie thought not. If Kay had been there, Miss Tank Top wouldn't feel quite so free and easy.

"She took off," Kitty said with a shrug. "The day after the party."

Sean frowned. "The day after?"

"That's what I was told."

"By Mr. Sheffield, I suppose."

The maid hooked a thumb in one of her straps. Slowly she dragged it up past her shoulder, giving Sean the eye. "By Mrs. Wells. Not that it matters."

"You're certain that she said the day after the party? That was the day we were fog-bound. I happen to know that Mrs. Sheffield was at home." Sean and Connie exchanged a worried glance, sharing the alarm that perhaps he'd only *thought* he'd seen her.

"I'm pretty sure that's when. All's I know is that I haven't seen Mrs. Sheffield since then."

Connie sighed. "Then I suppose Jilly Crosby is also gone. I'd hoped to say goodbye."

"Yup. She left this morning, on the yacht."

"This morning. *After* Kay." Connie didn't dare look

at Sean. "I'm sorry I missed her. I guess her husband went along?"

The other woman shrugged. "I'm just the maid, not the friggin' nanny."

Connie lifted her chin higher to catch a glimpse inside the house. The foyer floor gleamed under the chandeliers. Adjacent rooms were dark. There were no abandoned shoes or bloodstains or overturned wine-glasses. Nothing suspicious at all.

"May we come in to speak with Rachel?" she asked.

"She's not available." The maid's expression clouded. She pulled the door toward her body, as if they'd threat-ened to barge in. "You should go. Anders won't be back for at least an hour. He's gone for dinner at the yacht club." She pouted at that. "I was about to get out of here myself. Have some fun for a change, you know?"

She threw a flirtatious look at Sean, but he had stepped off the porch and was staring up at the second-floor windows.

Then Connie saw something that made her blood boil.

"Thanks for your help." She gave the maid a sketchy wave, then hurried down the front steps. She grabbed Sean's arm, saying beneath her breath, "Come with me. Hurry."

"I saw someone at the window upstairs," he said. "A woman. That house is *not* empty."

"Never mind. We've got bigger troubles." Connie waited until the maid finally closed the door before veering off toward the garden. "I just spotted Pippa and Josh sneaking into the maze with my garden spade."

"WHAT WAS I GONNA DO, sit on her?" Josh griped when Sean read him the riot act for allowing Pippa out of the house. "She's got this idea that there's buried treasure in the maze. Said now was the perfect time to find it, with everyone gone. I couldn't stop her, so I figured that at least I had to come with her."

"Keep your voice down, son." Sean put a reassuring hand on the boy's shoulder. "I'm sorry I blamed you. That was wrong. You did okay."

At first Connie had been simply relieved that they'd found the children so quickly, but now that the blood was returning to her head, she was becoming exasperated. "God, Pippa, do I have to handcuff you to keep you safe at home?"

"This was my last chance," the girl said stubbornly.

"What gave you the idea that there's buried treasure in the maze? Was it one of your mystery books?"

"No." Pippa was defiant. "I saw Graves with a shovel *two* times, but nobody would believe me. I just know he buried something here. It could be a body. Even Mrs. Sheffield's body."

Sean tried not to smile. "Do you realize how much digging is involved in burying a body? The maze isn't that big. The signs of a grave would be obvious."

Pippa wouldn't give up. "Then it could be money. Or jewelry. We won't know for sure until we look around."

"Yeah, maybe Pippa's right," Josh said, surprising them all. He waved at the hedges that surrounded them. "You could bury something pretty easy in one of the dead ends and scrape the gravel over the hiding spot."

"Oh, no," Connie said. "Not another one."

"Wait a minute." Sean held up a hand for silence. "Pippa, think carefully. Exactly what did you overhear the two men saying when we caught you in the maze the first time?"

"It's all in my notebook." Excitedly, Pippa raced over to one of the benches at the center of the maze, sat and pulled out her tablet. She flipped pages, found the one she was looking for and read it over with her finger tracing the entry. "They were whispering, so I didn't hear very good. One of them could have been a woman."

"We've been assuming they were both men," Connie said.

"Here's what I wrote—'They talked about the rock and splitting the money.' That's all." Pippa looked at Sean with little hope. "It's not good enough. I should have got closer to them, but I was scared they'd hear me."

"You did great, Pippa," Sean said absently. He walked over and sat beside her.

Connie picked up the spade. "Sean, I can see your brain working. What is it?"

"We've all heard the gossip that some of Mrs. Sheffield's jewelry is missing, right? A diamond ring."

"Yes, sir!" Pippa said. "That's how come I thought there might be buried treasure."

"And diamonds are often called rocks."

Pippa inhaled, her eyes like marbles. "Oh-h-h-h."

"We went off track," Sean said. "The two Pippa overheard never actually said they were *meeting* at the rock."

"A red herring," Connie observed ruefully. "And I followed it like a fool."

"It was an assumption," Sean countered. "Not your fault."

Josh kept looking from one to the other. "I don't know what any of you are talking about."

"I told you all about it," Pippa said. "See? Nobody listens to me." She pouted. "But I was wrong, anyway.

It was me who made the red herring. My fault. I thought they meant to meet at a rock."

Sean hugged an arm around her. "Don't worry about it, Pippa. If it wasn't for you and your notes, we wouldn't have figured out any of this."

"We still haven't," Connie pointed out. "This is nothing but conjecture. Personally, I'd rather not take it any further."

Sean glanced up at the house. The upstairs windows were all dark, but he was certain that earlier there'd been a light on in one of the bedrooms. And a woman looking down at them, until he'd spotted her and she'd disappeared. He hoped she hadn't seen them enter the maze.

He stood. "It's getting very dark and we have no flashlights. We need to start back."

"Can't we just dig in a few places?" Pippa asked. "Please, Mom?"

Connie shook her head firmly. She stepped aside and ushered them toward the closest opening in the hedge. Sean fell in line as compliantly as the children.

The sound of a car's engine stopped them. Sean listened. "Sheffield?"

Connie put a finger to her lips as the vehicle neared the driveway that curved around the maze. "I'd recognize that muffler anywhere. It's Graves."

Pippa reached for her mother's hand. "He's coming to dig up the maze!"

Connie shushed her. Sheltered by the high hedges, they strained to listen as the pickup pulled up to the front of the house. The truck door opened; boots hit the ground.

They heard more footsteps in the distance, growing louder, coming from the direction of the house. A man grunted hello.

"Watch what you say." A woman's voice, low and wary. "Kitty is still here. I couldn't persuade her to leave. With Mrs. Sheffield gone, she's parading around like she owns the place."

"We've got to get the loot out of here."

Graves, Connie mouthed to Sean.

"It'd be easier to wait until they close the house," the woman said.

Connie covered her mouth, then leaned to whisper to Sean. He couldn't make out what she said, but he assumed she'd also recognized the voice.

Graves grumbled. "That could be weeks."

"I finally have the key. They trust me, and they're too self-involved to see what's missing."

"Except the rock," Graves said.

"That was a risk, ayuh. But look who she blamed." Smugness filled the woman's voice. "All the fighting was just the distraction we needed."

Graves walked back to his truck. He swore. "Where's that damn spade gone?"

"Use your own."

"It broke."

Josh raised the spade he was still holding and grinned. Too cocky for Sean's liking; he covered Josh's hand with his own and forced the tool down.

"What does it matter?" hissed the woman. "Just dig the stuff up and get it out of here. I don't know how long Mr. Sheffield will stay away."

Graves muttered, sounding much closer now. He was cutting across the sloping lawn.

Pippa let out a terrified squeak, then clapped her hand over her mouth.

"Did you hear something?" the woman asked.

"Don't get squirrelly on me now. This one's gonna be our best haul yet."

"Keep your eyes open. Connie was here just a few minutes ago, with Rafferty. And you know how that kid of hers sneaks around."

"I'll take care of 'em if I have to."

"Don't be a fool. I'm not going to prison for murder."

Graves cackled. "Then it wasn't you who cracked the missus in the face?"

A muffled sob leaked out from behind Pippa's hand. Connie turned to Sean in desperation as she gathered her daughter close.

He dropped down to kneel beside Pippa. He spoke just barely above a whisper. "Stay calm, honey. We're not in any real danger, but I want you to do exactly what I say."

He waited until she nodded. Graves's footsteps were louder now, as he stepped from the lawn to the gravel paths of the maze.

"Good." Sean gave Pippa a brief squeeze. "All you have to do is to keep hold of your mom's hand, stay very quiet and follow her." He looked up at Connie. "Take the kids and head for the other exit. Stick close to the hedges, off the pebbles, to disguise your route."

"What about you?"

He rose and put out his hand. "I'll have the spade."

Josh's Adam's apple bobbed. He put the implement into his dad's hand.

Sean winked. "Go on with Connie. It'll be okay."

Graves was traveling the maze now, swearing oaths at the confusing, intersecting paths. Connie led the children in the same direction, but she seemed confident in her choice. He trusted that she knew the twists and turns well enough to avoid crossing paths with the gardener.

After they'd disappeared around one of the sharp turns, Sean stepped around a corner and found a dead end that seemed like a good hiding spot. He had no fear about the confrontation with Graves, but he intended to see that the man revealed his hidden stash first.

"Damn," he breathed. He rocked back and forth, loosening his muscles. Who would have believed that Pippa had been right all along?

There truly was a treasure buried in the maze.

CHAPTER SEVENTEEN

CONNIE BROUGHT JOSH and Pippa safely out of the maze but no farther. She didn't want to send them across the open lawn in case someone was watching. She felt safer sheltering them near the hedge, in the dark, where the lights from the house didn't reach. At the same time, that also meant they were stuck.

"I want to go back," Josh whispered. "Make it two against one."

"No. Your father wouldn't allow it." She hooked her arm through the boy's. "He can take care of himself, but Pippa and I need you with us." She squeezed Pippa's hand. "Right, Pip?"

Pippa nodded. Her face was wet with tears and nasal drip, but she was trying hard to be brave.

Connie wiped Pippa's cheeks. She gave her a hug. "Hunker down. Make yourself small." She wondered if that would seem scary and added in as normal a mothering voice as she could muster, "You'll stay warmer that way."

"I'm not cold," Pippa said, but she obeyed, folding herself into a ball. She burrowed her head against her arms.

Connie whispered to Josh, who was trying to peer through the hedge. "Can you hear anything?"

"There was a big thud. Now he's digging."

A thud? How much of a thud did a body make when hitting the ground? What if Graves had managed to sneak up on Sean and hit him over the head? Connie's mouth puckered at the sour taste of her fear.

She closed her eyes, her mind blank of everything but the need for her loved ones to be safe.

And that, she saw without any doubt, included Sean and Josh.

The suspense was terrible. "I hate this," she said. She wanted to run back to Sean, fight alongside him. But she couldn't. Might even be in the way if she tried.

Sean can handle it. He's a trained professional.

Connie gnawed the stub of her clipped thumbnail. Yes, his last day on the job had ended in tragedy, but this was different. Graves was strong for an older man, but not dangerous in a lethal way.

All reasonable assertions. But not particularly comforting.

She squatted beside Pippa. "You okay?"

"Uh-huh."

"Don't worry. It'll be over soon." Which didn't sound all that reassuring, either.

The scraping had stopped. "The hell with this," Graves said distinctly. There was a soft thud, a scuffling sound and then footsteps.

Connie raised her head. She swiveled to stare in horror at the garden shed at the edge of the forest.

He wanted the spade. He was coming their way.

SEAN STEPPED OUT into the open, the spade gripped lightly in his right hand. "Hold it, Graves. Stop right there."

The gardener froze at a point halfway along one of

the inner walls of the maze, still within sight of the center. The man had tipped over one of the stone benches there and had been digging beneath it, although not very successfully. The tire iron he'd used had been tossed aside. His hands were caked with dirt.

The man's bullish head swung around. "Who—"

"Lieutenant Sean Rafferty of the Massachusetts State Police. You're under arrest."

"Under arrest?" Graves sneered. "For what?"

"Theft, for one. I'm sure there will be other charges."

"I have every right to be here."

"And to possess stolen items?"

With a gloating chuckle, the gardener showed his grimy palms. "What have I got in my possession?"

"We'll worry about semantics later." Sean approached, keeping an eye on the man's open hands while staying alert to the possibility of the accomplice sneaking up on him from behind. "I want you flat on the ground, your arms stretched overhead. Don't fight or you'll be sorry."

Graves growled through clenched teeth. Sean reached for his collar.

The gardener lurched toward the abandoned tire iron. Sean yanked him back, using the spade handle like a nightstick to drop the man with one blow behind the knees. He knelt and shoved Graves face-first into the gravel.

"I'm the goddamn gardener!" he bellowed. "Ask Sheffield. Ask Rachel Wells, the housekeeper. She'll vouch for me."

"I'm sure she will." Sean patted the man down, discovering no weapons except a pair of pruners with Connie's label on them. He kept a knee in the small of Graves's back to prevent him from getting up.

The gardener struggled against Sean's control but soon ran out of breath. With a groan, he collapsed in surrender.

Sean called the all-clear to Connie. "I could use some rope."

He heard Josh volunteer. "I'll get it."

At the approaching footsteps, Graves writhed uselessly. He spat with anger as Connie appeared first, her face ghostly pale in the light of the moon. She took in the scene and motioned to Pippa, farther back on the path. "Stay there."

"But I want to see."

Sean smiled to himself. "Not right now, Pippa."

Josh ran up with a length of frayed rope. "From the shed," he said, panting. "It's all I could find."

"It'll do." Sean tied Graves's hands behind his back.

"I'll have you for illegal arrest." Graves heaved his upper torso off the ground and flailed a leg that Sean neatly overstepped. The gardener weaved his head back and forth combatively, hooded eyes glaring. The gravel had scraped his weathered face raw on one side.

Connie returned the man's stare, her posture tense, her fists propped on her hips.

Graves flopped down like a dying fish. "Assault, too," he grunted into the pebbles.

"You can try," Sean said.

"Yeah, just try," boasted Josh.

"Keep an eye on him, son." Sean walked back to the center area. The fountain was shut off, but the pool of water in the basin gleamed like glass, unbroken by the scuffle. He bent low to examine the spot of hollowed dirt, still not quite believing Graves had been stupid enough to bury stolen goods directly under everyone's noses. He rubbed the aching wound in his thigh. To what purpose?

Connie edged past Graves with Pippa tucked in behind her. They stared at the shallow hole carved out of the ground.

"That's it?" Pippa said, clearly disappointed.

Sean scraped at the dirt with the side of the spade. "There's a metal box in here. Looks to be about two feet wide. Might be a tool box."

"Can we dig it up?"

"Sorry, Pippa. This is a crime scene. In fact—" he looked at Connie "—you shouldn't even be here."

She nodded, nearly as wide-eyed as her daughter. "We'll go."

"Just a minute." Sean went to her and stroked the back of his hand across her cheek. "You did good," he said.

Pippa tugged at his sleeve. "What about me?"

He ruffled her hair. "You were great. Very brave."

"We caught a criminal, didn't we? Just like in my books?"

"Maybe." Sean glanced in the direction of the "buried treasure." "We'll see."

"What do we do with...?" Connie tilted her head toward Peregrine House.

"We turn her in and let the island police sort things out."

"Turn who in, Mom?" Pippa asked, just as the housekeeper and the maid burst onto the scene.

"My goodness," Rachel Wells exclaimed. She shone a flashlight in their faces. "We heard the clamor from the house. What's going on here?"

The maid, Kitty, gaped. "Is that Graves?"

"He's a criminal!" Pippa blurted. "I caught him!"

Rachel aimed her flashlight at the overturned bench. Her face went white, but she clamped her mouth shut.

Not incriminating herself, Connie thought. There

were still many questions to answer, but already she knew that as long as she lived she'd forever marvel over the fact that she'd once had tea and cookies with a cold-blooded thief.

"GRAVES AND RACHEL WELLS have been in cahoots for quite a while," Sean said, late the following day. He was sitting at the dining table in the Sheffield guesthouse, speaking to a rapt audience, a beer in hand. With interviews to give to the local sheriff's department, the Bradfords had wound up extending their stay another twenty-four hours.

"I still can't quite believe it was her." Connie stared at her hands, spread on the table. Compared to the previous evening, when she'd appeared furiously, fiercely beautiful to Sean, she was all buttoned up—pinned hair, neat clothes, careful voice. God knew that he, of all people, admired the control, but he was even more glad to know the Connemara beneath—the woman of passion and courage who had stood strong with him when the going got tough. He'd had the idea that opening his life to another person would only be a burden. But that didn't have to be the case, when they made as strong a team as he and Connie.

"That housekeeper was no Miss Trask," Pippa said sadly. By now, Sean recognized the comment as a Trixie Belden reference. He supposed he would have to get accustomed to those, until she moved on to more girlish teenage pursuits.

For now, that seemed unlikely. The day had been especially exciting for Pippa. Sean had explained to the Jonesport sheriff about the Book of Curious Observations and Pippa's part in uncovering the scheme of the Sheffield employees to remove valuable items from the house.

At Pippa's interview, which had taken place in a room at the Whitecap Inn, the sheriff had asked to see the notebook. He'd studied the entries with due deliberation and had declared himself impressed by her skills. Pippa had blushed with pleasure, leaving Connie to fret about evidence and testimony.

In the end, the sheriff had confided to Sean that neither the notebook nor Pippa would be needed to prove the case. Graves had confessed to both his and Rachel Wells's roles in the crime.

Sean took a drink of the beer. It had been a long day. "Mrs. Wells's motives were simple enough," he said. "Money. Apparently she's had a hard time making ends meet since the death of her husband. The temptation of all the valuable and essentially ignored items at Peregrine House was too much to resist."

Connie nodded bleakly.

"Mrs. Wells claimed that Kay was planning to ditch most of the things they'd taken anyway. She felt entitled to help herself."

While the loot buried in the garden had been only the latest items the larcenous pair had removed from the house over the past months, they still made quite a haul. A small oil painting worth thousands, a miniature scrimshaw boat, several pieces of silver and rare china and the diamond ring that had been the crooked pair's downfall. While neither of the Sheffields had noticed the gradual disappearance of other items from the house, the missing ring had caused an uproar between the couple. Guessing at her husband's infidelity with the maid during one of their screaming fights, Kay had accused Kitty of stealing the diamond. Anders had kept her from calling the police to protect his public reputation.

"I do feel for Rachel. She must have been desperate." Connie glanced at the children. "Of course, she was also dead wrong to resort to thievery."

Sean had pondered how much to tell Josh and Pippa, but he'd decided that it was an important lesson to learn. Maybe the close-up look at the results of breaking the law would put a good scare into his son.

"From what I know, the thefts began not long after the Sheffields hired Mrs. Wells as their housekeeper. At first, she took only minor items, passing them to Graves to pawn. Eventually, they got more greedy." Sean rested his elbows on the table. "The cops have a job on their hands, trying to identify everything that's missing. Since Sheffield used the house so infrequently, even after his current marriage, he was oblivious to the losses."

"Then they weren't burying the things all along?" Connie asked.

"Because that was really stupid," Josh said.

Sean explained. "No, Graves had always been able to smuggle things out among his gardening tools. But a couple of days before the garden party, Mrs. Sheffield noticed that one of her diamond rings was missing. The house was in a furor, with all the employees under suspicion. And there was the latest haul, stowed in an old tool box in the back of Graves's pickup, the diamond included. He'd planned to hide the things somewhere on the estate and come back for the box when the situation wasn't so hot, but he claimed that he couldn't get away from you " Sean nodded at Connie " long enough. You'd ordered him to finish laying the gravel in the maze, so finally he just buried the box there, knowing the spot would be covered in the gravel. A bad decision, but he was afraid of being caught with the stuff red-handed. Remember, the estate was already swarming with workers preparing for that night's cocktail party."

Connie gasped. "And so he's been trying to get back and dig it up ever since. Except we were always foiling him! Or, rather, Pippa was."

Pippa wriggled with barely contained glee. "I knew he was up to no good."

Connie grinned wryly at Sean. "While you and I were distracted by the Sheffields and their marital spats."

"Our suspicions weren't totally off-base. After their last, um, disagreement, Mrs. Sheffield did leave the island kind of abruptly." Sean tapped his eye, indicating to Connie that she had been bruised. "Mr. Sheffield admitted that, to explain his wife's sudden absence, he arranged to escort Jillian Crosby to the yacht in hopes that she'd be mistaken for his wife." Sean scoffed. "He was still concerned with saving face, particularly in front of his remaining houseguests."

"I'm just glad it's over and we're all in one piece." Connie pushed away from the table. "There is bad news, however. It's dinnertime and there's nothing left in the house to eat."

"There's not much at my place, either," Sean said. "I didn't remember to pick anything up."

"Man, and I'm starving," Josh said.

"I'm not much a dad if I can't remember to feed my kid."

"Nonsense," Connie said, giving him a pat on the shoulder. "You've had other things on your mind."

"I did hear that there's a clambake going on at the beach, sponsored by the inn. What do you say? We could go and have a special dinner out in honor of your last night on the island." He took Connie's hand and raised it to his lips, not even minding when Josh *sheeshed* and Pippa giggled. "You're still planning to leave tomorrow? I can't persuade you to stay awhile longer?"

"I think we've imposed on Mr. Sheffield long enough." Connie chuckled. "He'll probably be relieved to see the last of us."

"Rude of him," Sean murmured, "considering everything you did." Already he was thinking ahead, to getting some real private time with Connie. No children, no criminals, no sorrow, no regret. Only the two of them and a future that would become brighter and stronger with every kiss.

Connie's eyes were locked on his, liquid with desire. She squeezed his fingers.

"Jeepers!" Pippa's shrill exclamation made them pull apart. She put her elbows on the table and her chin in her hands. "I just realized—Mr. Sheffield should give me a reward. Trixie always gets one!"

Connie reached over to stroke her daughter's hair. "Don't worry, Pippa. I believe we're leaving Osprey Island with something a lot more valuable than a monetary reward." She included Josh in her smile, and her intent was so sweet and generous that not even he could scoff at the sentiment.

Sean's thoughts went briefly to the fatal shooting before he pushed the incident away. He would never forget what had happened and how the lives of innocents had been irrevocably altered. But it—*all* the events of his life leading up to this moment—had not only brought him to Connie, but back to his son, as well.

This is worth it. Worth the risk. He looked at them, Josh and Connie and brave little Pippa, his heart bursting with love. *This is worth everything.*

THE NEXT MORNING, Connie and Sean stood at the railing of the ferry, watching Osprey Island diminish to a blue-green hump on the ocean horizon. "I wonder if we'll ever be back."

"Together? We will." His gaze remained level even when the ferry pitched beneath their feet. He lowered his eyes to Connie's face and smiled. "I can't think of a better place for a…vacation."

She blinked, certain that his hesitation had been deliberate. The only other fitting word that sprang to her mind was *honeymoon*.

You're getting ahead of yourself. She turned her head to follow the island, her hair whipping in the wind. *It might be advisable to go on a real date before you start thinking marriage.*

"How far is Holden again?" she said.

"Just a hundred miles or so." He leaned down to put his elbows on the rail. "But I swear the distance is getting shorter every time I think about being away from you."

"Shorter! It seems longer and longer to me."

"Shorter," he repeated. "I can drive it in a snap."

"Well. Good." They couldn't seem to stop looking at each other. "And thanks for taking the ferry with us." She hugged herself. "It delays the goodbye just a little while longer."

"I was thinking about Josh." Sean glanced to where his son sat on a bench, trying to listen to his iPod while Pippa chattered away, brandishing her notebook and pen. "He needs a video-game fix real bad, and there's an arcade in Jonesport."

Connie nodded, though her gaze had lingered on her daughter. She was thrilled that Pippa had her spirit back, even if dealing with the consequences of her reinforced enthusiasm for detecting might not always be easy.

Unless they had a statie on their side. She looked at Sean again, her mouth curving at the thought of having him as a part of their life. They would find a way to make it work.

"Oh, all right," he said, teasing her a little. "You had *something* to do with getting me on the ferry. I've gotten to like having you around."

She put her hands on his shoulders and gave him a small shake. "You'd better not revert to your solitary ways after we're gone. As soon as the rest of your vacation is over, I'm expecting a call."

"You'll have it. If I didn't need the time alone with Josh, I'd probably be following you home today."

Sean opened his arms and she went into them, clinging to his solidness and warmth, her safe haven among the pitching deck and the bobbing waves and the throbbing engine.

"You stick with Josh," she said. "I can wait."

"I can't." With his arms wrapped around her, Sean tilted back his head and let out a moan, lifting her off her heels as he did. "Damn if I haven't been hoisted on my own petard. I came here to be left alone and now the only leaving I'll do is with a heavy heart." He set her down and took her face in his hands, kissed her through her wind-ruffled hair. "I promise, Connie, we've got plenty of good times to come."

"But next time less heroics required, okay?"

"Don't start with that. I did nothing extraordinary. I'm nobody's—"

She stopped him with a kiss. "You're *mine,* Sean." The true courage and honor of heroes came in many forms. Philip Bradford had been her first. She hadn't expected to find another so soon.

"You're my hero, and don't you ever forget it."

Pippa Bradford's Book of Curious Observations

MOM IS KISSING MR. RAFFERTY again. Maybe that's not too gross after all. Kind of, but I can get used to it if I try. I think he's going to be my stepfather, but Dad said I should be happy for Mom if that ever happened and he knew that it didn't mean we would ever forget him, so that's okay. The only thing is that then Josh would be my stepbrother. GLEEPS!!! But I can even get used to him if I really, really have to.

I wonder if my dad can see me now. I bet he can, and he's proud of me for solving the Mystery of the Midnight Maze just as good as Trixie.

Today's Curious Observations: I guess I forgot to make any, so I'd better get started.

1. There's a man in an overcoat with a briefcase standing alone by the railing. I think he's the same one I saw coming to the island on the same day as Mr. Rafferty. That *is* curious. I wonder if he's a spy?

* * * * *

Ladies, start your engines with a sneak preview of Harlequin's officially licensed NASCAR® romance series.

Life in a famous racing family comes at a price

All his life Larry Grosso has lived in the shadow of his well-known racing family—but it's now time for him to take what he wants. And on top of that list is Crystal Hayes—breathtaking, sweet… and twenty-two years younger. But their age difference is creating animosity within their families, and suddenly their romance is the talk of the entire NASCAR circuit!

Turn the page for a sneak preview of
OVERHEATED
by Barbara Dunlop.
On sale July 29 wherever books are sold.

Rufus, as Crystal Hayes had decided to call the black Lab, slept soundly on the soft seat even as she maneuvered the Softco truck in front of the Dean Grosso garage. Engines fired through the open bay doors, compressors clacked and impact tools whined as the teams tweaked their race cars in preparation for qualifying at the third race in Charlotte.

As always when she visited the garage area, Crystal experienced a vicarious thrill, watching the technicians' meticulous, last-minute preparations. As the daughter of a machinist, she understood the difference a fraction of a degree or a thousandth of an inch could make in the performance of a race car.

She muscled the driver's door shut behind her and waved hello to a couple of familiar crew members in their white-and-pale-blue jumpsuits. Then she rounded the back of the truck and rolled up the door. Inside, five boxes were marked Cargill Motors.

One of them was big and heavy, and it had slid forward a few feet, probably when she'd braked to make the narrow parking lot entrance. So she pushed up the sleeves of her canary-yellow T-shirt, then stretched forward to reach the box. A couple of catcalls came her way as her faded blue jeans tightened across her rear end. But she knew they were good-natured, and she simply ignored them.

She dragged the box toward her over the gritty metal floor.

"Let me give you a hand with that," a deep, melodious voice rumbled in her ear.

"I can manage," she responded crisply, not wanting to engage with any of the catcallers.

Here in the garage, the last thing she needed was one of the guys treating her as if she was something other than, well, one of the guys.

She'd learned long ago there was something about her that made men toss out pickup lines like parade candy. And she'd been around race crews long enough to know she needed to behave like a buddy, not a potential date.

She piled the smaller boxes on top of the large one.

"It looks heavy," said the voice.

"I'm tough," she assured him as she scooped the pile into her arms.

He didn't move away, so she turned her head to subject him to a *back off* stare. But she found herself staring into a compelling pair of green...no, brown...no, hazel eyes. She did a double take as they seemed to twinkle, multicolored, under the garage lights.

The man insistently held out his hands for the boxes. There was a dignity in his tone and little crinkles around his eyes that hinted at wisdom. There wasn't a single sign of flirtation in his expression, but Crystal was still cautious.

"You know I'm being paid to move this, right?" she asked him.

"That doesn't mean I can't be a gentleman."

Somebody whistled from a workbench. "Go, Professor Larry."

The man named Larry tossed a "Back off" over his shoulder. Then he turned to Crystal. "Sorry about that."

"Are you for real?" she asked, growing uncomfortable with the attention they were drawing. The last thing she needed was some latter-day Sir Galahad defending her honor at the track.

He quirked a dark eyebrow in a question.

"I mean," she elaborated, "you don't need to worry. I've been fending off the wolves since I was seventeen."

"Doesn't make it right," he countered, attempting to lift the boxes from her hands.

She jerked back. "You're not making it any easier."

He frowned.

"You carry this box, and they start thinking of me as a girl."

Professor Larry dipped his gaze to take in the curves of her figure. "Hate to tell you this," he said, a little twinkle coming into those multifaceted eyes.

Something about his look made her shiver inside. It was a ridiculous reaction. Guys had given her the once-over a million times. She'd learned long ago to ignore it.

"Odds are," Larry continued, a teasing drawl in his tone, "they already have."

She turned pointedly away, boxes in hand as she marched across the floor. She could feel him watching her from behind.

* * * * *

Crystal Hayes could do without her looks,
men obsessed with her looks and guys
who think they're God's gift to the ladies.
Would Larry be the one guy who could blow
all of Crystal's preconceptions away?
Look for OVERHEATED
by Barbara Dunlop.
On sale July 29, 2008.

SPECIAL EDITION

A late-night walk on the beach resulted
in Trevor Marlowe's heroic rescue of a
drowning woman. He took the amnesia
victim in and dubbed her Venus, for the
goddess who'd emerged from the sea.
It looked as if she might be his goddess of
love, too…until her former fiancé showed
up on Trevor's doorstep.

Don't miss

THE BRIDE WITH NO NAME

by *USA TODAY* bestselling author
MARIE FERRARELLA

*Available August
wherever you buy books.*

Harlequin® Historical
Historical Romantic Adventure!

From *USA TODAY*
bestselling author
Margaret Moore

A LOVER'S KISS

A Frenchwoman in London,
Juliette Bergerine is unexpectedly
thrown together in hiding with
Sir Douglas Drury. As lust and
desire give way to deeper emotions,
how will Juliette react on discovering
that her brother was murdered—
by Drury!

*Available September
wherever you buy books.*

REQUEST YOUR FREE BOOKS!

2 FREE NOVELS PLUS 2 FREE GIFTS!

HARLEQUIN®

Super Romance®

Exciting, emotional, unexpected!

YES! Please send me 2 FREE Harlequin Superromance® novels and my 2 FREE gifts (gifts are worth about $10). After receiving them, if I don't wish to receive any more books, I can return the shipping statement marked "cancel." If I don't cancel, I will receive 6 brand-new novels every month and be billed just $4.69 per book in the U.S. or $5.24 per book in Canada, plus 25¢ shipping and handling per book and applicable taxes, if any*. That's a savings of close to 15% off the cover price! I understand that accepting the 2 free books and gifts places me under no obligation to buy anything. I can always return a shipment and cancel at any time. Even if I never buy another book from Harlequin, the two free books and gifts are mine to keep forever.

135 HDN EEX7 336 HDN EEYK

Name	(PLEASE PRINT)	

Address		Apt. #

City	State/Prov.	Zip/Postal Code

Signature (if under 18, a parent or guardian must sign)

Mail to the **Harlequin Reader Service:**
IN U.S.A.: P.O. Box 1867, Buffalo, NY 14240-1867
IN CANADA: P.O. Box 609, Fort Erie, Ontario L2A 5X3

Not valid to current subscribers of Harlequin Superromance books.

Want to try two free books from another line?
Call 1-800-873-8635 or visit www.morefreebooks.com.

* Terms and prices subject to change without notice. N.Y. residents add applicable sales tax. Canadian residents will be charged applicable provincial taxes and GST. Offer not valid in Quebec. This offer is limited to one order per household. All orders subject to approval. Credit or debit balances in a customer's account(s) may be offset by any other outstanding balance owed by or to the customer. Please allow 4 to 6 weeks for delivery. Offer available while quantities last.

Your Privacy: Harlequin is committed to protecting your privacy. Our Privacy Policy is available online at www.eHarlequin.com or upon request from the Reader Service. From time to time we make our lists of customers available to reputable third parties who may have a product or service of interest to you. If you would prefer we not share your name and address, please check here. ☐

HSR08R

LAURA WRIGHT

FRONT PAGE ENGAGEMENT

Media mogul and playboy Trent Tanford is being blackmailed *and* he's involved in a scandal. Needing to shed his image, Trent marries his girl-next-door neighbor, Carrie Gray, with some major cash tossed her way. Carrie accepts for her own reasons, but falls in love with Trent and wonders if he could feel the same way about her— even though their mock marriage was, after all, just a business deal.

**Available August
wherever books are sold.**

HARLEQUIN
Super Romance

COMING NEXT MONTH

#1506 MATTHEW'S CHILDREN • C.J. Carmichael
Three Good Men

Rumor at their law firm cites Jane Prentice as the reason for Matthew Gray's divorce. The truth is, however, Jane avoids him—and not because he's a single dad. But when they're assigned to the same case, will they be able to ignore the sparks between them?

#1507 NOT ON HER OWN • Cynthia Reese
Count on a Cop

His uncle lost his best farmland to a crook, and now Brandon Wilkes is losing his heart and his pride to the crook's granddaughter…who refuses to leave the land her grandfather stole from them! How can he possibly be friends with Penelope Langston?

#1508 A PLACE CALLED HOME • Margaret Watson
The McInnes Triplets

It was murder in self-defense, and Zoe McInnes thinks she's put her past behind her. Until the brother of her late husband shows up, and Gideon Tate's own issues make him determined to seek revenge. Not even her sisters can help Zoe out of this mess. Besides, she thinks maybe Gideon is worth all the trouble he's putting her through…and more.

#1509 MORE THAN A MEMORY • Roz Denny Fox
Going Back

Seven years ago Garret Logan was devastated when his fiancée, Colleen, died in a car accident. He's tried to distract himself with work, but he hasn't been able to break free of her memory. Until the day she walks back into his pub with a new name, claiming not to remember him…

#1510 WORTH FIGHTING FOR • Molly O'Keefe
The Mitchells of Riverview Inn

Jonah Closky will do anything for his mom. That's the only reason he's at this inn to meet his estranged father and brothers. Still, there is an upside to being here: Daphne Larson. With the attraction between them, he can't think of a better way to pass the time.

#1511 SAME TIME NEXT SUMMER • Holly Jacobs
Everlasting Love

When tragedy strikes Carolyn Kendal's daughter, it's Carolyn's first love, Stephan Foster, who races to her side. A lifetime of summers spent together has taught them to follow their hearts. But after so much time apart—and the reappearance of her daughter's father—will their hearts lead them to each other?